# FLORENTINO RUSHED HIM. . . .

Rhiannon sidestepped just a handbreadth. Florentino's wild swing grazed his chin. Rhiannon's hands shot out, gripping and closing. Florentino let out a single lost wail as the hands closed on his neck and crotch, lifting him off his feet.

Then he was high above Rhiannon's head, helpless and kicking in that terrible grip. Rhiannon swung back and forward, putting out all his strength, letting go. Florentino's body smashed sidelong against the canyon wall.

It fell to the ground as limp as a rag doll. It did not move again. . . .

Other *Leisure* books by T. V. Olsen:
**DEADLY PURSUIT**
**LONESOME GUN**
**EYE OF THE WOLF**
**KENO**
**STARBUCK'S BRAND**
**MISSION TO THE WEST**
**BONNER'S STALLION**
**BREAK THE YOUNG LAND**
**THE STALKING MOON**
**BLOOD OF THE BREED**
**LAZLO'S STRIKE**
**WESTWARD THEY RODE**
**ARROW IN THE SUN**
**RED IS THE RIVER**
**THERE WAS A SEASON**

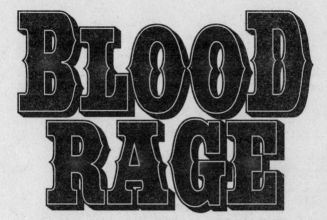

# BLOOD RAGE

## T.V. OLSEN

LEISURE BOOKS  NEW YORK CITY

A LEISURE BOOK®

March 1999

Published by

Dorchester Publishing Co., Inc.
276 Fifth Avenue
New York, NY 10001

ISBN 0-8439-4500-1

# CHAPTER ONE

CONSCIOUSNESS CAME BACK SLOWLY, ALONG WITH COLD AND the smell of dank earth. And utter darkness. With it came a rising explosion of pain that knifed through his head, his joints, his whole body. His cheek was resting on moist dirt. He tried to turn his head and could not. The slight movement caused a scrape of dirt along the raw side of his face.

He groaned.

Above the blood-pounding of pain in his head, he heard a faint sound, dull and whispery, somewhere at his back.

*God, what was that?*

He lay very still now in the total darkness. That smell of dank earth was all around, filling his senses. *Underground.* He was down in the earth somewhere. *Buried alive?*

He tried to think, but nothing was clear in the awakening sludge of his brain. The slicing pain dulled even a first edge of panic. In spite of the damp cold, his throat and mouth felt like a kiln. He tried to form sound with his lips. Nothing. Not even a parched whisper.

Christ . . . the thirst. His tongue was furred, without sensation.

Again, in an exploratory way, he tried to move. It touched off fresh bursts of pain here and there, all over him, but knifing hardest against sore ribs. Then he realized he was trussed up like a hog, hands and feet. Whether ropes or thongs, they were tight as hell, digging into flesh that had no feeling. Pain, except for the chill dankness and a gritty awareness of dirt against his face, was his only feeling. His hands and feet were like frozen clumps. Slowly he shifted his legs, pulling his knees up to his belly.

1

Again that ominous whispery noise—*or was it a slither-ing?*—somewhere behind him.

He waited, again not moving. Again the sound subsided.

He blinked his eyes and felt a flaking away of something that crusted his eyelids, his whole face. Like a caking of dried blood.

Overriding all of it was the crushing agony that filled his head. It rolled in like great combers of the gulf waters he'd once seen at Matagorda, crashing at the back of his skull in a pulse-timed rhythm, slugging and letting go and slugging back to his blood beat's roar.

He did not move again. He lay quiet and tried to think. Something at his back . . . but a silent something as long as he didn't move. And keeping still meant less pain.

Threads of thought forming like trickles of molasses. Shaping themselves into shreds of meaning. Of memory.

The last clear memory?

*The Englishman.*

The Englishman in the Roadbrand Way House. He'd only been starting to get drunk then and he remembered the Englisher coming in, last night.

Was it *last* night? How long had he been here? Was it day or night now? Nothing, not a least slit of light in the blackness, informed him.

All right. Start with the Roadbrand. Other things had happened. But they were a red-gray confusion, a jumble of violence and noise and pain. So start with that.

The goddamn Sassenach. The Englishman . . .


"I've heard it said that you've a touch of Comanche blood in you."

"That's what they cuss me with. Only it's rougher talk they use. A *touch* of it, indeed." Rhiannon chuckled in his chest and reached for the bottle. Squaw man. Red-nigger lover. Renegade. Ah, all the lovely names. Aloud, he said, "Not a jot of truth in any of it."

"Here . . . Bartender. I'll buy us another."

"No. You've bought me one, Sassenach. It's the custom." Rhiannon slapped coins on the bar and filled his own glass. "Drink up."

The Englishman raised his untouched glass in a mild salute, took the raw whiskey in a swallow, and did not even blink. But the twitch of his Adam's apple was a little convulsive.

Rhiannon, hunched with his big arms folded on the bar, grinned sideways at him. "Raises bristles on your gizzard, huh?"

"I should say so. Never tasted the like."

"We're even. I never drunk a bloody Sassenach's whiskey before."

"Come now. It's not my liquor." The Englishman nodded good-naturedly at Gooch, the proprietor, a stumpy ex-brush runner with a stove-up leg, as he came gimping over to sweep the coins into a scarred palm. "Just bought you a sip of his."

"Yours after you pay for it."

"That's a way of looking at it, I suppose."

The Englishman was slender but trimly built, with a lean, well-set-up look about him, and his face was ruddy with a well-seasoned burn from the sun. His nose had been broken once and rescued the face from being too handsome. He was about thirty. Eyes of a cornflower blue, quiet and unblinking. He wore wee little spikes of mustache as pale blond as his smooth cap of hair. A fancy pearl-gray Stetson rode on his head at a jaunty angle, and his black boots were as glossy as a cricket's shell. His riding breeches were white whipcord and his coat . . . Rhiannon liked his coat.

"Irish tweed, ain't that? It becomes a man."

"Even a bloody Sassenach?"

"Oh, aye." Rhiannon refilled the other's glass. "Clothes make the man, it's said. They'll make a bloody Orangeman of you, at the least."

Warrington's white smile flashed under the blond spikes. Richard Warrington, he'd said he was. Rhiannon hadn't encountered him before, but he knew the name. Warrington was the manager of the Cross W over northeast. Newly registered from Cross M since old Charlie Joe Manders had sold it to a British company. Big outfit and lush grass and plenty of water. As fine a spread as you'd find in the county, and all a man or a company had needed to take it and turn the bloody letter upside down was a small fortune and old Charlie Joe's desire to idle away his remaining years in St. Louis amid modest luxury. Charlie Joe was a tough old woolywhyhow who'd trapped with mountain men, then guided the soldier boys fighting against the Comanches and Kiowa till the Austin government had given him a headright league of land for his services during the Mexican War. Rhiannon wondered incuriously what this English chappie had ever done.

"What did you ever do, chappie?"

"Beg your pardon?"

Rhiannon grinned. "Nawthin'. Forget it, chappie. Drink up."

Warrington turned his glass between his fingers but didn't raise it. "If I may ask, just what *is* your relationship to the Comanche?"

Rhiannon took his drink, smacked his lips, and said, "Whooo!" He eyed the other askance. "Mostly I'm a brother-in-law to Stone Bull. We growed up together."

"Ah, yes. War chief of the Quohada Comanche. Quite a rum one, I've heard."

"He's a scrapper, to be sure."

Warrington swallowed his drink, then laid a crisp, new greenback on the bar. Rhiannon poured for both of them and rolled his gaze ceilingward, meditating. The pleasant fog of drink was only starting to heat his belly and head.

A hellhole of a dive, the Roadbrand. Hand-hewn rafters, stained by time and smoke, supported a canvas-and-sod roof that rested on fieldstone walls a foot thick. A dinky little roadhouse on the trail to Horsehead Crossing. Hardly anyone but teamsters, drifters, men from local outfits—one-loop outfits like his own—ever frequented it. What in Sheol was a curried Englisher like this one doing in it? Especially this late of an evening? He should be ensconced by his own comfy hearthside sipping a sporty Scotch-and-polly, whatever, but it would be imported firewater for sure, golden as sunset and smooth as a baby's arse. Warrington looked to be consistently immaculate in his habits. A little dust on his boots. Back at his hearthside, the flick of a silk cloth would swipe it away.

Yes, sir. High marks to the man for turning in here where it was known that Mike Rhiannon unloaded his cares and shipped on a goodly load of red-eye each Saturday night regular as clockwork, otherwise never leaving his place or his kids after dark.

And the first Comanche reference. Real sudden that had come out. Then another. Warrington said idly, "A Comanche raising, then? Odd how well the brogue of Erin has survived it, if you don't mind my saying so."

There it was. Rhiannon sighed, rubbing a hand over his face. "You ain't the first has wondered. My story's soon told. Born in County Roscommon's heart. My people took ship for America when I was two. Grew up in a good solid Irish slum o' Boston till my pa notioned to come west just before the war; the Mex one. Comanch' hit our wagon train north o' the Canadian and wiped it out to a man and woman, save for the kids. I was one o' six. The others . . ." He lifted his burly shoulders and let them fall. "Dead now, the lot, over the years. My wee sister . . . she wasn't long for the world."

"They take children captive?"

"And any young women."

There was an odd tightening of flesh along Warrington's jaw. Rhiannon went on, "They do, aye. Raise 'em as their own. I become as near Comanche as a white lad crowding fifteen ever can. He'll stay mostly white inside. That's the part that brought me back to a white man's world when I was a man growed. Leavin' the best o' me behind, I've ofttimes thought. But the blood of a man don't change. There now. Is it that you were digging so daintily for?"

Warrington's ruddy color deepened a shade. "To be truthful, I'd heard as much."

"And what was that Comanche-blood-in-me-ancestry blather about? Is it greenhorn curiosity, then?"

"Well . . . it was just by way of openers, you know. I wanted to talk with you."

Rhiannon glanced around the cramped room. A pair of out-at-the-heels punchers were playing cards at one of the two battered deal tables. At the other, a sleepy-looking teamster was wolfing down a late supper. A surly-faced Mexican was nursing a glass at the bar's other end. All were minding their own business.

"Me in particular?"

"Yes. I wanted to——"

"My turn, old chappie," Rhiannon said.

Warrington downed his drink and patiently waited as Rhiannon laid out money and refilled their glasses, not hurrying it. Warrington said, "Your neighbor, sir? Mr. Alec Dragoman?"

Rhiannon's jaw set hard and sudden under his beard. He swallowed his drink and banged the glass down. He said softly, ominously, "Aye?"

"I am engaged to his daughter. Perhaps you have heard that a week ago she was carried off by Comanche raiders."

The slow rise of Rhiannon's temper cooled back. "Ah. Is that the truth?"

"I'd have thought you'd—"

"Never leave me place save to frequent this blisterin' den. Once a week, as you seem to know. 'Cept when I got to trail cows over to the stockpens at Colton. Buy all me supplies here, too. Carried off, was she?"

"She and her maid. While the two of them were out riding not far from the Corazon headquarters."

Rhiannon gave a snort of derision. "At the time o' Comanche Moon? I'd think not."

Warrington said evenly, "But far enough, it seems, that the red devils discovered them. There was sign where they'd been taken, track all around. A band of ten or twelve. You *did* know the Comanches have been out hereabouts on their September forays?"

A slow smile began to split Rhiannon's beard. "They usually are, 'most any damn year. Way south o' the Palo Duro is still Comancheria by their lights."

"Is it?"

"Mmm. They don't like us down here. Mex or white, immigrant or born Texican. They ain't particular. At Comanche Moon, we're all meat for the slaughter."

"Well, that brings us to my reason for being here. You know the Comanches as well as any white man alive. You married a Comanche woman and had two children by her. It is said you are intimate with the Quohada band of the Comanches. And I have it from your own lips that you are brother-in-law to a chief. . . ."

Rhiannon's lip curled. "You heard more than that, bucko.

You heard the reddies have never touched my place, my stock, in any raid o' theirs. Hit all my neighbors regular as rain, but give my outfit a wide berth. Because I'm still chummy with 'em, eh?"

"Mr. Dragoman suggested as much, yes. He admitted it is speculation. Ordinarily, Mr. Rhiannon, I am a man who places no credence in rumor. But I am also, at this juncture, a desperate man. If there is a white man alive who might be able to rescue my fiancée from the savages, it is you." He paused, then burst out, "What the devil are you grinning about?"

"A joke," Rhiannon said, his grin broadening. "The greatest joke of me life. But you know what it is. Dragoman would be telling you that, too. He of all men."

"Yes. I know he misused you once. . . . But God, man. That was over ten years ago. Surely—"

"Did he tell you *what* he did? All of it?"

"Why, that some of his hands had caught you mavericking on range he claims. In the act of branding an unmarked calf. And that they used you badly—"

"Badly, was it." Rhiannon's voice dropped to a whisper. He picked up the bottle, took a long pull from it, shuddered, and set it down. "Man, I won't tell you. I'll show you. Fill your goddamn Sassenach eyes with this."

He shrugged off his brush jacket and laid it on the bar. Staring at Warrington, he peeled off his shirt and dropped it on the coat. Then he turned around slowly, full circle, the saffron light from an overhead lamp polishing his pale, massive torso as he turned.

"My God . . ." Warrington's face had lost its color; he could only stare and swallow. "Oh, my Lord."

Rhiannon's upper body was a criss-crossed map of old welts and scars. Dead white here, wrinkled like ancient brown leather there, they twisted over and around his shoulders, back, belly—his whole trunk. Some formed great puckered ridges where the flesh had been split so deeply that even Naduah's skilled needle hadn't been able to take stitches tight enough to close the wounds. Discolored knobs of flesh stood out in places; where the whip had lifted out whole pieces of skin, shallow white valleys had formed. His chest and belly were matted with crinkly red hair. Where the scars snaked across them, no hair grew.

The best of it had been saved for the last. On Rhiannon's left breast a letter *C* had been seared into the skin, three inches high and a half inch wide, as if to capitalize and claim the whole nightmarish terrain.

Once, working on a broiling-hot day with one of his crewmen as they'd set rafters for a new barn, he had stripped off his shirt against the heat. For a minute they had worked on in silence, his puncher's toughly weathered face as stoic as a mask. Then all of a sudden the man had bent over and let go the contents of his innards. Rhiannon had never again bared his body to any other, not even Naduah. Always he undressed after the lamps were doused and donned his clothes at first light.

Warrington, to the credit of his English guts, did not step back. He did not even flinch. But a nerve quivered in his cheek. His eyes were a wee glassy and his face was patched ruddy and white. He cleared his throat.

"I am prepared"—he cleared his throat again and went on in his even tenor voice—"to give you ten thousand dollars of my own money if you can secure the rescue of Miss Dragoman and her maid. Half will be paid to you before you undertake the mission, half upon your return with the two young ladies."

Rhiannon watched him in the dead stillness. He could feel the eyes of the men at his back. One of the cardplayers said in a mild croak, "Sweet Jesus A'mighty," and that was all. Rhiannon let the silence run between Warrington and him for a half minute. The Englishman's eyes had lost their glaze and they held to his as steady as stone.

Rhiannon picked up his shirt and pulled it on, then the jacket. He took another long pull from the bottle, set it very gently on the bar, and swiped a hand across his mouth. The fumes felt good, mounting to his head.

"You're a piker," he said quietly.

"Twenty thousand dollars. Same terms. Or take it all before you depart and place it in trust for your children." Warrington hesitated. "If . . . you shouldn't return, you know."

"A man faring forth to risk his ruined hide should ask if that's your highest bid."

"My father owns our London company. I will meet any

terms of yours that he is willing to grant. As quickly as transatlantic cable and cross-country telegraph can bring word, a draft for the amount will be in your hands."

Rhiannon smothered a yawn with his big palm. "Ah-hum. Well, leave me to think on it a spell. Say a week. Now toddle along to your nice bedtime toddy, there's a good lad."

"Don't toy with me, sir. Your answer now. Or not at all."

"You're still a piker, me lad."

Warrington's jaw rocked faintly and clamped hard. "It is my money I offer—"

"Your old man's."

"—not Mr. Dragoman's. You have no reason to bear ill will toward me. Or an innocent girl."

"Two of 'em. Suppose I can only fetch back the maid?"

"I believe I have your answer."

Rhiannon crashed his fist on the bar; the bottle and glasses jumped. "*No it is!* Not for all the gold in your bloody coffers! Not for all of it in Christendom!" His voice fell to a hoarse whisper. "A score of times I could've deadfalled the old son of a bitch. Laid for him and put him down dead. Just that—that alone, mind you—wouldn't add a drop of nectar to the cup I've borne for him. This now. Christ, it's the knife I prayed for. I couldn't twist it better if I'd placed it in his rich, stinking guts with my own hand. Now, mister . . ." His voice lifted to a sudden roar. "Take your bleedin' roast-beef face out o' me sight before I smash it!"

Warrington pushed his change across the bar. "Have a drop of nectar on me, sir. For your cup. A saddle cup? Or will you be drinking the night long? I daresay. Drown all sorrow at least till the morrow, what? Good night."

He turned and walked toward the doors, his back straight as a ramrod. With an oath, Rhiannon picked up the bottle and flung it. It burst against the doorjamb inches from Warrington's shoulder, exploding glass and sparkling amber across his tweed coat. The Englishman halted and turned his head, arching a quizzical blond brow.

"Yes?" he said politely.

"*Up your hairy hole, bucko!*" Rhiannon roared.

Warrington parted the swing doors and walked out.

\* \* \*

Rhiannon lay in the blackness on cold dirt, his thoughts drifting. Lying quietly made some of the pain subside. Some of the rest numbed as the chill that needled his flesh ate deeper into his bones.

Warrington and him. The last clear memory. After that?

They did not want him dead. Just short of it, maybe, but not quite dead. A rasp of humor in his throat. The way he felt, it was like after one of those monumental bouts when you woke up the next morning and were afraid you were going to die. After a little while, you were afraid you weren't going to.

They?

Dragoman had something to do with this. All right. That would figure. Dragoman wanted his daughter back. He would go to any lengths. Warrington wanted her back but was a passably decent Sassenach. Bloody code, he'd have. Playing fields of Eton and all that. So it was Dragoman.

Rhiannon squeezed his eyes shut hurtingly. Trying to remember afterward. After Warrington. He had gotten more pissed than he could remember in a long time.

*And then?* Goddammit, *think!*

He gathered the dregs of his faded will together and thought, *Move!* Get your blood up, get your head working.

Knowing it would hurt like hell, knowing it would have to because only real pain could clear his brain, he twisted his hips and rolled onto his belly.

Good. Plenty of pain . . .

Something else, too.

That dry slither of sound again. And with it, this time, a loud burring, a brittle warning that froze his blood.

Sweet purple saints. A rattler. The bastards had put him in this black hole with a goddamn rattlesnake.

# CHAPTER TWO

**I**NSTINCTIVE PANIC MADE HIM ROLL AGAIN, AWAY FROM THE sound. He was on his back now. The rattling trailed into a faint hiss. Then silence.

It should have struck him. It was that close. As he lay on his back, dead still again, blood pounding in his battered head, warm trickles of blood on his face from the sudden effort breaking the scabbed cuts, he knew why it hadn't. The bloody reptile was torpid with the cold.

Any more of 'em in here? Still greater panic thickened his veins as he fingered the notion around, briefly and carefully. One was enough. But don't move again. You might roll right onto one of the buggers. Christ.

Well, he could almost think again. Patches of dim clarity were sifting into focus. He almost wished they weren't. . . .

After Warrington had left the Roadbrand, Rhiannon listened to the drumming of his horse's hooves fade away. There was stillness broken only by the sound of the cardplayers' chairs scraping back. They left quietly, along with the teamster who'd left his meal unfinished. They were followed a moment later by the Mexican, who took his last drink quickly and tramped out with a vast chinking of his big *Californio* spurs.

Gooch watched Rhiannon with a quiet care. But he said only, "Another bottle, Mike?"

"I'm owing you for what the last one still held."

"On the house. This one, too." Gooch set a fresh bottle in front of him. "Good night for it, seems like."

"Gooch, me lad, you're a prince of your trade. But I'll pay for this one."

11

Rhiannon put down a huge slug, coughed, and shuddered, and then settled down to serious drinking. He didn't bother with a glass.

This night the old memories were mushrooming in him worse than ever, rising to his throat like black bile. He remembered the day as clearly as etching on glass. All the ancient fury of it surged back.

Down from Comancheria he'd come with his Comanche bride, and he was a pacific man. In fact, the ultimate reason that he had left the band was his refusal to make war on his own race. It had gotten to be an irksome thing, his tribesmen being more and more distrustful of his never riding out to raid with them, save for the forays against other tribes. If he was not a traitor with a white heart full of water, he was a woman. One to be spat on, though no man ever dared to try it.

Well and good, then. He would make the break clean, save for Naduah. But he had to start from practically nothing. A little gold to buy a little land. He hadn't realized the depth of the animosity held by the big cattlemen toward maverickers. A hatred so intense that it would soon result in the cattlemen's ramming the Act of '66 through the Texas legislature to make mavericking a first-degree crime. He'd carefully consulted land charts before staking his legal claim. Then he'd ranged out from his camp, looking for unbranded wildlings.

His first find was a mulberry-colored longhorn yearling, and he had chased it and roped it and tied it. He'd been branding it with a straight iron when he was discovered by four Corazon hands. All they'd told him was that he was on Corazon range and Mr. Dragoman had given orders as to how any long-iron artist found on his range was to be dealt with.

They had tied him up and gone to work. They lashed him with their doubled-up ropes till his shirt was in bloody rags. Then a big, yellow-eyed man called Herb took a coiled bullwhip with a blade-edged popper from his saddle.

It hurt like hell's fury at first, but he was barely, numbly conscious when Herb's arm grew tired. Worse than hell came pouring back when they used the Corazon iron on him, wisps of smoke trailing from it before it was slapped on. The stink of his burning hair and hide was his last clear sensation before he passed out.

Coming to, finding his horse driven off, he had started at once to crawl, trying to take the bearings for his camp by guess. After a while he got his feet under him and lurched on with nothing but the sense of setting one foot forward, then the other. The sun broiled him. Weak from the blood loss, he fell many times and passed out once more. When he came to, it was dark. He plodded on endlessly again till he fell.

When he revived he found himself only a hundred yards from his camp, it was a new day, and Naduah was washing his sand-plastered wounds. It took a long time, for sand left in such wounds would worsen the scarring, if that was possible. There was no whiskey to put down the agony. Then the stitching and bandaging and a week of thrashing fever.

Long after he was on his feet again, working with a will, the hatred remained fresh and open in his guts, unhealed. He'd turned over in his brain a hundred schemes of revenge upon the man called Herb. Till he learned that Alec Dragoman, in giving the order, had told Herb to a detail what was to be done. A lot of raggedy one-loop settlers were starting to infest the country. The first one to be caught on Corazon range wasn't merely to be rope-punished by whipping or hanging. He was to be made an example of. A piece of walking butchered meat, a live warning to all others.

It worked. Given all the distance between neighbors, word still got around like wildfire. It always did in this country. That Herb Mansavage, he was a crackerjack with a whip. But he was only a brawny arm. He was only cruel on direction. A few other little folks were pushed around, nothing serious. The point had been made nicely.

Well, he could clear out of the country, Mike Rhiannon could. Start his outfit elsewhere. Or find another trade. Or go back to the Comanches. The notions barely tickled his mind. He wasn't a running man. And there would always be Dragoman. Wherever he went, there would be Dragoman, burning in his head like a live coal. So he stayed, all the contemplated revenges upon Dragoman left to simmer, cooling a little over the years, hardening into a black iron lump.

Rhiannon lived with it. There was no fitting, no satisfying way to fetch Dragoman. Whatever was done, Dragoman must not die of it. *Not right away.* Bide your time, Mike me boy. It will come . . .

Rhiannon grunted and tipped the bottle again.

Had tonight been it? Some, he conceded. By his doing nothing at all instead of something. But, man, it left a hollow feel, not a satisfying one. Was it too small a revenge? Or wasn't Mike Rhiannon, at the last reckoning, a man cut out to suckle such a tit of vengeance?

He denied it with a flat, savage "Shit!" that made Gooch glance at him and then look away again.

Well, a man needn't think much for now. The whiskey would help. He called for another bottle. He was taking on his biggest load since Naduah's passing and it was going down as swimmingly as syrup, turning the black lump golden at the edges.

Not all bad, those years. Not while Naduah was with him. It had made up for all the hardscrabble living of those first years. His MR outfit had grown till he was breaking even and could even, finally, take on a couple of good hands, Elugio Centavo and Opie Childress. Good men. Even if Opie did have a weak stomach. And there was Norabeth, born in '64, and Cully, born in '67. A family, by God. The heart hadn't gone out of it till the pox caught them three years ago. A mild summer pox, but a touch of white man's disease was enough to lay a full-blooded Indian by the heels. Naduah had died after two days of fever.

*Ah, Naduah . . . Naduah!*

All the gold was melting. Rhiannon watched it melt in lamp-gilded tears down his shaggy beard and off its tip and puddle on the bar.

Ah, the blackness of it. The black loneliness . . .

Everything was spotty for a spell after that. He remembered, lying now in his dark, snaky hole, riding homeward bawling out "The Minstrel Boy" in his top tuneless form, riding all over the trail and off it and back again, his short-coupled bay, Donegal, taking on the imparted glow of him and careening almost as drunkenly as his master.

Rhiannon remembered seeing the lights of his house way up ahead, bobbing like saffron cubes in his blurred vision. Then . . .

They rose up on all sides of him, silent men who were waiting in the masses of dark brush along the trail. He had that brief picture, the black outlines of brush and rocks and moving men against a cobalt sky.

One seized Donegal's cheek strap, another came at Rhiannon from his left and grabbed his arm and gave a yank. Drunk as he was, he held fast to the saddle.

"Here, ye blasted—*goddamn!*"

He pulled free and knocked the man reeling with a back cuff of his hand. Another was rushing him now and Rhiannon backed his foot free of the stirrup and kicked out. He felt the boot meet flesh and bone—a man's head—bone or teeth crunch, and heard the man's scream as he dropped backward.

On Rhiannon's other side came the tug of a hand closing on his belt and a savage pull that dumped him from the saddle. He was slammed down on his back and shoulders and head. The shock cleared his brain a little; he roared an oath. Then two men were piling onto him, grappling him.

Rhiannon's right foot was hung in the stirrup. Donegal snorted in annoyance and shuffled sidelong from him; the foot came free. He flung one of the men away and gave the other a backhand that half stunned him. Rhiannon flung him off too, but another pair were on him at once. A third man fell on his legs, pinning them.

Each of the others got hold of an arm and had all they could do for a wrestling, grunting half minute to get a fast lock on him. Rhiannon fought them in silence, but he was securely taken. He let his body relax, his chest heaving, hissing, "Ye . . . goddamn . . . black-leg scuts."

The man on his legs rolled off, then clamped his hands tightly around Rhiannon's ankles. Immobilized like a steer for the branding—*God, the branding*—he was hauled to his feet. The crouching man let got of his ankles.

The one he'd kicked was letting go a steady string of obscenities, spitting them out with his blood. Then he was in front of Rhiannon, his arm lifting and falling. Blurred starlight slashed along a gun barrel. It slammed against Rhiannon's temple. He sagged down, his captors shifting themselves awkwardly to support his weight.

"*Sangre de Cristo!* Don't hurt him—only hold him fast, you *bastardos!*"

He knew the voice.

Corazon men they were. Agh. Who else? He threw back his head, the stars pinwheeling whitely above. They came into steady focus now. The blow had wholly cleared his head. Bloody offal.

Rhiannon suddenly reared up, legs braced wide and knees unhinging straight. With all his might, he smashed back against the grips on his right arm. His elbow sank into the man's belly and jolted him back a step. It was a child's effort to wrench that arm free. He pivoted in the same moment and smashed his fist into the left-hand man's face. A nose collapsed under his knuckles.

He was free, his hand diving now to the big Bowie knife at his belt. It all happened lightning-fast, taking the others off guard fleetingly, but already they were coming at him from all sides.

"*Por Dios!* No guns—no knives! *Don't hurt him!*"

But Rhiannon had a knife, the best of all weapons for close work. "Ah, scuts!" As they pressed in around him, he swung the blade in a glittering arc that met flesh shallowly once, struck another man and cut deeply.

They were yelling and cursing, three of them falling back. But the others were on him, trying to grapple with him. He brought the blade up underhanded, trying for a belly and fetching an arm instead. Again a hoarse scream was heard as the steel cut up vertically, elbow to shoulder, ripping deep.

Rhiannon kicked out at the next man, catching him in the thigh. The fellow's leg folded and he went down. The third one made a grab for Rhiannon's arm and he pivoted hard on his heel, throwing his weight behind his bunched shoulder, and smashed him high and hard in the jaw, click-snapping his teeth. The man collapsed without a sound.

Rhiannon made a rush at two others standing crouched a little apart. He feinted with his knife at one and, as the man stumbled back, veered enough to crash headlong into the other, bowling him over.

Rhiannon went down, too, somersaulted cat-quick, and rolled to his feet. Now there was clear open space at his front and he crossed it in two great bounds, plunging into a night-black mass of mesquite overgrowth, crashing through it bent over to make his body small, an arm upflung to protect his face.

Then he was free of brush, sliding down the cutbank of a steep wash and running along its pebbly floor for a half-dozen yards before he sprang up the other cutbank and into more mesquite.

Distance; he needed a little more. Not too much. He could move more carefully now, weaving quietly across stony terrain and between clots of brush familiar to him, knowing the ground near his place like the seams of his palms. Or the scars on his back.

Finally, winded and suddenly wobble-legged, he penetrated a thicket to its clear center and dropped onto his hunkers, head down.

His heart was laboring, slugging hard against his ribs, the blood roar in his skull drowning any other sound. Christ and all the saints. He held a hand to hs bleeding temple and wagged his aching head, sunk almost between his knees. That wallop was catching up to him of a sudden, that and all the poteen he'd consumed. His belly was churning.

His hearing picked up now, feeding into his senses the sounds of men, the crashing of brush. They were spreading out, fanning wide for the search, coming this way. He should clear out of here now. But all the sudden bursting effort by a man both hurt and drunk had left him depleted, momentarily done in. He must hold himself still until his strength came back enough so that he could move on without blundering into their arms.

For they were around him now, not close, but at his back and both flanks, beating the brush, swearing, shouting orders. Crouching in the faint starlight, he thought if he hugged the dark ground, he might be lucky. The familiar voice again. Bernal Rubriz it was. The *segundo* of Corazon.

Rubriz. He would not have thought it of that man. White-haired and courteous and seldom-spoken, he had never been an enemy of Mike Rhiannon. Rubriz had a gray, neutral way about him but was a man for all that. On chance encounters during the cow hunts or in Colton for the cattle trade, he and Rubriz would even exchange greetings, a spare word or a few, Rhiannon gruff about it, Rubriz quietly polite.

Dragoman had always kept a few bad apples on his payroll to handle his troubles, but Bernal Rubriz had never seemed

touched by that part of Corazon, only heading up the workaday
crew. Rhiannon had sometimes wondered why Rubriz kept his
place under a man like Dragoman.

And why would Rubriz, of all men, head up this party?

Rhiannon stirred his arms gently, rubbing them. He was a
little rested. The night was still clear at his front; his attackers
were moving off away from his flanks. And he should move,
too, move carefully while the way was open, get way back into
the deeper chapparal and find a place to lay low at a safe
distance from his house. If they couldn't find him, they'd put a
watch on the house.

But he'd be free. Embattled by worries for the children, or
Opie and Elugio. But free to make his plans and put them into
action.

His stomach was still churning thickly, and he rubbed it,
swallowing against a taste of vomit. Hold it down for now. Just
for a little.

But it would not stay down. Wave after wave of nausea
convulsed him. Suddenly it emptied sharp and sour from his
throat. He spat it out and bent his face nearly to the ground,
trying to fight it back at first. And then, finding he couldn't, he
tried to keep the retching as quiet as possible. Half choking, he
gave up the contents of his stomach in three surges of noisy
convulsion.

He was still fitfully dry-gagging when he heard a whisper of
parting brush at his back. Slowly and sickly, he turned on his
heels. The man stepped forward, a gun gleaming in his fist.

"How you doing, brush bum? Been awhile. Under the old
weather, huh?"

Herb Mansavage laughed. He was a high, big-shouldered
form in the starlight. He tipped his head back to laugh.

Rhiannon's full fury, the black rage that his father had
always called the curse of the Black Irish, broke and wiped out
his thoughts, made him even forget his Bowie. He lunged,
floundered on his hands and knees, and grabbed out. Mansavage grunted and was about to chop the gun on his head but
hesitated. Another floundering lunge on his knees and Rhiannon had the man, both arms wrapping around Mansavage's
thighs. He lifted with all his power, getting one foot under him,
then the other, as he reared upright, roaring at the top of his

voice. Mansavage was lifted bodily with him, twisting wildly against the hold.

Clubbing his gun down now, Mansavage fetched him a glancing blow above the ear. Rhiannon hardly felt it. He twisted the man's bulk high, using one hand for a second hold on his shoulder. Then he dashed Mansavage to the ground, headfirst.

A movement came from behind him. Rhiannon couldn't even begin to turn on his new adversary when the man hit him. Caught him on his bleeding temple with stone or steel or hardwood.

Whatever it was sent his world spinning away. He was falling, that much he knew, but it all went black before he hit the ground.

Time seemed to drag interminably in his dark dirt prison, but Rhiannon knew his mind was magnifying minutes into hours. His head was clear now and all he could do was wait. Wait with all the iron patience of his Comanche training.

What did Dragoman have in store for him? Rhiannon turned over the possibilities. Rubriz had stressed taking him unharmed. *But the rattlesnake.* If Dragoman wanted him alive—at least for now—why throw him into a black pit with a venomed menace? Maybe because it would stretch out the hours of his dying unbearably. The mind could hardly conceive of a worse way to die. Dragoman would like that.

But weighing that against Dragoman's larger stake, the rescue of his daughter, Rhiannon did not believe it. More likely the snake had already been here, torpid and unnoticed in the dark, when they'd dropped him inside.

Gradually, holding himself utterly motionless, Rhiannon felt the pounding pain of his head subside to an aching throb that he could tolerate. Saints, the bastards had worked him over something fierce after he was out stone cold. On top of a monumental hangover, he'd taken several good kicks in the head, in other places, too, and he guessed that was Mansavage's doing.

At last a vertical slit of gray was forming along one dirt wall, a dim thread of light that grew as the minutes passed. The coming dawn told him the nature of his prison. He was in a dugout on the side of a hill, an old sod-roofed dwelling or an abandoned root cellar. Aye, a likely hidey-hole for snakes and vermin.

His flesh crawled as, off to his left, he heard the scaly slithering again. It began and stopped. Soon enough the rattler would warm out of its lassitude.

He considered letting out a yell. But a yell might not bring help, while it would surely arouse the reptile all the more swiftly. And if help came, if the dugout door opened of a sudden, the rush of light and warmth would bring a strike of quick fangs for sure.

Taking a chance, he again rolled his body away from the snake. It hissed but did not strike, as if calculating its enemy now. He rolled once more and came up hard against a wall that sent dry earth crumbling down on his face, into his mouth. He choked and would have gagged but for the parched agony of his throat. He spat out the dirt and tried not to swallow.

Maybe he was a little out of striking range. Momentarily. God, but he hated those scaly bastards. To be like this with one of them! But only one, saints be thanked. Pencils of rose-gold were framing the whole door now, squaring it off, painting the dugout's interior with faint seeping light. He could just make out the wavy, ropelike outline of the reclining snake. It was a small one.

But even eight feet away was too damned close.

Rhiannon strained with a powerful care against his bonds, twisting all of his muscles to work the cold out of his joints. No use. He was lashed up tighter than a crawdad's ass.

A crunch of footsteps came from outside the door.

Now it would come. He tried once to make a sound, a warning. His neck corded and bulged with the effort. Nothing.

The door scraped and jammed. Then a strong wrenching effort yanked it wide, sun shafts of a new day flooding the dugout.

The rattler squirmed to life, stretching out and toward him in a long, lethal ripple, then coiling all at once to strike, the rattles loud in a brittle blur, the flat head drawn back.

# CHAPTER THREE

"**M**ADRE DE DIOS!"

The soft curse exploded from Bernal Rubriz as he dropped the knife he held. Slowly he eased a pistol from his belt and cocked it.

The shot boomed against Rhiannon's eardrums.

Headless, the thrashing reptile flopped across his chest, the bloody stump hitting his face. Jesus God. The stink of cordite filled his nose. He squeezed his eyes tight shut.

Rubriz grunted as he kicked the dying snake aside and dropped to a knee beside Rhiannon, who opened his eyes. A quick glint and slash of knife steel. His feet were free.

"Can you move?"

"Aye. But not to get up." Rhiannon's cracked lips only shaped the words. "My hands, if you please."

"No," said Rubriz. "Lift your shoulders. There. Now my arm under your back and we bring you up, eh?"

Rhiannon managed to double his legs under him and push up as Rubriz supported his weight. His knees threatened to hinge, but Rubriz took his leaning weight with a sinewy strength and held him upright as they bent over and climbed out of the dugout into the flush of a new day.

The flat sunrays hit his eyes, making them water and blink.

"Can you stand?"

Rhiannon heaved his shoulders, then nodded. The Corazon *segundo* let go of him and stepped away, eyeing him with a wary respect.

Rhiannon was built as thick as a bear and, standing upright on his braced legs, reached a good five inches above six feet.

21

His shoulders and chest had the rounded power of a bull's and columnar muscle bulged the sleeves and legs of his worn brush-popper's garb: fringed leather *chivarras* and a canvas jacket reinforced with leather patches at the elbows. Blue lightning lanced from his eyes and his square, bony face was weathered as brown as an Indian's where the tumbled curly shag of his red hair and beard did not hide it.

A jug stood on the ground. Rubriz bent and picked it up, pulled the cork, and tipped the jug to Rhiannon's mouth. He drank deep of cold water, sweet as Erin's milk, letting it stream down his beard and off his chest. Directly his burning thirst was slaked, he said, strong-voiced, "Pour the rest over me head. Ahhh . . . there's the ticket." He grinned through his dripping beard. "That's one thirst. Would you have a drop of dog's hair to cut the other?"

Rubriz showed a small, gray smile. "Maybe soon."

"Let me walk around, then. Work up me blood."

"Do not walk far."

Rhiannon tramped a slow, wide circle. As sore as his ribs were, nothing seemed broken. He swiveled his stiff neck back and forth, drawing in the sweet air of morning. Corazon headquarters it was. He had never seen the place but from a distance. It was a choice layout, for certain, a broad grass flat dotted with old cottonwoods and girdled by a cordon of low hills. The *casa grande* was a rambling, one-storied, white-washed building set in a shady grove of cottonwoods. On a grassless hard-packed area to the west lay a vast tangle of barns and sheds and corrals. A crumbling Mexican chapel with its distinctive cross and bell stood a little distance from the house. Probably it hadn't been kept up since Alec Dragoman had taken over the place.

That had been back before the Mexican War, talk had it, and Dragoman had bought it off a Spanish landowner whose family had held it for a century on a king's grant, and he had paid straight gold. Gold and the man's fierce, driving ambition had ground under what he couldn't reasonably buy off. Rumor had it that Dragoman had turned a young fortune by plying the slave trade off Galvez Island and the business had hardened his soul to iron.

Rhiannon halted, glancing now at Rubriz who stood hipshot,

hands resting on his hips. "Take the ropes off, Bernie. You got the hogleg."

Rubriz shook his head gently, speculatively. He was trim and wiry and dark as old leather. Not a large man, he carried himself like one without being aware of it. He was silver-haired and trim-mustached, with no frills about him. He wore scuffed *vaquero*'s duds, brown and all leather, and a flat-crowned hat that sat straight, with no crease or flourish, above his gaunt-boned face.

"You want to go to the outback, maybe."

"Believe I got it all up last night, thank you kindly."

Rubriz nodded. "You will bear the ropes on your hands a while, I think." He tipped his head toward the big combination cookshack-bunkhouse a little west of the *casa*. "There are men who will not go out today. They are pretty sick."

"Mmm. Combed a few of their coxcombs back, did I? I reckon they done me one better, though."

"It was not my orders. You got their hackles up, señor."

"Mansavage?"

"His head will hurt a long time. And the Tollander brothers. They are three, all in bad shape. I did not get on the scene fast enough. So they did a job on you." His tone was not unfriendly. "Man, even if I hold the *pistola*, you are too much of a bull to trust with your hands loose. But we let the *mayordomo* say." He motioned toward the *casa*. "*Ándale*, now."

Rhiannon spat. "Let the bastard walk here to say his piece."

"That he cannot. You did not know? Two years ago there was an accident. A wagon overturned. His legs were crushed. Mr. Dragoman does not walk now."

"Well, then." Rhiannon made no effort to conceal his pleasure. "The morning has a better taste than I knew. Lead on, old man."

"You lead," Rubriz said politely.

They tramped toward the *casa* and were passing near an outback when a young man came out, buttoning his pants. Rubriz came to a halt, eyeing him. It was curious how they watched each other, like a pair of stiff-necked dogs.

"My dear *bastardo*," Rubriz said in a voice of hatred. "*Por favor*, will you tell the curly wolf who leads your pack to come

to the *casa*? When Mr. Dragoman sees this man, I think he will
want to see Herb."

For a moment the ranch hand stood unmoving. He was a
slim whiplash of a youth in shabby puncher's clothes, his face
so ruddy from sunburn that maybe it never tanned healthily.
His eyes were the palest of wintry blue in the shadow of his hat
and the hair that showed under it was dead white.

"All right," he said mildly.

"A hundred thanks, *bastardo*."

"There's no call for that, Mr. Rubriz." The same mild tone.

"Is there not? It fits so well." Rubriz barked a short, ugly
laugh. He glanced at Rhiannon. "Blanco, they call this one.
That fits, too. Look at him. A bleached bone could not be
whiter. Or a snake's belly. Note the gun. He cannot go to take a
shit without the big gun on his hip. Do you take it off to shit,
*muchacho*?"

If Blanco's face flushed at all, it was hard to tell. He didn't
turn a hair otherwise, only wheeled and headed for the
bunkhouse. An evil tongue, thought Rhiannon, that you'd not
think a man of Rubriz's quiet-spoken caliber would use on
another man, even one of Mansavage's.

"And, *bastardo*," Rubriz called after him, "ask him where
Wilsie's snake is, eh? We will all wait to hear that."

Rhiannon murmured, "Snake?" as he and Rubriz walked
on.

"Wilsie Tollander keeps a small rattler in a big glass jar. He
has a game. If a man can hold his hand on the jar while the
snake stikes at it, Wilsie will pay him five dollars. If he cannot,
the man pays Wilsie. Maybe now he has only the glass jar."

"And why's that?"

"You kicked Wilsie's teeth in last night."

They went through the cottonwood grove and entered an
enclosed patio, the old stone walls of which bore the
unmistakable scars of besiegers' bullets, probably from a time
when the domain of the warring tribes had extended a lot
farther than it did now. Double doors, opened for the morning
warmth, led into the grand *sala*. It was a large room with big
comfortable furnishings of mixed Spanish and Anglo design.
Everything looked expensive but comfortably worn and home-
like. There were concessions to a woman's taste in the fancy

harpsichord and delicate pottery and the floral designs in some scattered carpets.

Mostly, though, it was a man's room, dominated by the stamp of one man's passion on the walls mounted with big-game heads of puma, jaguar, buffalo, grizzly, and bighorn sheep: the taste of a man who had ranged long and far to bag his trophies. There was also a collection of weapons, from old cutlasses and flintlock pistols and matchlock arquebuses to modern revolvers and hand-crafted rifles of an immense killing power.

The man all of it reflected did not look the part. Not any longer he didn't. Rhiannon had never seen Alec Dragoman up close and the sight of him now was a bit of a jolt. You expected a big fellow, and he was broad enough in the shoulders and chest. But most of the flesh had melted and gone to a suety paunch. His hands, clasped on the arms of his wheelchair, were shrunken so that the tendons stood out beneath the liver spotted skin.

Dragoman's face was slack at the jowls, though well browned from much sunning. If he was a husk or a near husk of the man he'd been, there was still a florid, well-fed alertness about him. Otherwise he wasn't what Rhiannon had expected. His features were small and fine in his big face. His pleasant brown eyes and thick shock of white hair almost gave him a look of spurious saintliness. He didn't appear particularly shrewd, just careful and appraising in the way he sized a man up.

Rhiannon hauled up in the middle of the room. "Top o' the morning, Mr. Drag-old-ass-man," he said cheerily. "Appears you'll not even be dragging it any longer."

Dragoman's gaze moved to Rubriz. "He's marked up quite a bit, wouldn't you say, Number Two? I told you to go easy."

"That was my order, *mayordomo*. He was hard to take. Some men got rough."

"What men?"

"Herb and the Tollanders."

"I want to see Herb."

Rubriz explained that Blanco had been given that message already. And he thought Herb would bring along the Tollanders, too. Last night a rattlesnake had somehow got into the dugout with Rhiannon.

"By accident?"

"It may be," said Rubriz. "Wilsie Tollander lost his front teeth taking this man. I don't know of anyone but Wilsie who keeps a rattlesnake near to hand."

Dragoman turned his mild gaze back to Rhiannon. "I ordered you put in the dugout so you'd have a time to think about things, son. The snake wasn't part of it."

"Thank you kindly. Cold and dirt and dark do stir up a man's thoughts. So does being trussed up as for a slaughter. I'll thank you again if you order my hands freed."

"If I have your word to hear me out and not create a ruckus. Not while you're under this roof."

Rhiannon hesitated only a moment. In this country a man's word was his bond, even coming from, or given to, a Dragoman. "Aye, if I've got yours that I'll leave this place of my own will with a good horse under me and no more pretty marks on me."

"All right. Number Two?"

Rubriz cut Rhiannon's hands free and he stood for a moment rubbing his wrists, getting the blood back and letting his gaze move to a mammoth walnut sideboard. He walked to it, picked up a wide, cut-glass decanter, pulled the stopper, and tipped it to his mouth, throwing his head back. When he set the decanter down, its whiskey level was lower by an inch.

"Agh." He blinked and smiled at his host. "An eye-opener fit for a king. Or even a son of a bitch if he can afford it. There's an auspicious start, Mr. Dragoman; your poteen don't turn my stomach. But I fear you're wasting your time."

"I don't reckon I am, son." Dragoman's voice held a benign patience. "A question, first. How are my daughter and the Rubriz girl likely to fare at the hands of them red niggers?"

Rhiannon glanced at Rubriz, who nodded quietly. ""Señorita Dragoman's companion was my daughter, Consuelo. It is my interest in this, if you wondered."

"I wondered." Rhiannon combed a hand through his matted beard. "Why, both will be worked hard. Handled a mite roughly, it may be. But not ill-used otherwise."

Both Dragoman and Rubriz were silent, eyeing him with a hard expectancy.

Rhiannon shrugged. "Not raped, then, if you need it said. To spare themselves rough going, they might find it convenient to be married soon. If they're comely, they'll not wait long."

He expected Dragoman to say something like "What, to a damned stinking savage?" but he only tapped his fingers on the wheelchair arms, looking thoughtful. Rubriz's face did not change.

"After young Warrington left you," Dragoman said, "he gave Number Two here your answer in more or less your own words."

"Well, I thought Bernie and the boys might've been waiting not far off," Rhiannon said dryly. "Sakes alive, gentlemen, but you want your precious wenches back something fierce. I've a curiosity as to why you'd think this'd turn the trick if the limey's wealth wouldn't."

"Well, son, money ain't all that makes the world turn. There's other considerations. Family, for instance. Eh, Number Two?"

Rubriz was building a cigarette. He took out a tinder cord and flint and a steel *eslabón*. He neatly struck a spark into the tinder cord, blew it to a fine coal, and lit his cigarette. His eyes lifted to Rhiannon's.

"That is right, man. The *mayordomo* and I each have a daughter. You—"

Spurred boots rang on the patio flagstone. Herb Mansavage came in, followed by three men. Herb had a bandanna tied around his scalp and was hatless. The other three took their hats off. They all halted in the room, standing a little apart, and only Mansavage didn't appear discomfitted.

"Hey, Rhiannon," he said genially. "How's your head this morning, boy? Mine's sorer than a big ol' bear with coal oil under his tail. Or, say, what about your back? How's that doing? How's that ol' brand?"

Rhiannon rumbled a chuckle. "Brand's a bit poorly, Herb. Aches a wee when the weather turns. But the back, there's a beautiful thing. Want a squint at it? Or have ye had breakfast?"

"Oh, man. Hey, that's prime." Mansavage laughed heartily. He slung a leg over a sofa arm and sat at his ease, a big man with a broadly handsome face, insolent yellow eyes, and a fine white smile. His long mane of yellow hair fanned over his shirt collar.

"Herb," Dragoman said gently, "right now I want a curb on your tongue except for giving out answers. All right?"

"Sure, Mr. Dragoman."

"I told you in plain English how I wanted Rhiannon fetched here. Lay hold of him amd tie him fast. Nothing rough. You had eight men at your back, your four and four of mine, counting Number Two. You was under his orders and mine. Now you tell me how all of you couldn't take one man without chopping him up raw. I'd admire to hear that."

Mansavage lifted and settled his shoulders. "He's an ole woolywhyhow, Mr. Dragoman. Took as much to bring him down."

"Did it? After a man's down, how many boots in the head does it take to keep him down?"

"Don't forget the rest o' me, Herb," Rhiannon put in, grinning. "That's some piece o' territory you covered, lad."

Mansavage shifted his butt on the sofa arm, glancing at the three Tollanders. "Don't allow I used no boots. Frank and Duane and Wilsie, they went a mite on the peck. Frank got cut bad and Wilsie lost some teeth and Duane's arm . . . Well, you see what he done, Mr. Dragoman. I had a time dragging 'em off."

Dragoman sized up the brothers, nodding slowly. Frank Tollander had walked in gingerly, and he kept a hand pressed to his side. He was bleach-eyed and gaunt as a famine wolf. Duane was chunkily built, pale-eyed, too, and his right sleeve was thick with bandage wrapping from elbow to shoulder. Wilsie, the youngest, was halfway in size between his brothers. His lower face was purpled and puffy with a vast bruise. All three were unshaven and bleary-eyed from lack of sleep.

"Them was pretty mean doings he fetched us, Mr. Dragoman," Frank said in a drawling, guarded twang. It labeled the Tollanders as plain as paint: Old South hill trash, the kin-crazy kind that clung together like burrs.

"About your pet snake," Mansavage said. "You got some'at to tell us about that, Wilsie?"

"Wilsie's mouth ain't fixed for talking," Frank said. "All

right, he eased ol' Curly, that's the snake, into the burrow with this here mick. Duane and me went along. You get to fetching blame, you fetch us all three."

Dragoman lightly drummed the knuckles of his right hand on the chair arm. "You knew what was at stake, all three of you. If that pet of yours had bit this man, he maybe wouldn't die—"

"That's for a fact," Mansavage put in . "Hell, you ever hear of rattler pizen killing a man? Might take him sick for a spell—"

"I told you just answers, Herb. Otherwise shut up." Dragoman didn't take his eyes off the Tollanders. "That's right. Damned sick and maybe for a damned long spell. I don't want this man laid up even a day. Number Two, pay these bastards off. Then send 'em packing out of here. On foot. Frank, you listen. You or your brothers ever show your faces inside ten miles of the Corazon again, you're dead. You hear me? You'll be shot on sight. Now get out. Herb, you stay."

Bernal Rubriz made a curt motion of his hand. Wordlessly, the Tollanders trooped out the door, Rubriz following them.

"Herb, take out your gun and hold it on Rhiannon. See you keep a distance from him."

Mansavage said softly, "Yes, sir," and stood up, slipping his Colt from its holster with a professional ease. His yellow eyes were as alert as a cat's.

Dragoman said to Rhiannon, "We were talking about family, I believe, son." He turned his head, raising his voice for the first time. "Margarita! Bring 'em in now!"

Rhiannon turned his eyes toward a dark corridor leading off the *sala*. A clot of phlegmy dread lifted in his throat even before the Mexican woman appeared in the entrance with the two children in tow.

Both cried "Papa!" and tried to break away. But the tall, lean woman had a grip on the wrist of each and she kept it tight against their struggles.

They hadn't been harmed. That's what he thought of first and it was all that held Rhiannon still in his tracks. His big frame gathered, he hung forward on the balls of his feet, and then settled his weight back slowly.

Norabeth's small brown face was streaked with tears. Cully

was dry-eyed, though his lower lip trembled. But neither made another sound. They strained quietly against the woman's hold, their large dark eyes fixed on him, and that was all.

Good, strong kids, both. Even in this. They would need all the toughness he and Naduah had bequeathed them, and he knew it would be enough. They could take it. But God, *could he?*

"Take the children back to their rooms. Lock the door and stay with them." Dragoman's voice was gently matter-of-fact, as if he were commenting on the weather. The Mexican woman turned, her stern face without expression, and whisked the kids out of Rhiannon's sight.

He could feel the black killing rage filling him, turning to a quivering white-hot, and he fought it with all his will. Now, of all times, he could not let it wipe out his rational mind. In his youth he'd been long in coming to that discipline. It had taken a lot of switchings by his father's strong arm to instill it. "Learn not to act till you think," the old man had patiently told him after each larruping. And he'd learned. A few times after, his temper had still slipped. But rarely.

Now, of all times, it must not.

"What will ye do?" His voice was hoarse in his ears, as if from a distance.

"I'll tell you," Dragoman said. He spoke easily and evenly in the manner of a man saying a thought-out speech. "Your children will be kept safely in the *casa* until your return. They'll have the best of food and care. Margarita will give 'em outings, short walks around the place, each day to keep up their health and spirits. Several armed men will be along at all times. Otherwise they'll be confined to a big room with all the comforts of home. Margarita will be with 'em day and night, to see that no harm comes to 'em."

Dragoman paused, drumming his fingers. When Rhiannon didn't speak, he went on. "You'll do nothing that would mean risk to their lives. We will not harm 'em under any circumstances, but anything you try might get them hurt. There'll be a couple of men on guard outside their room, more men on watch outside. You can try it by yourself, you can come with men, you can bring in the law. None of it will make a whit of difference. Anything you do will mean gunplay. You won't risk that, son."

Rhiannon sighed. He rubbed his nose and shifted his feet, never taking his gaze off Dragoman, who was silent now, waiting.

"Well—"

"Careful how you move!" Mansavage said sharply. His grin was amused and dangerous. He deliberately thumbed the Colt's hammer back to half-cock, the sound loud and crisp.

Rhiannon gave him a brief, indifferent glance. He knew Mansavage would have him dead before he took two steps. One well-placed slug from Herb's big piece would blast him halfway across the room.

"That lass of yours must be something for a son of a bitch like you to have sired," he observed. "The limey said he was desperate. Seems you're a sight more so."

"You know how it can be with a man's own blood," Dragoman said. He sounded almost complacent now.

"Aye, that I do. Well, then, if I fetch your daughter back in fair condition, my children will be released safe and sound, eh?"

"Not a hair of their heads harmed."

"Then I needn't tell ye how you'll fare if one is. I'll tear you down, Dragoman. I'll wipe out all you have, all you've built. And then I'll kill ye by inches. I swear by God's teeth I will. And all the hired guns in hell will not stop me."

Dragoman only nodded.

"Now there's a question," Rhiannon said slowly, "if I can carry out this grand undertaking. Maybe, as ye seem fixed on believing, I'm the only bucko that can. The rub is, even if I can find 'em in all of Comancheria—and that's a mighty if—it might not be I can fetch your lass back alive. In that case—"

Dragoman broke in. "Then you'll bring me proof that you found 'em. A trinket, a piece of clothing, anything I'll know. That will satisfy me."

"Ye have it thought out to a fare-thee-well," Rhiannon murmured. "But a man like you would. Suppose'n, though, I'll not manage even that?"

"Then it may be a long, long time before you see your kids again. I can hold 'em for weeks, months, years, if need be.

And your hands will be tied. You can worry and fret, you can plan and appeal. But, son, just what can you *do*?''

Dragoman let the words hang in a dead silence. Rhiannon didn't reply. They both knew the answer.

Sheriff Mullen was a friend of Dragoman's from way back. The whole county knew it. They came from the same stripe of sea beast that used to ply the slave trade in the Gulf waters. Jack Mullen had influence that reached clear to Austin and the U.S. Marshal's office. No help there, either.

Dragoman was running no great risk in holding the kids as long as he wanted. Even if they got hurt, he could cover it. The way things were, a man needed just one powerful friend. Rhiannon had none. Not even a coterie of friendly neighbors he could appeal to. He'd played the lone hand too well, too long. And his word-of-mouth reputation as a Comanche-raised renegade had done the rest.

Dragoman said, "What will you need? Guns, men, supplies, money? Anything.''

"It's a firm temper I'll need," Rhiannon said quietly. "Right now my thinking don't budge any further.''

Rhiannon strode from the *casa*, heading for the corral where his horse was. Mansavage followed him at a careful distance, his gun ready.

"You are some shuckins, Rhiannon," he commented. "You're man size. By God, I'm sorry for this.''

Rhiannon made an obscene sound with his tongue and teeth.

"Hey, boy, I mean it. I ever tangle with you again, I'd like it to be straight up, just you 'n' me. Man to man.''

Looking straight ahead as he tramped on, Rhiannon gave an icy chuckle. "You don't know what sorry is, Herb. Not yet, you don't. When the time comes ripe, I'll be obliging you. That's a promise.''

# CHAPTER FOUR

**I**T WAS PAST NOON WHEN RHIANNON TOPPED A SHALLOW rise of hills and saw the headquarters layout of his own MR ranch on the flats beyond. The buildings had a silent and deserted look, and by now he was filled with a deep worry for his two tough crewmen. Earlier, they had taken second place to his overriding concern for the kids. But the Corazon men couldn't have gotten to Norabeth and Cully without getting past Elugio and Opie.

Adobe wasn't common to this part of west Texas, any more than large building timbers were. MR's buildings had been laboriously constructed of big rocks hauled to the site, built to last forever. For what? Rhiannon wondered as he rode Donegal past the outbuildings toward the main house. Feeling utterly used up, even his hot edge of anger dulled, he stepped from his saddle by the veranda. His head pounded monotonously; he was nearly dead for lack of sleep.

"Opie," he said in a weary voice. "Elugio?"

The door was prodded open from inside, slowly and warily. A rifle barrel showed and then Opie Childress's bloodshot eye. Now he came out on the veranda, rifle pointed down, a slight, balding, scruffy-whiskered man in his stocking feet. He scrubbed a hand across his face, blinking.

"Hey, boss. Caught me nappin'."

"Where's Elugio?"

"Inside. He's poorly. They bored him through the side. Bullet went clean through and not too far in. Be laid up a spell, though." Opie blinked again. "Boss, they done a woolly-balled wowser on you."

Rhiannon said grimly, "In more ways than one," and tramped inside. Elugio was in the back room where he and Opie had their bunks. Lying on his blankets, the aging Mexican's face looked frail to gauntness. Fever burned in his cheeks and varnished his eyes.

"*Jefe*, they take the little ones."

"I know."

"Done it by surprise," Opie said. "Busted in through the door a-sudden. We got took before we knowed it. Elugio went for his smokehole. Damn lucky he ain't dead."

"That is nothing," said Elugio huskily, "if I take one dirty Corazon *puerco* with me. I could not."

Rhiannon slumped down onto a bench and scraped a callused palm over his face, trying to grind awareness back into his sluggish brain. Blood crusted on his cheeks and beard powdered away; his own smell was rank in his nostrils.

Slowly, in a voice leaden with exhaustion, he told the two men what had happened to him and how the situation stood now. Before they could speak of what had to be done, he needed sleep. Opie said that he'd caught enough of it to keep watch while Rhiannon caught some.

Rhiannon stumbled the last few feet, nearly falling as he sought his bed. He collapsed facedown across it and slept dreamlessly for six hours.

When he began to stir awake, his first impulse was to let the fog of sleep close over him again. He was still sluggish, and every bruise and cut came alive when he moved. But the edge was off his exhaustion. Setting his teeth, he rolled painfully out of bed and peeled off his filthy, blood-stiffened clothes. Afterward he grabbed a bucket and a piece of soap and tramped out to the horse trough. He scrubbed his beaten hide unmercifully, sluicing bucket after bucket of cool water over his head. Finished, he felt as raw and tingling and edgy as a sore-assed porcupine.

Returning to the house, he got into clean duds and then hauled an old possibles sack from his commode. From it, he took a Sharps .45-caliber buffalo rifle and its loading accouterments. Rhiannon hefted it in his hands, getting back the feel and weight of it, memories built into his nerves. He hadn't used it in a good while, relying on his lighter Winchester to fetch small game for the table. Now he dug out his 1860 Colt Army pistol, which had remained in the bag just about as long. He checked it to be sure it was hound's-tooth clean, free of any fouling, then bit the ends off six paper cartridges and loaded its chambers. He drove the .44-caliber balls into place with the loading lever and crimped percussion caps on the nipples.

While it was still light, he would burn a little powder on targets. Besides testing his shooting eye, it would work off enough of his hard-banked fury to let him think more clearly.

Right now, though, he was feeling light-headed with hunger. Opie had laid out a sketchy meal of cold steaks, cold biscuits, warmed-over *frijoles*, and a pot of fresh coffee. Ravenous as a baby buzzard, Rhiannon ate his way through seconds and thirds.

Afterward he lit a cigar, poured his fifth cup of coffee, and mulled over what must be done. Comancheria was a lot of territory for one man to cover. Being known as a brother-in-law of Stone Bull might make him welcome at some fires but would, like as not, make him a live target at others.

Though the Comanches mingled freely at the big councils, members of one band even switching allegiance to another if the spirit moved them, the five major bands—Ponetekas, Noconis, Kotsotekas, Yamparikas, and Quohadas—had their violent differences at times. Stone Bull was no outstanding favorite even among his fellow Quohadas. The Comanches had both civil and military leaders, each one chosen for particular qualities. A peace chief won his position by his wisdom and kindliness and good sense, and only incidentally by his valor. Stone Bull was a war chief whose cross-grained social behavior complemented his aggressively brilliant tactics in the field. But it had won him few friends around the lodge fires.

Regardless, the obvious place to begin his search was with Stone Bull and the Quohadas. Even with the raiding bands out, they'd be deep in the Staked Plains this time of year, likely between the Palo Duro and the South Fork of the Canadian. A long way to travel through hostile land occupied by the southern Comanche bands. But odd bits of news ran through all of Comancheria like quicksilver, and the Quohadas might have the information he sought.

If they didn't, trying to find the Dragoman and Rubriz girls could be like seeking a pair of needles in a very large hayfield.

Rhiannon remembered the last time he'd seen Stone Bull, sitting awkwardly, white man style, at this very bench, his black eyes laughing as he'd pretended to scold his sister for serving his braves and him only coffee, never whiskey. Naduah had a healthy respect for what American firewater did to an Indian's sensibilities, and she'd quickly hide any suggestion of it when her relatives came calling. Rhiannon's neighbors were correct in their assumption that he entertained his Comanche friends when they were in the district. Yet he'd never given them aid or comfort of any sort when they'd come as hostile raiders.

It was no easy thing to live on a tightrope between two peoples. Only a man of stubborn and go-to-hell independence could manage it. Maybe only a crazy man would try.

He went to the back room and found Elugio fully awake and resting comfortably, and asked if the sound of gunfire would bother him any. Elugio, eyeing the Winchester Rhiannon carried and the Army Colt snuggled in a homemade holster at his hip, smilingly said it would be music to his ears.

Rhiannon went outside. The light of the sunset fading from the sky shed a sandy glow across everything, dulling dark objects to black. But enough light remained to shoot by. He collected some small chunks of wood from the open-sided woodshed and set them up as targets a distance from the house. Then he began to burn powder. He emptied the Colt at a chunk of wood at a fair range but hit it only once. He reloaded and checked his impatience now, firing slowly and carefully. His first three shots smashed the chunk to splinters. He scored on a second chunk with two out of three shots.

Opie, looking on, said, "There's some peart shootin'. Don't take a man long to get back the feel."

"Not if he keeps his mad damped."

Rhiannon felt better already. Just making believe each chunk was Dragoman's face helped. He walked off a long-gun distance and gave the Winchester a try. Out of fifteen shots he knocked over thirteen chunks of wood, missing the last two. Good enough. A man made a lot bigger target. Tonight he'd prepare some cartridges for the buffalo rifle. Couldn't know but that he'd need some heavy firepower for a job like this.

Opie wagged his head. "Tall shootin'. You must notion to fetch some tall game."

"Only the kind that'd notion to fetch me first, Opie lad."

There was a chance, the very thinnest of chances, that he could bring off this fandango by negotiation, without gunplay. But it was a dim hope. If he could even locate those girls, there was the problem of getting them away. Comanches didn't give up their captives lightly. Already Rhiannon felt a bloody fey premonition, the kind that gloomed many an hour for Celt folk of the old blood.

Opie cleared his throat gently. "Boss, that's a mean task you're setting yourself. Might be needing a man to side you."

"I won't. It's best undertaken by a man alone. You'll be needed here, Opie, to look after Elugio and the place. But I thank you for the offer. Would ye set up them targets again?"

After pacing back to Colt distance again, he tried for a bit more speed. He sent five out of six balls true to their marks. As the echoes died in the soft twilight, a voice said quietly, "Capital shooting."

Both Rhiannon and Opie came around on their heels, fast. Richard Warrington was sitting a big roan horse about ten yards away, just short of some thickets that had covered his approach. A loaded packhorse was attached to his saddle by a lead rope.

Rhiannon felt the blood thunder to his head. It took him a moment to find his tongue. "You got your damn and blasted gall, Sassenach! And that's a handy way to get a ball in your brisket, coming up on a man's back."

"Quite so. Same might be said of you, setting up such a racket and never troubling to check what's behind you." Warrington's tone was mild but not apologetic. He started to step down, then settled back into leather with a wry smile. "Forgot. A man doesn't 'light down' without an invitation."

Rhiannon's head was still congested, but he checked his first impulse. He said thickly, "First things first, limey. Did ye know about my kids?"

"Beg your pardon?"

Rhiannon told him in a few splenetic words about the

kidnapping of his children and for what. Even as he talked, though the light was bad, he could see a blanch of shock in Warrington's face.

"My God. I didn't know. That the Corazon men meant to take you if I failed, yes. But not that. I—I can't believe it. That a man would—"

"You got a few things to learn about your maybe daddy-in-law-to-be. Now"—Rhiannon began to reload the Colt—"you got an invitation, all right. To get the hell out of here while you're in one piece."

"One moment. I have come to offer my services. I had no real hope you'd accept them, but I hardly thought you'd shoot a man in cold blood for offering."

"What services?"

"Whatever you might require for your mission. I wish to accompany you."

Rhiannon eyed him, scowling. Warrington was wearing the rough garb of a brush rider, and that packhorse had enough gear lashed outside the pack to show that he was outfitted for a rough and lengthy journey.

"Dragoman sent a man to tell me he'd secured your agreement. No details, just that. I thought you could use some extra talent. It's my idea."

Rhiannon gave a hoot of laughter. "And *what* talent, pray? I need a goddamn greenhorn dogging my steps like I need another hole in my head!"

"Well, I'm a fair shot and—"

"Bless me. *This* I got to see. Do light down, Sassenach. The light's poorly, but . . . ."

Warrington stepped to the ground and accepted the Winchester Rhiannon held out. He checked its action quickly and expertly and peered at the targets. "Quite. Mind if I try for something higher, against the light? Say that farthest corral post yonder?"

As he spoke, Warrington brought the Winchester to his shoulder in a smooth motion, cocked the hammer, and fired. The bullet made a clear *thwack* of impact.

Opie whistled. "*That's* a prime piece of country shootin', now."

"Thank you. I aimed at the knothole in the approximate center. Bit far to tell if I scored, with an unfamiliar piece."

Opie loped off at a half run to have a look. Rhiannon squinted. By straining his eyes, he could barely make out the knothole. He spat at the ground and said nothing. Opie came back, shaking his head. "Dead center."

"It's a job I can best do alone," Rhiannon said in a chill voice. "Last thing I need is a damn greenhorn dogging me back. Fancy shooting's a small part of my need. Luck and experience is the most of it."

"No doubt," Warrington said coolly. "But one way or another, Rhiannon, I'm coming along. I'll follow you at a distance if I have to. I happen to be a fair country tracker, too. And I'm not altogether bereft of experience—"

"Shut your face," Rhiannon said wearily. "All right, damn your eyes, cut your girl's chances that much finer if ye wist. I'll have the trouble of watching out for you, too."

He believed that, but privately he allowed that a sharp-shooter of Warrington's caliber could be a considerable asset, too. Damned if he'd say so, though.

"Come along, then," Rhiannon growled. "We'll put up your nags and talk about it."

They headed for the holding corral that adjoined the stable, Warrington leading his horses. The twilight was furring gently into dusk now, fading from sand-colored to a soft purple.

"Can a man be asking where you learned to shoot? At Chamston-Hedding, no doubt, with beaters in white smocks to flush out the pheasants? Eh?"

Warrington smiled. "I'm an indifferent wing shot, I've been told. But I've hunted in India, Africa. Lion, tiger, cape buffalo, rhinoceros."

Rhiannon snorted. "From safely in a howdah on an elephant's back? Or a nice high tree perch? With white-smocked natives to drive the game?"

"Afoot in the bush, too. Veldt, savannah, jungle. If I didn't know better, Rhiannon, I'd swear that you're prejudiced—"

A shot crashed across Warrington's words. It shattered the stillness like a whip crack. Even before the sound was heard, a bullet kicked up floury dust against his boots.

Rhiannon didn't pause to check for the source of the shot.

Not even glancing around, he let out a roar. *"Hit cover! Come on!"*

The stable was a little off to their right, and there was no other cover nearby. Rhiannon veered for the barn at a run, Opie right behind him. Another shot came and it was close, smacking into the barn just ahead. A third shot came right on its heels.

The three shots had come from different positions, though all were close by. At least three assailants. Rhiannon's mind registered these facts in a flash. Thrown off momentarily by the bad light, they'd have the range in another moment.

Rhiannon reached the stable door and slammed it open, wheeled, and stepped aside to let Opie pile in past him. Warrington was yards behind them, tugging his horses along.

"Let the nags go, ye damned boghead!"

Warrington let go of his bridle, but he paused another moment to wrench a rifle from its saddle scabbard. Then he ran for the doorway, a clear target for the next bullet. But it wasn't fired at him. The slug bit into the door frame inches from Rhiannon's side.

Then Warrington lunged inside and Rhiannon dragged the door shut and spun away from it. Just as he did, two more bullets crashed through the door, square center to where he'd been standing.

Rhiannon murmured, "Stay low, both of ye. I'll look at the back." Leaving his companions crouched in the dank gloom and the sharp ammoniac stink of dung, he moved swiftly down the runway between the stalls to the rear door.

As he did, he heard a man's voice bawl from outside, "Get around back, Duane!"

Frank Tollander's voice. Frank and Duane and Wilsie. Any others? Not likely. This would be their private vendetta. Dragoman had ordered the Tollanders off his place on foot, and they must have tramped all day to get here, maybe in a rambling off-course way if they weren't sure how to reach his place by daylight.

If they get both doors covered, thought Rhiannon, we'll be in a trap for sure. He got to the rear door, wrenched at it, and swore when it resisted his strength, scraping slowly open against the packed-clay floor.

He paused, Winchester in hand, pivoting his head to the left and right, trying to probe the dusk. He saw a man's chunky form coming at a crouching run around the corner of the breaking corral to the right of him. Rhiannon pulled off a hasty shot at him. Duane pulled to a halt and fired back.

Both men levered their rifles at the same time and fired again. Rhiannon saw his bullet chew splinters from the corral's corner post; Duane's shot made a screaming ricochet off the stable's fieldstone wall. Jesus! Trying to take a bead in this fuzzy light was like—

A terrific boom of gun roar almost in his ear. He saw Duane flung over backward as if smashed by the fist of the Almighty. A mist of pale dust moiled up around his still form and then settled.

Warrington was at Rhiannon's side and he slowly lowered the big rifle, staring at the broken shape of Duane Tollander.

Rhiannon, his ears still ringing and hurting from the deafening roar, found his voice. "What in the name of Sheol is *that*?"

"A Martini express." Warrington's voice rasped as if his throat were clotted; he swallowed hard to clear it. "I've killed big game with it. Under night conditions. But never a . . ."

"That was no man. It was a sidewinder." Rhiannon shook him by the shoulder. "We'll split, then. You go right, I'll go left. Draw their fire, but don't show yourself less'n they do."

They moved apart toward the corners of the stable. Rhiannon halted and peered around his corner. Two dark forms were leaving the massed brush that bordered the open compound around the buildings, coming at a dead run from widely separated positions. They were heading at deep angles for the stable's front and side. If they reached the front entrance, the unarmed Opie would be helpless.

Rhiannon snapped a shot at the left figure, but it kept running. Then a rifle spoke from the scrub brush somewhere behind the Tollanders. The man on Rhiannon's side pitched forward, skidding on his face in the dirt.

At the same time, Warrington's express rifle boomed again. Caught in a crossfire now, the remaining man pulled up fast, then turned back toward the brush at a wild run, crashing into it and out of sight.

Rhiannon made a dash across the compound, skirted the

twisted body of Wilsie Tollander, and raced for the thicket
where Frank had vanished. He thrashed his way through into
the open and stopped, peering and listening. He could see
nothing and he heard nothing. More banks of heavy brush lay
beyond and Frank Tollander would be snaking among and
around them, making his escape. As had Rhiannon himself,
the night before.

There would be no finding him out in that black and gray
jungle of chapparal. Blundering after him to search, a man
would only make himself a target.

Rhiannon tramped back to the yard. Opie was edging
cautiously out the stable door while Warrington was coming
stealthily around the stable's far wall. Rhiannon called to them,
"Stay where ye are. I think we've a friend out there. Show
yourself, friend!"

Brush rattled softly. Rhiannon turned his rifle on that spot,
waiting. The man emerging from the brush was a dim, lean
figure.

"I am Bernal Rubriz," he called, "and I do not want to be
shot."

"You're alone?"

"*Sí.*"

Rhiannon walked to met him, and Opie and Warrington
joined them. Rhiannon felt a mite shaky on his pegs, and what
man wouldn't?

Quietly, Rubriz said that after he'd discharged the Tollanders
this morning, he had got to thinking that given their vengeful
natures, they might make another try for Rhiannon before they
quit the country; also they could get some mounts at his place.
The feeling had grown strongly on Rubriz throughout the day.
Finally he'd saddled up and set out to pick up the brothers'
trail, wanting to be sure.

"We're owing ye," Rhiannon said.

"*Por nada.*" Rubriz showed his small gray smile. "I have
an interest in seeing that you stay alive. But one got away."

"Frank," said Rhiannon. "You got Wilsie and the limey got
Duane. Now it's only Frank I'll need to keep a weather eye out
for."

"Reckon he'll stampede clean out of the country now," Opie

said. "Lay low till he can sneak himself a horse some'eres and light out."

"I might," Warrington said, "lay you a small wager on that."

Opie chuckled. "Seeing how you shoot, I wouldn't take no bet goes against you. No, sir."

Rubriz looked questioningly at the Englishman.

"It's a thing we've settled between us," Rhiannon said. "He'll be coming with me, the limey will, on the search."

*"Bueno,"* Bernal Rubriz said. "I have thought about it today. So will I."

# CHAPTER FIVE

**R**HIANNON SAT UP LATE, PREPARING THE BULLETS FOR HIS buffalo rifle. He did it all methodically, washing a batch of old spent shell cases in vinegar and hot water, drying them with flannel, checking the fit of the bullets and reducing the mouths of loose shells with a crimper, and setting the new caps. He worked smoothly and absently, out of habit. Meantime his thinking ranged afar and ahead.

They would be a party of hide hunters, he and Warrington and Rubriz. It would be the most believeable cover ruse to put across, though a dangerous one. There was no choice, seeing that the Englisher and the Corazon *segundo* couldn't be dissuaded from accompanying him; otherwise they'd only trail him up and likely get their hair lifted for their pains. On the other hand, both were cool-tempered and determined: not a bad pair to have siding you if worse came to worse.

Danger was, the Comanches were hell-down on the hide hunters. The buffalo was their way of life. Meat for food, hides for robes and lodge covers, and chips for fuel were primary among their hundred uses of the buffalo. For years they had smoldered about the inroads on the herds made by whites who'd collect three dollars a hide up at the Dodge City railhead north of the Cimarron. The great northern herd had been virtually wiped out by this autumn of 1873. Any party of hunters encroaching on the southern herd of the Llano Estacado, the Staked Plains, was courting sudden extinction.

Rhiannon's hole card was that, thanks to his Comanche upbringing and marriage to Naduah, he could harvest a small quota of hides in the Quohada country and draw only grumbling objections here and there. He'd done as much several times during the early years of trying to scrape up money to develop his outfit. Now he would go to the Quohadas as a supplicant, asking a special favor for two close friends—Warrington and Rubriz—who were down on their luck, asking if he and they might be permitted, later on, to return with wagons and the necessary gear for a small buffalo kill. Now, if the Comanches were agreeable, they would only scout the country for likely stands.

Ye'll be riding the edge of your luck even so, he thought glumly as he seated bullets in a brass loading tube, poured powder into its funnel-shaped top, placed wads of drafting paper in them, and completed the operation by tamping the slugs down gently with a ball starter.

Allowing that twenty rounds were enough, he leaned back on the bench, stretching his arms and yawning as he gazed moodily at the row of finished cartridges on the table before him. The mild snores of Warrington, coming from the dim corner where he'd spread his blankets, rasped along Rhiannon's tired nerves.

Rubriz had returned to Corazon to secure a leave of absence and to outfit his own gear for the journey. Dragoman wouldn't like it, but neither would he deny an insistent request from his highly valued *segundo*. Rubriz would return to the MR by first light, and the three of them would be on their way to . . . what?

Rhiannon let his gaze range the big familiar room, wondering if he'd ever look on it again after tomorrow. It held too many memories. The two kids, black-haired and brown as nuts and hardly favoring their daddy at all, cavorting in and out. Naduah moving quiet and graceful about her ordinary tasks. And the best memory: Naduah sitting by lamplight, her quick fingers plying fine-bone needles at weaving, sewing, mending, God . . . *There would never be the like again.*

Rhiannon's eyes stung as his glance moved across the pieces of furniture he'd painstakingly hand-fashioned, bright rugs that Naduah had woven . . . and the shelves of worn books that lined one wall. Reading had always occupied most of his few idle hours. He'd taught Naduah how to speak and read English with those books. Together, far from any school, they had begun to give the kids an education to equal any town-bred American's, one they could carry without shame into the wide world they'd never seen but must one day cope with.

Rhiannon cursed with a savage softness. *God damn the way things went.* And here he was sitting and indulging in memories when he should be getting all the rest he could against the morrow.

He blew out the lamp and went to bed.

In the predawn light Rhiannon and Warrington and Opie set to digging a common grave for Duane and Wilsie, locating it well away from the MR layout. With three men on the job, it didn't take long. They were setting the last stones of a burial cairn in place when Bernal Rubriz arrived with a packhorse. Rhiannon assembled his own gear, and they went over their supplies and equipment, balancing these out among their three pack animals. If the search stretched long and food ran short, they could always bag enough game.

By the time a full flush of sunrise was topping the horizon, the three-man party was on its way, heading for the place on Corazon's top range where Melissa Dragoman and Consuelo Rubriz had been captured.

Rhiannon didn't expect to find much there after a week's time. The track was no longer fresh, and Dragoman's riders, fanning out in futile search parties, had pretty well trampled what there was. Rhiannon's best hope was to find anything that might identify the Comanche band that had taken the girls and thus narrow things down a bit. They found nothing, not even a clear moccasin print that might have helped. Farther north of the scene, all sign had been wiped out by a drift of sand across the flinty ground.

Warrington had brought a map of the country into which they'd be heading, and Rhiannon gave it a careful study. It was a fairly accurate piece of charting by U.S. government surveyors, but it wasn't much help, either. He knew most of the places named on it and was mostly interested in the locations of military garrisons, which he intended to give a wide berth. The army had standing orders to keep parties of buffalo hunters or other whites out of the Comanche country loosely framed by the Colorado River to the south and the

North Fork of the Canadian to the north. The Brazos and Clear
Fork agency posts could easily be avoided, but they would
have to watch out for cavalry patrols in those vicinities.

They covered twenty miles by sunset and camped beside a
shallow creek. Rhiannon, who had ceaselessly scanned the
horizon all day, had twice spotted the dark speck of a rider far
to their backs, keeping a steady distance. He told the others
about it as they crouched on their heels by the fire, eating.

"That would be Frank?" asked Warrington.

Rhiannon nodded. "You'd have won that wager plain.
Didn't take him long to find a horse and other needs."

"What do we do?"

"A pity we cannot bait him like a coyote," Rubriz said.
"He's a *loco* one. *Loco* enough to follow each of us to hell. But
he will be careful; watch for his chance."

Rhiannon scraped his plate clean and wiped his beard.
"What we can't do," he observed, "is try to run him down.
Need the horses kept in good condition. They'll likely have
their fill of running later. Nor will I brook the delay it would
mean trying to lay a trap he more'n likely would smell out."

Rubriz agreed. "They were mountain people, his brothers
and him. Woodsmen. Very good on track, as I know, and Frank
was the best. He will not make a fire by night to lead us to him.
He will live on jerky and cracked corn or roots and nopal fruit,
if he must. If he comes for us, he will come like a snake."

"What do we do?" Warrington repeated.

Rhiannon weighed the question. "Camp always in the open
so he'll find it hard to steal up. Take watches, by turn, every
night. Douse our fires after dark."

"And if we get a chance . . .?"

Rhiannon gathered up the supper utensils, walked to the
river's edge, and hunkered down to sand-scour everything
clean. Over his shoulder, he said, "Kill him like a lobo wolf.
He's that, but with a human brain. Don't be forgetting it."

Three days of monotonous travel followed. The autumn
days were warm, the nights cold. The landscape was mostly
rolling and the horizons were limitless. Unending winds
combed the buffalo grass that lay brown and curling now with
sun blast and the summer's end. They kept to open country

wherever they could, avoiding hills ragged with brush. The only cover they sought for rest stops were thin, isolated stands of post oak and pecan and hackberry. Several times they saw distand bands of pronghorn, but no other large game.

Again and again in the distance, Rhiannon saw the lone rider pacing them. He was even warier than they in avoiding dense patches of trees or brush mottes, wary of ambush by them. If there was a way to throw him off . . . but there wasn't.

Rhiannon drew on an arsenal of tricks, holding to stony ground or following behind low ranges of high ground that would break the follower's view of them for a while, then cutting away suddenly. None of it worked. Along with his crazy, patient tenacity, Frank Tollander was as wily as a weasel.

Sooner or later, it must come to a showdown. More than once, Rhiannon was tempted to double back by himself and go on a lone hunt for Frank, just the two of them in an open field, one man's cunning against the other's. But he didn't. Besides the probability that Tollander's wilderness craft was a match for his, he felt an overriding spur of urgency. It would mean time lost, hours or even days; already his failed ruses had made for small delays.

They were three stoical men, but the slow knife edge of tension began to build in each. Rhiannon took his out on Warrington with an occasional remark of a brutal, baiting nature. The Sassenach was starting to wear fine, he couldn't help noting with satisfaction. Doubtless Warrington had never endured a sustained roughing on his bush forays in the tropics. Served hand and foot, a man could keep his fastidious ways even in the back of beyond. There'd be short marches from a main camp with obedient native guides and gun bearers, then a return at day's end to a hot bath in a canvas tub, a body servant ready with fresh linen, an excellent supper and tall cool drinks, a tented cot, and a mosquito bar. No saddle-sore butt, no dirt, no evil smells about the person, no composing one's self for sleep on pebbly ground that gouged every sore spot.

At sunset of the third day, they made camp on the south bank of the Colorado River. They were a worn, tired, dirty trio. Warrington took a bath in the warm river shallows but afterward had to climb back into his sweaty, filth-grimed, smoke-pungent brush clothes. He tramped around the fire, trying to loosen his aching muscles; he coughed and wiped his eyes. Finally he burst out, "Why in hell does the blasted smoke have to follow a man everywhere?"

Rhiannon, sitting on his haunches as he tended the cooking fire, glanced up innocently. "Don't trouble the man who's got the sense to lay down"—he nodded toward Rubriz, who was reclining on his soogans—"or the one who stays on his hunkers."

Warrington halted and looked at him balefully. "And why is that, pray?"

"Smoke makes for the biggest object around. A rock or a tree or a man who keeps on his feet, even if he moves. Smoke goes for a vacuum, ye see. That's you, limey. You're the biggest vacuum around."

Warrington came to the fire and settled down on his haunches across from Rhiannon. His face was boiled past its former ruddiness; his jaw was hard beneath a blond burr of stubble. "Your quaintly oblique way, I take it, of saying there's nothing inside me?"

"No-o." Rhiannon turned the sizzling bacon over with a fork. "There's worry enough in each of us, I reckon. We each got reason for it, Sassenach. Riding it to an edge don't help."

"If only I could *know*," Warrington muttered. "If only I could be sure of . . . anything."

"Well . . ." Rhiannon grasped the iron handle of the small skillet in a callused palm that was impervious to heat and gave the cake of pan bread a dexterous flip. "Ain't likely your lady has got her precious whatchadinger busted by a buck. Not till she takes a husband, that is. Y'see, the Comanches—"

At first speechless, Warrington broke in hotly, "My God, Rhiannon! Haven't you any decency at all? To speak of a pure woman like a—"

Rhiannon gave a hard snort. "It was what ye were asking, wasn't it, coming at it from the side? Words don't varnish truth, however it's put. I'm telling ye that most precious jewel of a woman's dowry is most likely intact. What more d'ye want?"

Warrington's mild eyes had taken on the cold blaze of blue steel. His hands were gripping his knees, and now they tightened, the flesh ridging out whitely, as if he were poised to spring.

"I believe," he said in a distinct and icy voice, "that you have a saying that your St. Patrick drove out all your snakes. In England we have a saying, too. That he drove out all but the Fenians. They came over here. You're a rotten Fenian, Rhiannon. A traitor to queen and country. Rotten to the guts."

Rhiannon had grown so accustomed to his casual baiting of the Englisher, and Warrington had accepted it so patiently, that it hadn't occured to him that in the long pull he might be rubbing a wildcat against the fur. He had gone too far. Christ . . . him and his dumb mick tongue.

Even if it wasn't too late, could he brace himself to make an apology?

Rubriz broke the moment very simply. He rose to his feet, walked to the fire, squatted down, and picked up a tin cup. He filled it from the bubbling coffeepot and held it out to Warrington, who didn't look at him. Rubriz nudged his arm with the cup. Not taking his chill stare off Rhiannon, the Englishman accepted the cup. Then he got up, walked off a way, and stood with his back to them, his shoulders stiff and high.

Rubriz poured a cup for Rhiannon and one for himself. He sipped his coffee and made a wry face. "*Dios*. Did you dump in half our Triple X?"

"No more'n what's needed to float a horseshoe nail."

"What are these 'Fenians'? People? Or are they snakes?"

"Irish revolutionaries in America. I ain't one. But a snake? Maybe."

"*Quién sabe?*" Rubriz shook his head gently. "That was a cruel thing, *amigo*, and you're not a cruel man. You and the *Inglés* are both men. What your people fight about, what does it matter?"

Rhiannon sighed. He pulled the skillets of bacon and pan bread away from the fire. "It don't matter a damn piddle of mouse pee, Bernie. Man gets harried, his tongue gets the worst of him. It don't make a flyspeck of sense. No more than a man like you giving his hire and his loyalty to a man like Dragoman, it don't."

Rubriz pursed his lips and blew on his coffee. He let his gaze idle roundabout, as if studying the bare, rock-studded, and lightly brushed landscape that would allow no enemy to steal up while daylight held. He looked again at Rhiannon.

"*Hombre*, the heart has its ways. Corazon, the very word means heart. I have lived on it all my life and my father and grandfather before me. For a hundred years the Rubrizes have served the people of Corazon. I have buried a good wife and two sons on it. All my memories are there."

"And so is Dragoman, now."

"It is a thing a man does not question," Rubriz said. "It is the land. It is there, always. It will be there when the *mayordomo* is gone. When I am gone. I am the last man of my line, and Consuelo . . ." He paused and shrugged. "She is a woman and maybe she will not stay. There will be a man and where he goes, so will she. But I will die on the land of Corazon."

"If ye live so long."

"Yes." Rubriz's eyes crinkled at the corners, almost smiling. "There is that."

The three men ate in silence. The shadows strung out as the sun flattened to a red stain and was gone. The afterlight would go fast, and they chose the night's watch. Warrington was the most tired—it would take him a time to harden into saddle ways—but he asked for the first watch. He was still hotly rankled, and Rhiannon guessed he'd better let him cool out a bit before offering an apology.

Men on a common mission couldn't afford an open sore festering between them and, besides, damn and blast, he liked the Sassenach. Maybe Warrington didn't like getting dirty, but, fastidious or not, he had his own brand of bottom and grit.

The fire had died to a mound of cherried coals. Rhiannon doused it with sand, then stretched out on his blankets and lit a cigar. Cocking a folded arm under his head, he studied the sky and automatically took his bearings by the constellations as he did each night, while just as unthinkingly his senses combed the ordinary night sounds.

The time ahead . . . how would it be? He hadn't seen Stone Bull in three years. Or Bull's little brother, Kicking Bird. The kid must be coming to sixteen summers by now. Both were good friends and there were others, too, whom he hadn't seen in even longer. Naduah's younger sister, Sumah . . . How long had it been? He and Naduah had last visited the lodges of the Quohada in . . . what, '67? No, '68, a year after Cully was born. They'd wanted their relatives to see their two kids, and it had seemed worth the long trek.

Sumah . . . Warrior Woman, they'd called her by then. Rhiannon blew out smoke in a quiet chuckle. There was a fine unfettered filly for you! Riding out on raids with the men, a practice not uncommon with Comanche women. They'd stand offside at a battle and shoot arrows at the enemy, often with deadly effect. Not Sumah, though. She'd plunge into the thick of a fray, a fighter, strong and active. How had she fared? he wondered sleepily. Had she taken a man yet?

He jerked out of his doze as the cigar began to scorch his fingers. He stubbed it out, cocked his ear to the soft noise of Rubriz's snoring, then rose from his blankets and stretched. Afterward he crossed to where Warrington sat in a covert of rocks, watching the faintly moonlit terrain. He was as alert as usual, a good man on guard.

Rhiannon moved up beside him and sank down on his hunkers. "I don't know how to say it, English," he said quietly, "except only to say it. I owe you an apology. And my hand on it, if ye'll accept it."

Warrington turned his head. His face was hidden in shadow and he was silent for a long time. Rhiannon was about to withdraw his hand when Warrington took it.

"I'm sorry, too. Afraid I'm worn a little raw."

"Well, I can rise and bow a bit on that one." Rhiannon took out two cigars. "Have one? It's a particularly foul brand of me own favor."

"Is it safe?"

"I doubt it." Rhiannon grinned. "You mean to make a light? Aye, safe enough in these rocks, if we bend down a bit."

They lit up and smoked in silence for a minute. Finally Rhiannon said, choosing his words, "About your lady, now. Ye needn't fear for her honor. I . . . well, the Comanches, y'see—and I was partly raised one—got different ways. The young people, some of 'em, get a sight loose in their courting. It ain't regarded as the ideal—they got marriage customs as fancy fine as ours—but some think it makes for happier unions, in the end, than the arranged ones. A man may ask the girl's father or brother for her hand, or they'll seek him out even, and the girl will be brought to him that very night."

"Interesting," murmured Warrington. "But not altogether 'loose,' even by our standards."

"Well, but a Comanche lad and his girl may meet in secret by night. No great onus attached to it. Only if they're caught together, they're considered married. No fuss on't, but there you are. And they got what you call taking many wives—"

"Polygamy. I've seen it in Africa."

"Mmm. They loan out wives, too, though only on the husband's say-so. Woman's got none."

"Interfamily exchange marriage. Of course." Warrington rubbed a hand across his eyelids wearily. "I know it's foolish to beat one's brains about it. I'll be thankful if she's alive and well. Humbly thankful."

"That's the ticket." Rhiannon paused. "What ye'll do best to consider is her toughness. She'll face hardship enough. Is she strong? Has she spunk? That'll weigh most in the long pull."

"Physically, she's rather on the frail side," Warrington said slowly. "But spunk? I guess she has that." A wry, oddly bitter note entered his voice. "Oh, yes. Melissa has her own peculiar kind of toughness."

Rhiannon said nothing. It was up to the Englishman if he wanted to say more. Or not.

"It was her supervision as she grew up, I suppose," Warrington said at last, almost abstractedly. "She received practically none. Her mother died when she was three and old Alec, believe it or not, was a highly indulgent parent. Melissa was a lone girl of her race and position on a great ranch. She had private tutors, no outside schooling. She became—is— willful and imperious in her soft, strange way. Hard to explain. A strange girl."

"But worth a man's strong feeling, eh?"

"I don't know." Warrington shook his head slowly, looking both tired and baffled. "Melissa gets a man . . . set up strangely. She appears to be an angel. But at times it seems"— he made an attempt at a faint, embarrassed laugh—"she's a fire-in-the-blood devil. And the fire's contagious. God help a man if it touches him. . . ."

"Hst! Drop your voice."

Rhiannon, his ears attuned to the night, spoke in a sharp whisper. His gaze raked the clots of rock and brush. "Something, Sassenach . . . something's not right."

"What?"

"The coyotes."

Warrington listened, then shook his head. "I don't hear any coyotes."

"And there's what's not right. We've got a night bird calling on us or I'm a liar. If we could snare him . . . that would be a thing now, wouldn't it?"

# CHAPTER SIX

**R**HIANNON TOLD WARRINGTON TO STAY WHERE HE WAS. Then he cat-footed over to wake Rubriz, quickly and quietly telling him that somebody was reconnoitering the camp. He meant to go and find out who. Best chance he'd have was to go it alone. If Rubriz would stay with Warrington, carry on some chitchat in normal voices, it would encourage the skulker to continue his stealthy approach. They'd never have a better chance to take him.

"So you will get all the fun." Rubriz's whispered objection was only half-humorous.

"Bernie, this is my kind of game. I was raised to it. So was the lad out there, or I miss my guess."

"Tollander, yes."

"Or a reddie. Or several. They don't like moving by night, but old Texas hands got a saying . . ."

"Yes. When the coyotes stop. All right. If there is a ruckus, do we come?"

"No. It might be a lure to draw you. There's cover enough here, the rocks. Keep tight among 'em."

Rhiannon strapped on his pistol belt; the big Bowie was already sheathed at his hip. He slipped out between a pair of boulders and bent over deeply as he made his way into the forest of rock and brush, a shadow among shadows. Ceaselessly he combed the night for every hint of a sound, weighing it.

The half moon shed a milky glow that cut mild contrasts between light and dark, but it was impossible to pick out anything for sure. Scattered patches of open ground and the tops of boulders were faintly pale; everything else was black as a bat's groin. He moved only a step at a time, pausing to assess the terrain, the noises of nocturnal insects, and found nothing amiss. His sole advantage was that he was knowingly on the stalk, while his enemy was aware only of stealing onto a night camp. The drift of Rubriz's and Warrington's voices was low, almost conversational.

Nothing . . .

A gunshot split the night, sharp and shocking. It was damned close. Rhiannon froze till its echoes racketed away. He listened for another sound. Rubriz and Warrington had broken off talk.

That was all. The one shot and then silence. The insects picked up again.

As Rhiannon prepared to move on, he heard a whisper of foliage. It came from almost dead ahead and not a hundred feet away. He waited till he caught the sound again, only nearer, telling him the enemy was still moving in and giving away his line of approach.

*Now I can cut him off.* Rhiannon went down on his belly and hitched himself along by his elbows, slithering between vegetation and rocks like the granddaddy of all rattlers. An aisle of moonlit ground lay open ahead of him and he edged between two clumps of brush till he merged as one with them. Then he drew up on his haunches, gathered and ready.

A man's dark, lean form came dead silent around a wedge of chaparral, bent low, steel gleaming in his fist. He paused, conned to right and left, and came on.

Rhiannon surged up and out and hit the man side-on with an impact that drew a hard grunt, grabbing for his wrist above the steely glint. The revolver was on cock; it went off in a lurid spurt of flame. Rhiannon bore the man to the ground, kicking and thrashing. He was slight but wiry, and Rhiannon, immobilizing the stalker's gun arm with his right hand, aimed to end it fast.

He smashed his right fist square into the face. Felt the man relax, only feebly struggling now. Rhiannon pitched the gun away and dragged the man to his feet. His hat was off; the moonlight shone silver on his hair and only a little darker on his gaunt young face.

An enemy, all right. But not Frank. This was the young one

Rubriz had called Blanco. Feeling a baffled anger, Rhiannon gave him a hard cuff.

"Talk, damn ye—and keep it soft. What's your business?"

"Yours, I reckon." Blanco shook his head as if to clear it. "Frank Tollander's been trailing you up. I trailed up Frank."

"Did ye, now. And where is Frank?"

"Back there." Blanco tilted his head. "I got the drop on him. He tried to beat it."

"Show me."

Rhiannon relieved the boy of a knife and picked up his gun, then motioned with it. Blanco retrieved his hat, being careful not to move suddenly, and led the way.

Completely nonplussed now, Rhiannon was ready for anything. When they came to a man's body, he kept half his attention on Blanco and struck a match, shaking off the sulphurous flare of sparks. The flame picked out Frank Tollander's face. He was on his back across a big boulder, his body arched over it, arms dangling. A revolver lay near his right hand. His shirt was soaked with blood, his head flung back, mouth open and eyes staring.

Rhiannon dropped the match. "Why?"

"He notioned to come up on your camp and fetch you. I aimed to stop him."

"Your friend, wasn't he?"

Blanco stirred his head in negation. "Frank was never that. Me and the Tollanders never set each other well. They been with Herb Mansavage a long time. Me, I hired on a couple months back."

"Hired on your gun."

"It's my trade," Blanco said calmly.

Rhiannon shook his head, still baffled and not much less irritated. "I need some answers that make sense," he growled.

"Long story."

"You got any horses by?"

"Frank left his a little way from here. Left mine in the same place."

"We'll fetch 'em in. Then you can talk a streak, boy. We'll all listen."

Warrington and Rubriz had held to their post as he'd ordered, but they must have chafed against the restraint. As

Rhiannon and Blanco came tramping back toward the camp,
leading the four horses, Warrington called in a strained voice,
"Rhiannon, dammit! If that's you, give us a halloo!"

"Halloo," Rhiannon said dryly.

"What was that shooting?"

"Damp your powder and build up the fire, boys. I got us a
friend. Maybe. There'll be some palaver. Let's all see each
other plain."

He and Blanco hauled up at the camp's edge. Warrington
touched a match to some brush laid for the breakfast fire. As it
flared up, Rubriz, standing warily with a hand on his gun,
hissed, *"Dios!"*

"You stay set, Bernie. This lad done in Frank for us."

Rubriz took a step forward, his stare burning on Blanco.
"What are you doing here?"

"Took a fancy to see the Llano Estacado," Blanco drawled.

"Blood of Christ!"

"Bernie, just cinch down now," Rhiannon said warningly.
"It's a damn sore burr you're riding for this boy. Seen that
before. Now I'm wanting his say on this, and we'll hear it
out."

Blanco told it in his mild, matter-of-fact way. He had aimed
from the start to follow their party and had waited to pick up
their trail on the morning they left. But Frank Tollander had got
ahead of him, and once Blanco had spotted him, he'd let him
stay ahead. Frank had never caught sight of him, never realized
that he was being distantly trailed as he was trailing their party.
Blanco, camped a way from Rhiannon's MR headquarters on
the night the Tollanders had made their try, had heard all the
gunfire but hadn't investigated then. As one of Mansavage's
men, he'd likely be shot as one.

Next morning, picking up Frank's lone trail, he'd figured
that Duane and Wilsie had bought it and that Frank still meant
to even the score. So he'd hung back since, keeping a watch on
Frank and waiting for him to make his move. It would give
Blanco a chance to prove himself a friend.

"To murder a man was the best way," Rubriz broke in. "For
you, *por Dios*, it would be."

"Didn't make my move till Frank did," Blanco went on
patiently. "When I seen him going afoot for your camp tonight,

I followed and came up on his back and pulled a gun. Told him to drop his. He rounded on me and I had to shoot. He got it straight up front, facing me."

"That's so," Rhiannon said. "Frank's gun was out and he took it in front. Well, then, we're obliged. Only why—"

"Well, sir, because Miss Consuelo's pappy would fetch me dead on sight otherwise. Had to wait for the right time."

Rubriz made a strangled sound in his throat. But he didn't move. Just looked at Blanco as if pure murder was still in his thoughts.

"What I meant to ask," Rhiannon said, "is why you aimed to join us." He glanced sharply at Rubriz. "Now I've an inkling, I think."

"This gunman *puerco*," Rubriz said tonelessly, "this whelp of a misbegotten coyote dared to approach my daughter. I warned him once. He did it again. I told him once more, and I would gut-shoot him."

"True or false, lad?"

"Right as rain, far as it goes," Blanco said mildly. He stood with his hands resting lightly on his hips, a slim and relaxed figure in the firelight. He seemed as gentle-mannered a youth as you might wish, but there was something about him, all right. Maybe his near-albino look and those chill bleached eyes gave it an edge. But it was deadly. Blanco might not be quite topping twenty years, but only a fool would read his sign the wrong way.

Rhiannon said, "And what'll be the rest?"

"Miss Consuelo and me aimed to stand up in front of a preacher and have him say the words. Mr. Rubriz didn't know that."

*"You lie!"*

Rubriz's face was mottled with rage; his neck muscles corded against the brown flesh. His fists closed and unclosed. "You lie in your throat, you filthy *cabrón*!"

"No, sir. We met together times you didn't know of. We have a feeling for each other, Connie and me, and we are bespoke. Mr. Warrington there, he reckons that's reason enough for him to come along. I reckon it's enough for me."

Bernal Rubriz moved quick as thought, crossing the few steps between Blanco and him, going past Rhiannon too swiftly for the latter to throw out an arm. Rubriz's bony fist swung in a short savage arc, and it connected. Fast as he was, Blanco was quicker yet. He moved only his head, turning it back and sideways, but it was enough to half slip Rubriz's blow. It glanced off his jaw, rocking his head a little, and then his left arm shot out.

Rubriz was leaning off balance with the force of his aborted blow, his right shoulder forward. Blanco's hand closed on it and whirled him partly around as his right hand dipped and wrenched Rubriz's Colt from its holster. His left hand thrust the older man aside; the gun blurred level in his other hand.

The gun crashed three times, bucking in Blanco's fist as fast as Rhiannon had ever seen a man work a single-action revolver. The coffeepot sitting near the dead fire leaped into the air, jetting black fluid. It had barely touched the ground when the second shot kicked it a dozen feet onward, still wobbling crazily as the third slug sent it spinning end over end beyond the rim of firelight.

Rhiannon stood as he was, his ears ringing. A shroud of powder smoke hazed away, leaving a bite of cordite in the air. *He could have taken out three men as easy.* Rhiannon let that thought settle in his marrow, then tried the first words that came to his tongue.

"Lad, that is plain hell on a party's one coffeepot."

"Got one of my own, sir. You'll be welcome to the use of it." Blanco held the Colt balanced lightly in his hand. "Mr. Rubriz, I'll keep this a little while. Mr. Rhiannon said you-all would listen. Can't get up much wind for talk if it's leaking out of a hole in me."

Rubriz stood flat-footed, his eyes fixed on Blanco with a glittery glaze. He was less than a yard from the boy, and neither looked ready to take a step back. Both were very still now, waiting, their gazes locked.

"All right, lad," Rhiannon said. "You have put on your little show. You got more to say, it better be to Rubriz here."

"No, sir. He will hear, but he won't listen. I'll say it to you. I'll come with you square alongside or I'll trail you some more. Either way it's to be, I'm going where you go."

"If it's with us," Rhiannon said flatly, "you better make medicine Bernal Rubriz will listen to."

Blanco hesitated, then gave a guarded, reluctant nod. "Mr. Rubriz, I know what I been. I won't be that no more. Not after this is over. Believe that or don't. It won't change nothing. Me and your daughter are pledged."

"She would have run off with you. . . ." Rubriz shook his head, his lips barely brushing the words. "I do not believe it."

"Didn't allow you would. I had no hankering to just sneak off with her, but had a sight less for letting her pappy gun me down. It would've been that way if we'd asked your consent, for I wouldn't pull a gun on you no way. Didn't leave us no choice. By now, if things 'ud gone otherwise, we'd be long gone from Corazon."

"Yes," Rubriz said tonelessly. "Gone off to your stinking way of life. I would not be dead. But she would be worse than dead."

Blanco lifted his shoulders in a faint shrug. He looked at Rhiannon now, as if for judgement.

Rhiannon sighed. "Goddammit, Bernie. He said you wouldn't listen."

"You believe this young pig? This stinking *puerco*?"

"Well, I know what I heard. It don't strike me amiss. Would a man hazard his life for a girl he hadn't a mighty feeling for?"

"It is the thing he is," Rubriz said bitterly. "Does a rattler change because it sheds its skin in season?"

"A rattler ain't a man. A man can change—aye, change his whole life quick as an eye can wink. He can if he's got a reason. A damn strong reason."

Blanco reversed the gun in his hand and held it out. "Mr. Rubriz? Here you go."

Rubriz was silent for a moment. Then he slowly took the Colt and turned it in his hands, gazing at it as if he'd never seen it before. Shaking his head, still bitterly, he dropped it in his holster.

"Now it is whatever I say?"

Rhiannon nodded.

"Then he will come. We know how he uses a gun." The red hate in Rubriz's stare was unabated. "There will still be afterward. If we both live, there will be time to settle this thing."

# CHAPTER SEVEN

**T**HEY RODE NORTHWARD. THE PLODDING MILES FELL BEHIND and the days settled into a pattern. The men did not push hard or fast. They made short rest stops and long noonings, always with an eye to sparing the horses. At sunset they made camp and split the night into four two-hour guard watches. In gray morning light they were on the move again.

Rhiannon knew the country and how to deal with it. Most important, he knew the streams and waterholes. His companions watched and learned, and they asked questions. He encouraged them. If anything happened to him, they'd need to know all they could just to survive.

They were an ill-assorted quartet, bound together only by a common mission, and the private strains between them canceled any feeling of comradeship. Rubriz's hatred for Blanco burned silent and unabated, and Rhiannon had a dark sense of being used by all of them. Still, the rough edges smoothed off a bit as time and distance crept by with a drudging monotony. Talk was the only way to break it.

Rhiannon rode beside Blanco a lot of the time, and it didn't take much talk to fill in the boy's harum-scarum past. He was of Tennessee hill stock, with all of that breed's toughness and pride and independence. His ma had died of milk sickness when he was two; his pap got killed in the bloody revival of an ancient feud. Blanco's large brood of brothers and sisters had been scattered to the care of various kin while he, twelve years old, had drifted and made his own way, most of it in bad company. He hadn't gone looking for trouble; it picked him up as a magnet did filings and he wasn't a kowtowing sort. You fought or you folded. Fighting, you took your bruises and you learned.

Blanco was polite and guarded; very early he'd learned to say little about himself. Mostly a man had to read between the words to cut his sign. But Rhiannon thought he read it right. The scarring and bitterness hadn't touched that part of the boy that wanted something more and better. He'd found it in Consuelo Rubriz. And he would take on wildcats to keep what he'd found.

Bernal Rubriz knew it; maybe he even accepted Blanco's sincerity. But he saw no good coming of it. And he would go the dead limit to stop it. Nothing would change his thinking.

That was *their* problem. It meant little to Rhiannon while the worry for his children ate deeper all the time. Suppose he was killed. Or they failed to recover the Dragoman girl. Even if they succeeded, what could he expect? Knowing that his action in seizing Rhiannon's children would double the bitter fury of Rhiannon's old grudge, Dragoman might decide to take no chances. Even if his daughter was restored to him, would he keep the bargain? Or did he have other plans for Mike Rhiannon?

Rubriz and Warrington and Blanco had played their parts in the action that had placed his children in Dragoman's hands. That cold fact sat in Rhiannon's brain like a stone, but he kept a mental fist clenched around it. Given the black turns of his nature, he feared it might brood into a bursting rage that would spell disaster.

It was Bernal Rubriz who put the matter to rest, quietly and simply. At the nooning of the fourth day, out of the blue, he said what needed saying. "*Amigo*, we took your children. It was I who gave the orders. I want to say I am sorry for it."

Rhiannon, sitting on his hunkers with coffee cup in hand, didn't glance up. "Dragoman give the orders."

"I carried them out. The stake was large, for me. I do not say I wouldn't do it again." Rubriz shifted on his heels. "Still, it was a bad thing to do a *muy buen hombre*. I am sorry for it."

Rhiannon raised his eyes. He watched Rubriz for a moment, looked at Warrington and then Blanco, who shook his head.

"It was plumb wrong. I been thinking on that."

"So have I," said Warrington. "Been wondering how to say

it, old man. If you spat in our faces, I wouldn't blame you. But there it is. I'm sorry as the very devil."

Rhiannon spat at the ground between his boots. Each man would do the same thing again, sorry or not. But Christ . . . would he have done different in any of their places? Would any man?

"Well"—he looked up and around him—"it's a fair and sunny day to be hearing the words. Only I'm wondering what they come to."

He told them what he feared for his children, for himself. And for their fate if the attempt to recover Melissa Dragoman failed. He laid it down flat and hard, asking for nothing, expecting nothing.

Warrington spoke first, quietly. "I cannot promise anything else. But this much I can give you, Rhiannon. Whether or not Melissa is rescued, no matter what comes about in that regard, you will have your children back."

"Yes." Rubriz spoke just as quietly and positively. "That much will be. You will go free with the little ones. I swear it on the altar of God."

Blanco only nodded once, slowly and soberly.

Rhiannon swigged the rest of his coffee. He got to his feet and took off his hat and batted it against his thigh a few times, dusting it off. He knew as sure as seasons turned that each man had given him a pledge that nothing short of death would break. He cleared his throat.

"A'hm. All right, now." He pointed with his hat toward the northeast and a rim of tan hills. "Boaz Tucker's post is that way. He trades a lot with the reddies. Tonk, Caddo, Comanch', Kiowa. Maybe he's gotten wind of something."

"How far?" asked Blanco.

"Maybe ten miles. It'll fill up our day to make it by dark." Rhiannon clamped on his hat. "We best be hustling."

It was nearly full dark when they came in sight of the squat stone buildings of Boaz Tucker's post, the largest of them showing window squares of light.

Boaz Tucker heard their approach and came out with a lantern and a shotgun. He knew Rhiannon, and his gruff voice held a real warmth, greeting them. He ordered a dark-skinned boy, one of his sons, to put up their horses. Boaz was short and broad, weathered brown as a coffee bean, his bushy chestnut hair and beard frosted with gray.

They were late for supper, but Boaz's still-faced Caddo wife heated up some cold steaks and beans and a fresh pot of half-chicory coffee. They sat on benches at the long puncheon table and ate while Rhiannon, between mouthfuls, told Boaz about their going north to look for buffalo. Afterward they sipped gingerly at the tin cups of pale liquor that their garrulous host set in front of them.

Bernal Rubriz said with a grimace, "*Qué es esto?* This is to take the bluing off a Colt *pistola*, eh?"

Boaz said complacently, "That's what I whup the stuff up for, ye guessed it," as he set a pitcher on the table and settled his bulk into a chair at its head. "Water there. Cut 'er if ye want." His shrewd gaze passed across their faces and came back to Rhiannon's. "Looking to cut buffler sign smack in Comanch' country, are ye? Now there's a case."

Rhiannon nodded. "If we can find Stone Bull. Need some good word to go ahead of us if we come back next spring."

"Ye might need more'n that. Army could be out in force this fall dustin' off red asses. Maybe not. Pret' late in the year. Once a ruckus gets kickin' up, the Llano Estacado'll turn hot as hell's hinges for any white man gets caught in the middle. Even me."

Rhiannon raised his brows. "You been stuck smack here since Adam was a pup."

Boaz glanced at his brood of half-blood children, four boys and three girls, ranged around the big room in the firelight, solemnly eyeing the newcomers. Boaz snapped his fingers and one small boy ran over to the fireplace.

"This child's never smelled trouble like what's makin'. Quaker peace policy ain't worked out worth a piddle of goose grease. Mackenzie stirred things to a boil last year when he run Quanah Parker's people out o' Blanco Canyon and took a lot o' prisoners. More come straggling in and give themselves up. Now the Fort Sill Agency can't supply the beef to feed 'em all. Injuns starving all over. Killing their horses and mules for food."

"They seen lean times before," Rhiannon said.

The boy ran over from the fireplace with some hot coals in a

clay dish. One of the girls brought tobacco and brown papers to
make cigarettes. Everyone but Warrington rolled their own; he
preferred his pipe.

"Right ye are on the lean times," Boaz Tucker said, picking
up a ripe coal in his callused fingers and holding it to his
cigarette. "But there's more. This spring the Comanch' joined
the Kiowa in their yearly Sun Dance. Ye ever hear the like o'
that before?"

"Not ever," grunted Rhiannon. "That's invoking the Great
Power. Mostly the Comanch' got no such use for such falderal.
Making medicine like that, they got something powerful in
mind."

"Sure," Boaz agreed. "Like pulling their bands into an
army that'll sweep the white man from the land. Ain't but talk I
heard, Mike. But I heard a heap of it these last months. And
the Comanch' got themselves a messiah now, too. You hear
anything of that?"

Rhiannon shook his head in genuine surprise. "Not a word.
What's this now, a Comanche Christ?"

Rubriz scowled. "*Maldad* . . . that is a blasphemy."

Boaz rolled out a plume of smoke. "Right as rain by their
lights, who's to say? This 'un's a young *puhakat* that claims his
medicine will turn bullets and make his followers soo-preme in
battle. Says the Great Power has promised if they rub out all
their enemies, the buffalo will come back, darken the plains in
numbers never dreamed of, and so on." His bearded lips
parted in a faint, sly grin. "Calls hisself Ishatai."

Rhiannon began to grin, too. "Is that some o' your blarney,
now?"

"Nope. That's his handle. Coyote Shit."

"Good Lord," Warrington said. "Honestly?"

"Or dung. Or droppings. Whatever ye wist for the translating. Shit's shit." Boaz puffed complacently. "What's doin'
down your way, Mike? Suppose that brother-in-law of yours
come down for Comanche Moon"

"It might be," Rhiannon said. "He didn't pay a call on me.
On some of the neighbors, maybe. You know old Alec
Dragoman?"

"By reputation. Who don't?"

Rhiannon reached for the jug of tiger tonic, poured some in

his cup, and added a splash of water; his movements were casual as he replied, "Well, *he* felt the wrath of the Great Power or some'at. His daughter and her maid were out taking a bit of sun when some Comanch' bore them off. No clue to what bunch it might be or where they went. Aye, the whole country's up in arms about it."

"Do tell." The wiry tufts of Boaz's brows drew together. "Wait . . . there was a Quohada and his family come in to trade a week back. He'd come from the Palo Duro. Braggin' on recent spoils of his band, he said they picked up an Anglo woman and a Mex one. Raiding way to the south they were. Didn't say much more. 'Ud that fit?"

Rhiannon shrugged and said, "Like enough." Sipping the liquor, he shuttled an idle glance at his companions. Rubriz's face was like brown stone; Blanco's was a mask with the color leached out of it. Neither, in other words, looked perceptibly different. Warrington, though, was struggling not to react and it showed some. He covered it neatly by shaking his head and saying in a splenetically English manner, "Jove, that's a damned rum show! A white woman in the hands of those bloody beggars! I say, surely you've gotten word to the army? If they know the whereabouts of the ruddy bounders, they can have a go at rescuing the ladies, can't they?"

"Well, I ain't exactly on fare-thee-well terms with the soljer boys. Tend my garden, let 'em tend theirs. Anyway, be a damned sight more to getting back that *white* woman, not to say the other, than you seem to reckon, mister." Boaz's eyes twinkled as he jerked a nod at Warrington and lifted his brows at Rhiannon. "Where'd ye pick up His Dukeship?"

Rhiannon grinned and winked. "Don't be letting that toffy accent fool you. Sir Richard is an old hand in the West."

Boaz, who could spout Shakespeare by the yard when the mood was on him and a few drinks were in him, said jovially, "Ho, then ye be not a peer of the realm? But high enough, I wot, that the serfs give ye a bow and a scrape and a tug of the forelock? Eh?"

Warrington let a broad smile break his sun-reddened face. "Oh, decidedly, old cock. Yes. Have to keep the hoi polloi to heel, you know."

Everyone showed appreciation at the good-humored

chafing, even Rubriz and Blanco bending their lips up at the corners. They had gained a pearl of information and it was time to turn the subject a bit, which Rhiannon did. He felt in a mood to celebrate a little. Well after his companions retired, he stayed up drinking and bullshitting with Boaz Tucker, who fortunately had a solid streak of Irish in him.

There it was. As easily learned as a turn of the tongue could make it. The Quohadas were at the Palo Duro and, it seemed dead certain, so were the two girls. Rhiannon felt the elation that came with sure knowledge but no real surprise. The range of the Comanches was vast, but the Palo Duro had always been a cynosure for council and trade among the bands, the more so since the encroaching whites had forced them into retreat and enclave.

Rhiannon was now willing to cast a loop of speculation wider: that a party under Stone Bull's own leadership had taken the girls. The Comanche Moons of many a year had seen the war chief directing his raids deep into the country where his sister and brother-in-law lived. The fact that he hadn't called on them in recent times—not at all since Naduah's death—didn't mean his activity in the region had ceased.

After leaving Boaz Tucker's, they took up the trek with a deepening watchfulness. By now they were in little danger of being sighted by Army patrols but faced an increasing likelihood of running into a party of hostiles. Rhiannon warned the others to keep a fresh alertness on night watch. They were bound to be discovered, but they must not be surprised.

Their first contact with Comanches was a friendly one. A large clan of Kotsotekas was on the move, looking for good hunting but not trouble. The two parties spotted each other at the same time, made signs of peace, and halted for a smoke together. The clan had just come from the Palo Duro. It was only two suns away. Rhiannon's gifts of tobacco and sugar and his fluency in the Comanche tongue yielded him a sketchy picture of the situation at the great canyon. Many Quohadas were there and, yes, Stone Bull's family was among them; and there was a band of Comancheros led by a white man.

That was interesting. Was he a Spaniard of the old blood? The Kotsoteka leader said he did not think so. The man spoke the American tongue, but not like a *Tejano*. His name? It could not be said in the tongue of the People. No white men's names could be spoken truly since they did not mean anything.

They traveled for the rest of that day and all of the next. Rhiannon's alertness sharpened with his recognition of the terrain, landmarks. They were well into the Palo Duro country.

By midmorning the following day they cut their first sign of buffalo. Before now they had come up on dusty wallows, plenty of track, and, of course, the ubiquitous chips, the plainsman's fuel. But now, coming over a low hill, they had their first sight of the great shaggy beasts. A small bunch of them was grazing near a pecan grove.

"God! Look at them!" Warrington was almost twitching with the avidity of the inveterate hunter. "American bison! The only big game of your North America I've never had a go at. Gadfrey, I'd give anything to dust one."

"Wipe off your chin, limey darlin'," Rhiannon said dryly. "There'll be no killing for killing's sake while I'm on hand."

Warrington was incredulous. "Do you mean to tell me you don't *hunt*?"

"For food. For a living. That alone. If you don't know what the difference is, Sassenach, I'll explain it to ye at a better time."

Warrington shook his head, smiling. "You're a strange one, Rhiannon. Rough as a bear. Yet, at times, as soft as butter. It wouldn't surprise me if you've a warmer spot for the lower orders than for your own kind."

"At times I don't find it a goddamn bit difficult," Rhiannon said. "If ye need a practical reason for holding gunfire, we're hard on to the Palo Duro and I don't want any action of ours to set off animosity. We come in peace. That means we don't show guns in our hands and we sure as hell don't kill a buffalo."

"At least not without permission, eh?"

"That's right. We—"

Rhiannon broke off as his gaze, never ceasing to search the horizon, found the string of riders coming up over a distant rise. They were to the northeast, somewhat above the grass flat that Rhiannon's party was crossing, and then came to a halt skylined, at the brow of the rise.

Rhiannon halted, too, right hand upraised. It brought his companions to a stop and also showed the distant party the universal sign of peace.

They were motionless on the rise. A party of ten—or a dozen. Wind ruffled their ponies' manes; sun held on their dark faces. They were not painted for war. The loaded pack animals suggested a hunting party.

None of them raised a hand in reply.

Rhiannon's hope of a peaceful encounter had begun to fade even before the first wild whoop drifted to their ears. One of them raised a feathered lance and kicked his pony forward down the rise. The others boiled after him, whooping, too, brandishing lances and rifles.

Ah, Christ, Rhiannon thought sinkingly. There it goes. If we live or if we die, there it goes for us in a trice. The whole damned mission . . .

# CHAPTER EIGHT

**T**HERE WAS NO REAL COVER CLOSE BY EXCEPT FOR A shallow hummock a hundred feet away where a prone man might at least make a small target of himself. Rhiannon told his companions to grab their weapons, pile off their horses and throw the reins, then get behind the hummock and belly down.

As they ran for it, the oncoming line of howling riders opened fire. Bullets kicked up clods of dusty earth way wide of the mark. They dived behind the shallow rise, crowded close, and settled their rifles on bead, waiting for Rhiannon's word to fire.

Coming in fast and close, the targets were easy to single out. As Rhiannon opened his mouth to give the word, the lead rider threw up his hand. The line came to a pounding, milling stop less than a hundred yards away.

*"Haint!"* the leader called. *"Haint!"*

The Comanche word meant friend. It also meant brother-in-law. Rhiannon did not recognize the voice—it was that of a young man—and he couldn't clearly make out the rider's face at this distance. But another rider was pulling up next to him now, shouting, too, and Rhiannon knew that voice at once.

"Redbeard! Is it you? *Kumaxp!*"

"My God," Warrington said. "Is that a woman?"

Rhiannon's beard split in a wide grin as he eased to his feet, waving his lifted hand. "Sumah, that is. Aye, she's woman enough for any . . . 'hem. Lay down your damn guns, boys, and stand up slow. We've run a rare spot o' luck. Likely they'll hooraw us a bit, so stand fast and stay calm."

A Comanche welcome was always predictable in its unpredictability, even if it was a friendly one. The riders' whooping had ebbed off, but suddenly they were yelling again, driving their heels against their ponies' flanks, urging them forward. They bore down fiercely on the four men, split apart when they were nearly on top of them, and then circled wide of them at a breakneck run, cavorting and stunting with a centaurlike grace. Dumpy and ill-gaited on foot, a Comanche brave was an incomparable sight on horseback.

Rhiannon stood hipshot as he watched, a lazy grin on his lips, but he didn't blame his companions for plain freezing to the spot. Just funning, his former tribe fellows were enough to scare a shitload of bejesus out of the bravest soul if he wasn't familiar with their ways.

Sumah was the first to rein up by them and drop easily off her pony. "Redbeard! *Kumaxp!*"

Her smile flashed white and fine in her handsome face. Sumah had the best teeth Rhiannon had ever seen among her people. Heavily fringed and flared, her loose buckskin blouse and skirt hid her tall, lean figure, but she moved with the grace of a young willow. The general height for a Comanche woman was about five feet. At five feet eight, Sumah stood a little taller than most Comanche men. As much as her height, her strong, even features made her appearance impressive, sort of like a female sachem of the tribe.

Sumah, always one to disregard ceremonial etiquette, showed exactly what she felt: a deep pleasure at seeing him again. And Rhiannon's own pleasure was unfeigned.

This somewhat relaxed the tense attitudes of several braves, strangers to Rhiannon, who were still eyeing the three whites and the Mexican suspiciously. But the others were already off their horses and gathering around, greeting him according to their feelings toward him, friendly or not so friendly. To them he was still the familiar "Redbeard," as he'd been since he'd been old enough to grow a beard and had refused to pluck it in the Indian manner.

A wiry youth in his late teens gripped Rhiannon's arm. *"Haint!"* He was the youthful leader and he was grinning broadly. Now Rhiannon could recognize him as Kicking Bird, his younger brother-in-law. The boy had grown up, but his impish demeanor, the moods flashing like swift minnows behind his face, hadn't changed much.

"My brothers are well?" Rhiannon said. "Stone Bull?"

"He will be better for seeing you, *haint*!"

Gravely now, Rhiannon went the rounds of final greetings and introductions, giving his companions elaborately faked names, gigging at his memory for names of the Comanches he knew, storing the new ones away in his mind. Comanches had names that meant something. Each had a secret name that couldn't be spoken aloud because if bad spirits got wind of it, they could do him mischief. But just the given names could tie a white man's thinking into knots. Rhiannon liked the liquid beauty of Comanche women's names but always found himself mentally translating the men's into English; such as Skinny and Wrinkled, who was an elderly brave, and Ten Bears, who claimed to have killed that many in a single week in his youth, and a phlegmatic fellow called That's It. In all, there were nine men and three women in the group.

This was a party returning from the hunt, as was clear from the four packhorses. Each was equipped with a double-oval rawhide packsaddle to which were lashed the butchered slabs of meat, wrapped in the hides. Sumah was armed, like most of the men, with a laminated strongbow made of layered strips of horn glued together and sinew-bound. The other two women, doubtless the wives of one or two of the braves, carried light bows of Osage orange, but their duty on this outing probably had been to skin and cut up the slain buffaloes and otherwise serve their husband or husbands.

One brave offered no greeting at all. He neither hung back nor stepped forward, only scowled darkly. He was huge and barrel-chested, not much taller than most of his fellows, but a near caricature of brute power. His massive arms corded and bulged with muscle, the fingers reaching almost to his knees. Naked to the waist like his companions, clad in breechclout and leggings and moccasins, he was unusually hairy for a Comanche. The men's facial and body hair was pretty sparse and most of them kept it plucked. But when you were as shaggy as Breaks Something, too much plucking was painfully out of the question.

Rhiannon had known him since boyhood. They'd been sworn enemies even then.

"Jove," muttered Warrington, "that one's a rum-looking devil. Nearest thing to a gorilla I've seen outside of East Africa."

Rhiannon grinned. That was it. Old Breaks Something surely had the aspect of a gorilla. He'd seen a picture of one in a book written by a fellow named Du Chaillu.

When he and his companions climbed back into their saddles, the Comanches prodded their own horses in easily around them, though they made no threatening motions. Some might count Redbeard as a friend, some might not. But he had come with others they did not know, and so a loose guard was formed around them as the party took up the trek toward the Palo Duro. It was not far away and from here Rhiannon could make out a fawn-colored bulge of rock that marked its rim at this point.

The Comanches had not asked why they had come here or where they were going. They were simply herding the newcomers toward their own destination. Only Kicking Bird was full of questions to which Rhiannon made evasive replies. The kid was brimming with teenage ebullience and didn't much care. He and two youthful cronies fell into a game of racing their ponies around the party, each hanging from his pony's offside with a leg slung over its back, pretending to shoot at the others from under the pony's neck.

Sumah fell in beside Rhiannon. They chatted in a friendly way about times that had been. But a kernel of good-humored tension lay between them and he couldn't remember when it hadn't been that way.

"So you are still Warrior Woman," he said. "I can see you have not changed."

Sumah laughed shortly. "Did you come so far to tell me that?"

"It is a visit to friends."

"Is it?" She gave a toss of her head. "And these others? Did you bring them to visit? Why are you here, Redbeard?"

"Those words are for Stone Bull."

"Maybe you will tell me later, eh?"

"Maybe."

Sumah's eyes flashed darkly. She was both amused and irritated by this sparring with him, an old story to both. Ordinarily she did not spar. She was strong and lithe and had a temper and did pretty much as she pleased. She was also completely tactless, overriding most rules of tribal courtesy, and nobody had to guess at how they stood with her. Since she was as handy with weapons as most men, hardly anyone ever complained—to her face.

Rhiannon said, "You have not married yet?"

"So many times." She held up two fingers, then bent one back against her palm. "Satank. You remember him?"

"He was a friend."

"He died in war. I saw him die. After him there was Paha-Yuka."

"Did he die, too?"

"No. He left my tipi. I would not bear his child. I beat my belly with stones."

That was the standard Comanche abortion, frowned upon because their usual birthrate was low. He could easily picture Sumah doing exactly what she'd said if her relationship with a man soured, and he didn't press for details. A question crossed his mind, and he thought it would sound sly but asked it, anyway.

"Breaks Something has no wife?"

"He has three."

"Long ago he wanted you to be one."

"He still wants it. That one will wait forever."

Yes. Breaks Something might have it in him just to wait. Rhiannon no longer remembered the cause of their childhood discord. Could be that being the two largest boys of their age in camp, they'd naturally given each other a wrong-way rub. Later on when they were older, no need to guess at why animus was preserved between them. Breaks Something had wanted Sumah and she'd wanted Redbeard, who'd preferred her sister.

There it was, thought Rhiannon. Always. Didn't matter if it was the height of Boston's Beacon Hill or the breakup camp of a Comanche band. Everyone wanted something. Let 'em fail to get it and they'd want it all the more and never let go of the hope. It had been a very special thing with Naduah and him, the sort of thing that lots of men and women never found in a

lifetime. Even as a gawky girl, Sumah had yearned to be part
of it. And she never could be, and never could forget it or
entirely forgive it. Neither, on her part, could her gorillalike
suitor of years ago. On that account, Breaks Something could
still hate Redbeard's guts.

And now, Rhiannon thought resignedly, now that Naduah
was gone forever and he'd returned to the band, nothing would
do but old wounds must be reopened and hopeless hopes
revived. Didn't matter what bloody mischief might come of it.
That was people. Especially a stubborn and single-minded one
like Sumah and a knot-headed one like Breaks Something.

Exactly as if she'd read his thoughts, Sumah said in a slyly
humorous murmur, "You could have had me, too, Redbeard."

Rhiannon felt the slow heat rising under his beard. Indeed,
nothing in Comanche custom could have prevented him from
taking Sumah as a second wife. And Naduah would not have
been averse to it.

"It's not the way of my people. Long ago I told you that."

"Ah," Naduah said silkily. "But you were of our people
then. Maybe you didn't want me."

"I could not take more than one wife. If I did not take you as
a second wife, neither did I take any other."

"Maybe you did not want any other. But you wanted me,
*kumaxp*."

Christ's blue eyes. It was true, and she remembered. He felt
a squirm of shame in the recollection of how he and Naduah
and Sumah would go off to disport themselves when they were
kids. On the surface it was mostly tussling and fun and
laughter, little that was too overtly sexual. But it had been
damned sexual all the same, and the three of them had been
intensely aware of it. Remembering, feeling his face grow
hotter, Rhiannon guessed he was wearing a high brick color.

Sumah said, "The ways of your people are hard ways," and
began to laugh. She laughed so hard that she had to clutch her
saddlebow to keep her balance.

Kicking Bird rode up beside them, demanding to know what
was so funny. Sumah explained and Kicking Bird broke up,
too. So did Rhiannon, finally. Nothing like having cuckoo kin
to melt whatever savage or civilized reserves a man could
claim. But there was a coiled tension in him, too, and he'd do

well to stay wary. Especially with Sumah giving the old familiar tug to his senses. Twice she'd called him *kumaxp*. Like *haint*, the word could mean brother-in-law, for which the Comanche tongue had no exact equivalent. But usually *kumaxp* meant husband. . . .

The party skirted the fawn-shaded bulge that cut the canyon rim from view and pulled up at its brink. The Palo Duro yawned away and below, a vast and precipitous chasm that slashed the plains for hundreds of feet across and hundreds of feet deep. The far end of the colossal crevice crooked away out of sight. Scores of tipis ranged along the canyon floor, far more than Rhiannon had ever seen at any encampment. From this height they were miniature pale cones and there was a hive of activity around them, people moving like ants.

Saints alive, thought Rhiannon. A good fifth of the Comanche nation must be down there. The Palo Duro had always been a place of council and ceremony, of trade and powwow. And now it may have become a stronghold of sorts.

Where they had halted, the age-old limestone cliff was broken down in a gigantic spill of rubble. Down it, a precarious zigzag path led to the bottom of the seven-hundred-foot-deep cleft. Steep and treacherous with crumbling shale, it was the only negotiable way down into the great canyon, Rhiannon knew. Indians had used it for centuries and so had deer, antelope, and mountain sheep, for there was water below.

The Comanches slipped off their ponies and stood waiting. The visitors were to go ahead of them. Leading their mounts, they went one by one over the rim and down the trail, picking their way with infinite care.

Some of the people by the tipis were moving toward them, their attention caught by the presence of strangers in the returning party. Ribbons of smoke from the fires were drawn along the cliff face by upcanyon drafts, fraying away as they rose, but the smell of burning mesquite and some cooking odors reached Rhiannon's nostrils with a rousing familiarity. He could even single out a whiff of dye stuffs being steeped in a cookpot somewhere. It conjured up an immediate image of his late Comanche mother squatting on her heels, patiently stirring a mixture of roots and leaves and trade vermilion.

It seemed like an hour, though he knew it was less than half that, before the uneven drop began to gentle away. The last two hundred feet of trail was a fan of outwash rubble. Finally they stood on the irregularly flat bottom of the Palo Duro.

The people who were curious had gathered at this end of the encampment and more were joining them. Rhiannon could make out only a few faces that were familiar and he knew it wasn't entirely because of his long absence from the Quohoda fires. Other main bands and possibly stragglers from the lesser ones were in evidence. God A'mighty, but this was one sweet passel of the Nenema to find in one place.

Some were jabbering eagerly. Seeing three strange whites and a strange Mexican, they were probably laying wagers—and a Comanche would place a bet at the drop of a war feather—as to their status: prisoners or visitors. Since any adult male captives taken were usually killed on the spot, the possibilities were narrow but tantalizing.

Suddenly a barrel-chested brave who was outstandingly tall for a Comanche, a strapping six-footer at least, came striding through the loose crowd. Stone bull. Usually grim, his face was now a show-nothing mask and in this moment Rhiannon felt a jab of real uncertainty. Stone Bull was nobody's fool; you'd have to get up early to run a sandy on him.

*Can we truly bluff it through?*

"Jesus Maria—"

The low oath came from Rubriz at his side. The Corazon *segundo* and Blanco were staring at some women at the front of the crowd, a little to the side.

"It sure is her," whispered Blanco. "For sure it's Connie—"

Sixty feet away now, Stone Bull's face broke into a welcoming smile and Rhiannon returned it with a rich, warm one of his own. At the same time, he hissed between his teeth, "Eyes front, ye goddamn chuckheads—or you'll have us all dead!" And he raised his voice out of his chest to answer Stone Bull's friendly shout of greeting: *"Haint!"*

# CHAPTER NINE

**T**HEY WERE ACCEPTED AS VISITORS, NOT PRISONERS. Nobody had to say so. A visitor knew he was one when, directly upon his arrival, a feast was thrown in his honor. Comanches had no set hours for meals. They ate when they felt like it, but everyone in a clan pitched in when a feast was in the offing.

During a brief ceremony of greetings and introductions, Stone Bull's wives got the pots boiling. The odors were savory and belly-tightening. Thinking that Warrington, Blanco, and Rubriz might be chary of the contents of the pots as they were served up, Rhiannon considerately identified the edibles by pointing to each vessel and saying the name of a food in English, then in Comanche. It seemed to the Indians that he was merely translating for the benefit of his friends, and nobody took offense. He was sure that Stone Bull, Sumah, and Kicking Bird caught on right away to what he was doing, but they'd only be amused by it, he knew. Three birds of a quirkily humorous feather.

It was damned good fare from Rhiannon's seasoned viewpoint, as he'd lived with the Comanches through fat times and lean times. The buffalo meat, wild turkey, and fish were fresh because all were plentifully available just now and the Comanches were consuming them at once against spoilage. The boiled corn was delicious, the vegetables, fruits, and nuts freshly gathered. Rhiannon filled his belly with gusto, seeing, to his amusement, that his companions were straining valiantly to show appreciative acceptance of the Comanche style of serving—Stone Bull's *pasaibo*, his chief wife, who was the

head cook and serving lady, fished food out of the vessels with
her fingers and solemnly dropped it into their bowls.

Everyone was seated cross-legged in rough groups. The
surrounding babble of conversation, gossip, funny stories, and
laughter meant that you had to raise your voice to be heard.
Stone Bull said loudly, "It is all good, *haint*, eh? After so many
years of eating as Americans eat?"

Rhiannon swigged the last of his coffee and politely belched
to show how replete he was. "It could not be otherwise."

"I hope your friends find it so."

"Look at their faces," Rhiannon said gravely. "Can you
doubt it?"

Stone Bull's black-stone eyes twinkled; he nodded with
equal gravity. "Let them eat on, then. We will speak apart."

His middle wife brought a vessel of water; each rinsed his
mouth and washed his hands. Rhiannon gathered his legs under
him and stood up, telling his companions, "Private powwow
with the chief. May take a spell. You stay set, hear? Eat up,
enjoy yourselves."

Stone Bull led the way to his tipi, a big one that dominated
the nearby cluster of Quohada lodges. No less than thirty poles
of skinned cedar supported the tanned and stretched covering
of twenty or so buffalo hides sewn together with the flesh side
out. The covering across the four-foot-high door opening, fixed
to its windward side with wooden skewers, was already thrown
open in welcome. Rhiannon ducked deeply, following his host
inside. He made a warm salutation to Stone Bull's youngest
wife, who was stirring up coals in the round central fire trench.
The two men sat down cross-legged facing one another while
Topah filled a soapstone pipe with tobacco, lit it, and handed it
to Stone Bull. He puffed briefly, informally, at the ornately
carved, hollow bone-shank stem and then handed the pipe to
Rhiannon, who did the same.

"Brother, it is good to see you again. Why have you come?"

Stone Bull was like his sister, Sumah. None of your
elaborate ceremonial preliminaries for him. Make it brief and
then to brass tacks. This, stemming more from self-assured
habit—or arrogance—than from impatience, had been known
to upset even his nearest friends.

Rhiannon, liking bluntness himself and being partly Anglo-

Irish raised, never minded in the least. He explained that he'd come to ask a favor: that he and his friends be permitted to scout the area for the presence of buffalo stands and, further, that if circumstances warranted, they be allowed to return with wagons, equipment, and skinners to obtain a modest harvest of hides. He realized it was a large favor to grant. Three times in years past he'd made such requests on his behalf alone. Now he asked for others. But these men were close *haints*, and times were bad for all of them.

Stone Bull handed the ceremonial pipe back to Topah. She brought tobacco and limp cottonwood leaves and a bowl of red coals. Each man built a cigarette while Stone Bull appeared to meditate.

Maybe he *was* meditating. Rhiannon suspected that his decision was already framed and his real ponderings ranged beyond it—to questions not yet spoken. His face was square and heavy-jawed, beetle-browed and not too short of ugly. You'd never catch a hint of what really played behind it till it suited him to let you know.

At last he said, showing his teeth in the friendliest of smiles, "I will think on it. How are things with you, Redbeard?"

"As I have said. The times are bad."

"I did not visit your lodge this season."

Rhiannon smiled. "Maybe Stone Bull was too busy." They were grinning at each other like Cheshire cats. "The soldiers have made it hot," Rhiannon added. "That is why you are all here. So many of the *Nenema*."

"You found us easily?"

"It was luck. We heard of your whereabouts as we journeyed."

Stone Bull sucked deeply on his cigarette and blew out smoke, squinting against it. "You know that we took two women in your country?"

Rhiannon nodded. "It was told all over. There it has never happened before."

"No," Stone Bull agreed. "There was never the chance. Like you and your friends, we were lucky. The women were riding too far from the *hacienda*. One is the daughter of Drag-a-man."

"This I heard. The other was her servant."

"Yes. I think it should give you pleasure, Redbeard. Drag-a-man did a bad thing to you many summers ago. Once you showed me your back. What he did you will wear forever."

Rhiannon shrugged. "Wounds heal, *haint*. Scars remain. Sometime I will settle this thing with Dragoman. I have nothing against his lodge people. But their women are their business."

Stone Bull grunted what might be a sound of satisfaction and lowered his gaze to his cigarette. It was nearly scorching his fingers; he ground it out. "The Mexican woman is in our camp. I sold the other one to the Comancheros."

The remark was casual enough, if sudden. His move of picking up the makings to fashion another cigarette was just as casual. But it was Rhiannon's face that he watched. For what? A tightening of the jaw, a flicker of the eyes? Any reaction at all?

What even he couldn't detect was the sensation of crushing cold in Rhiannon's belly. *The Comancheros!* Sweet purple saints.

Why was Stone Bull still riding an edge of suspicion? He might have seen the brief break of expression in Rubriz's and Blanco's faces when they'd recognized Consuelo among the group of women. Rhiannon had hoped so slight a lapse would go unnoticed, even by Stone Bull, in the pleasant hurly-burly of greetings.

Rhiannon let his right brow crawl upward mildly, quizzically. "Comancheros? The Quohada I met spoke of them. It is a long time since they came to the Palo Duro."

"They are here still. There is a white man leading them."

"The Quohada said so. And he is not a *Tejano*."

"No. He is an *Inglés*. Like your one friend. They do not talk the American tongue alike, but it is close."

"It is not the right order of things, *haint*. The Americans speak their tongue," Rhiannon said.

"Ah? Well, an Anglo is an Anglo. We have seen both kinds, a few, with the Comanchero bands. But before this we had not seen one who leads. It was to him, the *Inglés*, I sold the woman."

"It is interesting."

Stone Bull let a laugh rumble out of his barrel chest. "I think she would have done better to stay with the *Nenema*. But the trade was fair." He pointed to a low platform of cottonwood boughs that held an assortment of weapons. "There. The shiny new gun. I took that for her. It is very fine. Have you ever seen the like?"

Rhiannon singled out the Enfield rifle. "Yes. Very fine. The English make those."

His gaze shuttled back to Stone Bull, whose eyes were sparkling with sly humor. "Do you think it was a good trade, Redbeard?"

"I have not seen the woman."

Stone Bull laughed again. "Maybe you will see her." The laugh was wholly, and this time Rhiannon almost believed, genuinely friendly. "Do not believe all the things a brother says to you, Redbeard."

"I do not. The *Nenema* love games."

"It is so. A game to test you. But I was right to wonder. You have always been in a strange place between our people and yours. The American part is stronger or you would have stayed with us. I have sold an American woman to a Comanchero. Even if you hate Drag-a-man, you could not like that. We have our ways. With us, she would become as one of us. A few beatings from the women, but then she would wed one of our men and only he might beat her. Maybe her life with the Comanchero will not be so good. Eh?"

"To a *Comanchero*? To a damned lawless, murdering *cutthroat*?"

Warrington looked apoplectic. On the heels of the revelation, he'd come swiftly to his feet, fists clenched at his sides, staring at Rhiannon.

Rhiannon nodded wearily. "Aye. It will make our task much the harder. We—"

"*I wasn't thinking of that!* Oh, God. Melissa in the hands of . . ."

Warrington's voice trailed off; his hands unclenched slowly. He scrubbed one across his face in the grinding way a man might to rouse himself from a nightmare. A white, pinched look of despair formed around his mouth in his sun-boiled face.

Rubriz and Blanco were still seated tailor-fashion on the earth floor of the tipi, listening gravely. Blanco said, "I don't know a heap about these Coman-cherries."

Bernal Rubriz said with steely quiet, "You should know them. You would find a rightful home with them. *Cabrón!*"

"Mr. Rubriz—"

"Now, then," Rhiannon cut in ominously, "you agreed no more o' that, you two. By God, I hear it again and I'll be breaking a head or two. Remember where you are. And keep your damned voices down, way down. Tipi covers ain't walls. If one were listening outside and he knew a mite of English . . ."

Rubriz bit his upper lip, glowering. Blanco looked down at his lap and the pistol he'd been cleaning.

Rhiannon didn't blame any of them for breaks in their composure. The pent-up tensions of these past days had shaved all their nerves fine. For Rubriz and Blanco, a tantalizingly brief glimpse of the girl they both loved could only sharpen the knowledge of the appalling magnitude of what lay ahead, of what must be done.

Their horses had been turned into the Comanche *remuda* pasture; a tipi had been prepared for them and all of their gear brought to it. They would be honored guests of the People, and Comanche courtesy dictated that no limit be placed on a visitor's stay. Meantime, Stone Bull had vaguely reiterated that he'd think about the request. With any luck they'd have all the time they needed to make their plan and set it in motion.

And that was damned well it for just now.

For Blanco's benefit, and to give Warrington a chance to compose himself, Rhiannon explained who the Comancheros were. Not just Mexicans, as a lot of folks believed. They were the offscourings of various races and peoples—Mexicans, Americans, Europeans, blacks, and Indians of various tribes, scum of all stripes—and they were rightly regarded as the offal of the plains. For nearly a half century they had traded with the Comanches and Kiowas, giving them illicitly acquired white men's goods in exchange for horses and mules and cattle the Comanches drove off from *Nuevo Méjico* ranches beyond the Pecos River; the Comancheros in turn drove the livestock into Mexico and sold it.

Nobody knew just when this strange, gypsylike federation of renegades originated on the Western plains. The first American to make recorded note of it had been Zebulon Pike, back in '32, and he'd had no direct contact, just a sight of the deep wheel ruts left by the Comancheros' goods-laden *carretas*. They might have been legitimate traders to begin with, *ciboleros* or Mexican buffalo hunters who brought stores of dried meat, an important item of commerce, back to Mexico. Gradually they'd established trade relations with the Comanches, and it was the Indians' warlike activities that had turned trading for innocuous articles into a market for stolen livestock and other plunder. This in turn had given a spur to the Comanches' continual raiding against the border ranches.

At first the bands of Comancheros had been random wanderers of the Staked Plains, trusting to chance meetings with the nomadic Comanche bands. Then they had begun to establish regular rendezvous where the two people exchanged goods. Occasionally these included Comanche captives whom the Comancheros would hold for ransom.

Back in the early forties a Comanchero band led by a French-Portuguese outcast called Old Musketoon had made the Palo Duro what they'd hoped would be a permanent stronghold. A daring raid by Texas Rangers under the command of Captain Herrion had wiped out Musketoon's band. Thereafter, the Comancheros had avoided the Palo Duro like the plague for many years, holding their rendezvous at other places, most notably Rio de Las Lenguas and the Valle de Las Légrimas near Quitaguq, Texas, where the trade in white captives was particularly lively.

"They're a ruthless and wily lot of cutthroats," Rhiannon said soberly. "It's an evil hitch of luck, Sassenach. Bad that Stone Bull took a shine to your countryman's rifle, bad that the Comanchero leader took a shine to your girl. Bad you took a shine to her in the first place, if it goes that far back. There's a chance it's for ransom this limey wants her. A better than fair one if Stone Bull told him who her daddy is, knowing Dragoman would pay a pretty penny for her."

Warrington blinked. His mouth relaxed enough for him to say huskily, "That's true. Is it likely, do you think?"

"A body can hope. Pray if he's a praying man. But, lads,

patience is the word now. We say as little as possible; we ask no questions. Not direct, we don't. Leave that to me. I told ye Comanches don't rape or torture as a rule. But I've known exceptions. I'm thinking Stone Bull's suspicions are allayed. Doesn't mean he won't keep his eyes and ears open, you can bet. Let him catch a hint of what we're really about here, and God help us. You, Bernie. And Blanco. I'd not know your girl if I saw her. But she, by God, had the sense to show nothing when you near spilled it. Don't you be seeking her out. We'll go slow. Watch and wait. Lay our plans with care. When the time's right, when I tell ye, we'll all break out under their noses."

A fair speech to the troops. Words to brace them for what Rhiannon wasn't half sure himself could be done. And even if they didn't believe it, either, it seemed to settle their spirits. All three men nodded, keeping their dismal thoughts in check now.

"You're right, of course." Warrington spoke briskly, at the same time giving a distasteful hitch of his shoulders under his filth-ingrained clothes. "If a chap could clean up a bit, his state of being might improve his state of mind."

Rhiannon agreed. They were a sorry-looking crew. All four were raggedly bearded, grimy, and gamy as sin and smelling to high heaven. Bernal Rubriz looked haggard-eyed, not unfit otherwise. Same with Blanco, except that his face was blotchy and peeling. Warrington had seasoned out well and his skin had taken on the deeply ruddy darkness of any fair-complected man. All could stand a laving of their persons, a scrubbing of their clothes. They could do it here in the tipi, to which Stone Bull's wives had already fetched *ollas* of water, if they wanted privacy.

For himself, though . . .

# CHAPTER TEN

**R**HIANNON PASSED THROUGH THE SPRAWL OF TIPIS, HEADING downstream toward his goal. It was an unhurried stroll because he stopped often to greet old friends and enjoy a little powwow. Finally the main cluster of tipis was behind him and he turned out of the trunk canyon and tramped up a narrow, twisty side gorge that bent upward. Down it ran a stream of pure water that nourished greenery along its path, a choke of dwarf cotton-woods and willows.

Not far from the gorge's end, the source of the stream erupted from an underground spring. Just below, the water prowled through a rock basin to form a broad, deep pool, a well remembered retreat of his boyhood. The surrounding cover of trees and willow brush gave it a leafy seclusion. It was a place to be alone with your thoughts and to relieve the hot tedium of a summer's day. Often as not he'd had to share it with others, but today he was lucky. Not another soul was about, no doubt because the fall afternoon was seasonably cool.

Rhiannon stripped down, piled his clothes on a shallow ledge, and, armed with a sliver of strong yellow soap, entered the pool with gusto. He walked out until he was waist-deep and sloshed the pool water over his head and trunk, sputtering like a winded walrus. He dug his toes pleasurably into the smooth-pebbled bottom and began to scrub, doing justice to his matted hair and beard. Beset by worries, he'd looked forward to this. Not just for the relief of a cold bath. Here a man could bring back memories, good memories, and let his mind have its ease for a time.

Lord, all the days of old, the fine times of youth, cavorting

here with the other kids. Youngsters noisily diving and
splashing like shiny brown tadpoles, boys and girls alike. In
adolescence the girls had gotten weaned to more decorous
ways; there were times and places for them to bathe apart.

Save for him and Naduah and her kid sister. Sumah would
follow them here when they wanted to be alone. Wildly jealous
of their closeness, she'd wanted to be a part of it. One time,
when he and Naduah had congratulated themselves on slipping
away from Sumah and were enjoying the occasion to the
fullest, they'd been found together by her brother, Stone Bull.
The Comanches were highly practical in such matters. The
formal wedding ceremony was forgone, but that evening
Naduah's father had shown up at Rhiannon's adoptive family's
lodge with gifts. He and Naduah were considered married and
the young Rhiannon had gathered up his traps and moved in
with his new relatives. . . .

A single twig snapped; it was a sharp noise above his mild
splashing. It came from just past a down bend of the gorge,
bringing him out of his reverie with a shock. Rhiannon sank
neck-deep in the water, grinding his teeth. What a devil of a
time for someone to—

Sumah came into sight, tall and graceful, her smile flashing.
"Greeting, *kumaxp*!"

She walked to the edge of the pool, stirred his clothes with
her foot, and stood grinning at him. "I did not mean to disturb
you, Redbeard."

*Like hell!*

"I, too, had a thought of bathing. You do not mind, I hope."

"It is not the best time." Rhiannon was suddenly aware of
how cold the water was; his teeth began to chatter. "If you will
be so good as to let me finish my bath, Warrior Woman, the
pool is yours."

"You mean you would have me go away and not see you
naked as a buffalo's rump in the spring shedding?"

Bless his sister-in-law's charming candor, very much of a
piece with her following him here. "I had this thought."

Sumah toed off her moccasins and sat down on the ledge
where it projected above the water. She was wearing a loose
buckskin camp dress and no leggings. She dangled her long
coppery legs in the water, idly kicking riffles of foam at him.

"How your face hair shines in the sun, *kumaxp*! Is it as prickly as ever? I would like to know if it is."

Rhiannon's beard had been rich and full by the time he was seventeen. It had always fascinated the girls. Remembering those adolescent years, he felt the violent wave of embarrassment sweeping him again.

"God*dammi*t, Sumah!"

"You did not use to say that American word," she observed. "We know what it means. We call the white men *gottams* because they say it so much. Is it true it has to do with your Great Power? Do you call on him thus?"

"Yes, and on all the black grinning imps of Sheol!" Rhiannon shouted. "Try your English on that, you brazen brown baggage!"

"I don't understand those words. Why are you angry, *kumaxp*? We are alone here. Who cares what passes—"

"And will ye quit calling me *kumaxp*!"

"Speak the tongue of the People, *kumaxp*, if you would have me understand."

"You damned well do understand, enough to take my meaning. Go on with ye now. Or you'll see what you'd rather not."

Sumah rounded her eyes. "What would *that* be, Redbeard?"

Rhiannon glowered, hesitating. Then he straightened up slowly, water rustling off his arms and trunk. The mockery in Sumah's face died. Her eyes stayed round and wide, and her lips remained parted. After a measureless time, she spoke, her voice almost a whisper.

"That is what they did to you? Your people? What Stone Bull told me of?"

"Fill your eyes with it, Warrior Woman," he said between his chattering teeth. "Have you seen the like from any war wound?"

One thing had always been constant about Sumah. Unlike her gentle sister, she had a talent for small cruelties and was not averse to displaying it. But sorrow? Compassion? He'd never detected much capacity for such in her nature. Now he saw her fine-planed face stir with these emotions and wished he had not. Better, maybe, than the revulsion he might have expected at the sight of his hideously scarred torso. But still . . .

Rhiannon suddenly felt vulnerable in a way that only Naduah, quiet and accepting, had ever made him feel. It was a way to a man's inner being, that look on a woman's face. Anything that could push inside him that way was a jeopardy to his mission.

But in the rush of hot feeling through him, he couldn't help himself. *Maybe he didn't want to.*

"Do not move, Redbeard."

"Sumah . . ."

"There is no need to move. I will come to you."

She was on her feet in a lithe motion, her fingers at the thong fastenings of her dress. Christ's blue eyes! His thoughts were in a panic. Yet he didn't move. . . .

The grate of feet across pebbly ground broke the moment. Sumah whirled about, her shoulders bare, clutching the loosened dress to her. What they saw coming around the gorge bend, hulking and huge and with a bounding swiftness, was Breaks Something. His dark face was contorted, his bared teeth a stained slash of fury.

Rhiannon had seen it often in the war parties of old: a Comanche warrior suddenly possessed by a berserk rage that swept aside all reason, all restraint, all fighting craft. Smashing and hewing his way through the heart of a battle so that his own fellows scattered before him. That was Breaks Something in this moment—a very ape of vengeful jealousy—huge, knotty arms swinging, eyes red and unfocused, spittle flying from his mouth. A knife glittered in his big crooked fist.

He was coming on fast but was still yards away, and Sumah had the time and good sense to throw herself out of his path. Rhiannon stooped to duck under briefly, closing his hand around a sizable rock his foot had brushed. He came up with it, snorting a wet reply to Breaks Something's bellow as the big Comanche lunged into the water without pause, floundering toward him.

Rhiannon's head was still cool. He held the rock just underwater until Breaks Something was almost on him. The Comanche's knife flashed up and down. Timing his move to an instant, Rhiannon took a step back, at the same time bringing the rock up in a curving spray of water, checking his overhand swing, then smashing down with all his strength.

Breaks Something's aborted swing only stabbed water. For the moment he was wide open, arm extended. The rock met flesh and bone with a terrible impact. And a fierce crack of breaking bone.

Breaks Something was stopped in his tracks. The knife fell from a nerveless hand dangling on a broken wrist. But he did not even stagger. Did not utter a sound. As Rhiannon swung the rock back for a second blow, Breaks Something's good hand shot out and seized his arm in a crushing grip.

They surged together, went off balance, and toppled sideways. Rhiannon was ducked; he choked on water. Rolling hard, hooking one leg around one of the Comanche's, he kept them turning in the water. His head came up; he snorted his nose clean and, briefly topmost, tried to tear his arm free. He might as well try to break a vise. Now Breaks Something's head was underwater, but he hung on like death.

They turned over and over in the water, locked in a savage struggle. First one man's head was submerged, then the other's, and once they both sank to the bottom. Rhiannon tried clumsily and vainly to hook his free fist into his enemy's face, but it was buried against his shoulder. His arms were full of a slippery, thrashing behemoth. He had met his match, and he knew it, knew that his only edge was his enemy's injury. And for terrible moments, putting out his whole strength, he wondered if it would be enough.

Breaks Something's knee found his groin. Rhiannon felt the flare of agony splay his nerve ends apart, his muscles going loose. He knew dimly when the rock slipped from his hand. He didn't know the moment when he ceased to think. He was vaguely aware of strangling on water, rolling over and over in it, straining to fight free of the massive crushing arms.

He had no awareness of breaking the Comanche's double-armed grip, of wrestling free. Later he would reckon that only the debilitating pain of his enemy's shattered wrist and useless hand had enabled him to do so.

All he suddenly knew, as if a wind had blown through his brain and cleared it, was that he was standing up in the water. Breaks Something was bent over backward, his face just clearing water, Rhiannon's left hand clutching his throat, his right fist pumping great sledging blows into the Comanche's upturned face. Breaks Something had gone limp, his blood reddening the water.

With a kind of dazed shock Rhiannon let go of him. The bloody wreck of the Comanche's face turned over as his body did, loose in the water and starting to sink. Rhiannon turned his head to look at Sumah. She stood on the ledge, fists clenched at her sides. The suggestion she voiced was predictable.

"Let him drown," she said.

Rhiannon grabbed Breaks Something by the fastening of his breechclout. He slogged to the bank with the Comanche in tow and dumped him on his side in the shallows, a vast lump of sodden flesh. With a thrust of his foot, Rhiannon tipped his face up and clear of the water.

"That is stupid," Sumah observed. "Next time he will not give *you* a chance. Not even a little chance."

As always when the onset of a black rage drained away, Rhiannon's mind was empty and calm. He began to pick up his clothes and pull them on. "That's likely so," he agreed. "If there is a next time. And I've a thought that ye'll go right on working it up, making it so. Ain't that right, Sumah darlin'?"

# GET YOUR 4
# FREE* BOOKS NOW—
# A VALUE OF BETWEEN
# $17 AND $20

## Mail the Free* Books Certificate Today!

# FREE* BOOKS
# CERTIFICATE!

**YES!** I want to subscribe to the Leisure Western Book Club. Please send me my 4 FREE* BOOKS. Then, each month, I'll receive the four newest Leisure Western Selections to preview for 10 days. If I decide to keep them, I will pay the Special Member's Only discounted price of just $3.36 each, a total of $13.44 ($16.35 in Canada). This saves me between $3 and $6 off the bookstore price. There are no shipping, handling or other charges.* There is no minimum number of books I must buy and I may cancel the program at any time. In any case, the 4 FREE* BOOKS are mine to keep—at a value of between $17 and $20!

*In Canada, add $7.50 US shipping and handling per order for first shipment. For all subsequent shipments to Canada the cost of membership in the Book Club is $16.35 US plus $7.50 US shipping and handling per order. All payments must be made in US dollars.

Name _____

Address _____

City_____ State_____

Zip_____ Telephone_____

Signature_____

## Biggest Savings Offer!

For those of you who would like to pay us in advance by check or credit card—we've got an even bigger savings in mind. Interested? Check here. ☐

If under 18, parent or guardian must sign. Terms, prices and conditions subject to change. Subscription subject to acceptance. Leisure Books reserves the right to reject any order or cancel any subscription.

Tear here and mail your FREE* book card today!

# Get Four Books Totally
# F R E E* —
# A Value of between
# $16 and $20

PLEASE RUSH
MY FOUR FREE*
BOOKS TO ME
RIGHT AWAY!

LeisureWestern Book Club
P.O. Box 6613
Edison, NJ 08818-6613

AFFIX
STAMP
HERE

# CHAPTER ELEVEN

**R**HIANNON'S COMPANIONS HAD CLEANED UP, SHAVED, AND changed to the least grimy of whatever spare duds they had. Stone Bull's middle wife had taken the rest of their clothing and Rhiannon's to the stream for washing. They were curious about Rhiannon's skinned and bleeding right hand and quietly surly manner. But they asked no further questions after he growled a reply to the first one.

The late sunlight was mellowing to a rich dun color along the rimrock, and purpling twilight already filled the Palo Duro's shadowed depth. They were all exhausted and agreed they wouldn't be averse to sleeping the clock around, if there were anything like a sense of civilized time in the incessantly busy, hugely populated Comanche encampment.

Rhiannon was wrapping a cloth around his hand, the others spreading their blankets, when a man appeared in the open doorway of their tipi. He bent to look inside, scratched politely on the lodge cover, and said in an amiable, mincing way, *"Buenas tardes, señores.* Or is it *noches?"*

They gazed at him in mild astonishment. Damn my eyes if it ain't a bloody fop, though Rhiannon. The man was light-skinned, Spanish-looking, with a surprisingly high voice. Long and lean and mustachioed, he wore a white silk shirt and a fancifully embroidered *charro* outfit along with bench-made Justin boots bedecked with cruel Spanish spurs. The nearest thing to him Rhiannon had ever seen—it had been during a cattle-selling trip to New Orleans—was a Creole pimp he'd encountered in a low-caste dive in the French Quarter. This fellow had no particular resemblance to that pimp, but he had the same kind of priggishly dandified air.

"I am Florentino Diaz, *segundo* to Captain Harry Trevelyan. He begs to the pleasure of your company at dinner." The fop's English was excellent; he waved a languid hand downcanyon. "At the Casa Grande."

Rhiannon felt his spirits suddenly restored. "We're well fed, thank you. All the same, we accept the invitation. If your boss has something wet and ring-tailed on hand?"

"*Qué?*"

"*Aguardiente, pulque,* tanglefoot, booze. Anything to wet the whistle, y'know?"

Diaz's smile gleamed yellowly. It did not extend to his black eyes, which were beads of cold obsidian. "How exquisitely blunt and down to earth you *Yanquis* are! Truly, diamonds in the rough. Liquor is always the first amenity of which you request knowledge. Oh, my, yes. Of a certainty we have plentiful booze."

Rhiannon lunged to his feet, wincing at his sore ribs. "Why, then, lead the way, my good fellow. Here, let's be introduced first." He gave his name, then turned to his companions and said their names, winking as he added in a roguish stage whisper to Warrington, "Sink me, if it ain't a bloody fop!"

Warrington wasn't amused. He wore a look of deadly concern. He whispered, "Are these the Comancheros, then?"

"Who else?" Rhiannon murmured. "Straighten out your face, Sassenach, and leave me to do any talking's to be done."

They set off downcanyon through the deepening twilight. Rhiannon supposed their destination would be the old *casa* built by Musketoon and his crew decades ago. As a boy he and the other youngsters had played there, hunting the small animals that used its deserted walls as a lair.

Rhiannon strolled beside Diaz, asking few questions, mostly letting the dandy talk as he whisked away flies with a scented handkerchief. For all his pimpish looks, Rhiannon doubted he had much taste for women. At the same time, from the look of the two Colt pistols and the two wicked-looking knives he carried in the scarlet sash around his narrow waist, and also from the nasty scar that made a puckered pink slash down the left side of his gaunt face, he'd not be a bucko lad to take lightly.

"Directly Captain Trevelyan learned of the presence of *Americano* hunters in the Quohada camp," Florentino lilted, "he was most curious. They are not known to frequent the haunts of the Comanche. You, we have now determined, are a brother-in-law of Stone Bull, which explains a great deal. But it has only served to heighten *el capitán*'s curiosity."

"Dearie me," Rhiannon said mildly. "My death-dealin' renown does seem to precede me. And *you*, my fine *caballero*, are truly second in command to the muckymuck who heads this darlin' band of ruffians?"

Florentino slid him a wicked sidelong glance. "Of a certainty," he murmured, irked enough to walk a little faster, enabling Rhiannon to fall idly back into step with his companions.

"Listen, Sassenach," he said softly, "there's a more'n good chance ye'll be seeing your lady mighty shortly. No matter what ye see, what ye hear . . . mum's the word. You say nothing, you do nothing, you *show* nothing. Understand?"

"Of course," Warrington whispered irritably. "Do you think I'm a complete idiot?"

"Why would I be thinking that? Trevelyan," Rhiannon mused aloud. "What's that handle, Cornish?"

"English upper middle class, also."

"Ah, that could be a case. Could put ye up against a brother of the blood, eh? One fallen to Lucifer."

"Yes," Warrington said icily. "The name could easily be an assumed one as well."

"Likely, likely."

Rhiannon realized he'd best be chary of his residual tendency to stir the Sassenach's hackles. Warrington would be treading a tighter edge than any he'd had to before this evening. However it went, what lay ahead was an unknown quantity. A zestful prospect in its way, but all the more reason for Rhiannon to put a special curb on his own too-ready tongue.

If all went well, the situation would prove an unexpected stroke of luck. A chance to size up the Comanchero defenses outside and, to a degree, inside as well. Rhiannon's own knowledge of the old *casa* was solid in his memory. As soon as they'd learned that Melissa Dragoman was in Comanchero hands, he'd known that knowledge would be vital to even a slim possibility of freeing her . . . but they'd need still more.

The Comanche lodges were behind them. The canyon cliffs began to narrow, beetling to overhang rims that sheltered the numerous nooks and crannies below. Tucked inside these were old crumbling huts, wretched flat-roofed affairs like those Mexican peasants built.

And there were people, the scruffy and ill-defined bastard lot that comprised a gang of Comancheros. Villainous-looking men, sullen black-haired women, and broods of dusty, near-naked children came out to watch in blank silence as the party trooped by, a scurvy stew of mixed races and nationalities.

What Rhiannon saw next made the short hairs stand at the back of his neck. Warrington let out an audible gasp.

Musketoon's old stone council house was in use once more, its roof freshly thatched with cedar bark. And it was still a place where a Comanchero chief could pass justice, swift and ruthless and unquestioned, on any of his transgressing subjects. A new cedar-post gallows had been erected alongside and from its cross pole the bodies of two men hung dark and limp in the twilight, still suspended by the nooses in which they had kicked away their lives.

There had been a good deal of barbarous and drunken carousing last night, Florentino Diaz explained pleasantly. Two men had died of gunshot wounds and a woman had been knifed to death. When his pack of cutthroat curs grew quarrelsome and tensions boiled over, *el capitán* meted out extreme justice without hesitation. The killers' bodies would be left thus for a couple of days to impress everyone. Fear kept the jackals at heel.

By now the purple shadows had darkened to near blackness in the lower recesses, lending a peculiarly ominous cast to the tortured bulges of rock above and below. They came to the beginning of a broad path, and here a guard, bearing a rifle and two bandoleers of cartridges crossed on his chest, was posted. He let them pass without a glance or a word.

Florentino led the way up the path, which was almost stairlike and first ascended the lower slope, then twisted sharply to follow the cliffside at an upward angle, climbing higher toward the big, two-storied Casa Grande. It was built on a wide shelf about halfway below the canyon rim, which projected in a great sheltering swell of very solid limestone. The second story, Rhiannon knew, contained chambers for the Comanchero chief's immediate family or following; its lower story was mostly occupied by a large *sala* as well as cooking and dining facilities. The whole was built of the biggest boulders that two men could lift between them, chipped or naturally formed to fit closely together with patches of mud chinking here and there. In Rhiannon's boyhood all of the chinking had fallen out and there had been no roof on the second story. Everything looked restored and shipshape and the several windows were warm with lamp glow.

Florentino gave three spaced raps on the door. Another armed guard opened it and passed them through an antechamber and into the *sala*. It, too, was restored: the walls were freshly whitewashed and the furnishings were both plain and rich. Like Alec Dragoman, Captain Trevelyan had a taste for antique firearms as well as modern ones. Every wall was hung with them. No big-game heads, but there were several battered but well-polished morions, helmets such as the Spanish *conquistadores* had worn, and Renaissance cuirasses and halberds, as well as a collection of swords and knives ranging from a Scottish claymore to an *épée* dueling blade.

A Mexican *mozo* in white cottons admitted them. An olive-skinned boy of tender years with soft liquid eyes, he indicated a big trestle table laden with bottles and decanters and invited them to partake at will until *el capitán* made his appearance. Then he padded from the room, silent on his soft-hide sandals.

Rhiannon promptly picked up a decanter, lifted the glass plug and sniffed it, and—again calling on memories of his New Orleans sojourn—identified the contents as Napoleon brandy. The reigning toff had taste, bless his bloody soul. He sloshed some into each of four glasses.

"Liquid courage, Rhiannon?" Warrington said acidly.

Rhiannon dropped into a comfortable wood-and-rawhide armchair, saluted his surroundings with a circling motion of his glass, and downed a hefty snort. "Best kind the Lord made provision for, seeing he gave the most of us such rabbity bellies. Drink up, gents."

"And do not be nervous," Florentino said amusedly.

The others picked up their glasses but only stood holding
them stiffly. There was a delicious waft of cooking odors from
a rear archway. And from an upstairs chamber came a sharp
squeal, a girl's giggle, the great hearty boom of a man's
laughter. Warrington gave a kind of sharp twitch but otherwise
held himself still. Rhiannon finished his drink and poured
another. Blanco took a small sip of his and made a face.

Florentino poured himself a glass of wine, piping, "My
heavens. Obviously it is too rich for the dear boy's blood. Are
you afraid of it, *niño*?"

Blanco's chill bleach gaze studied Florentino's mocking one.
"Could swallow it straight down to show I ain't," he said
mildly. "Only I don't prove things for the fun of it, Mr. Diaz."

"Bravo! He speaks, he hides the teeth, he sheathes the
claws! Bravo, my—"

The clatter of boots on a stairway could be heard. A man
entered the room like a gust of wind.

"Trevelyan's the name, ye'r honors!" he boomed. "Harry
Trevelyan it is. Christ, I'm dry as a duck's oily arse! 'Ere,
Flory, don't be hoggin' all that berry pee. . . ."

He plucked the demijohn from Florentino's hand, tipped it to
his mouth, and drank with a steady, pumping convulsion of his
Adam's apple. When he slammed it down, a half inch of wine
remained.

Rhiannon, slackly at ease in his chair, gave the demijohn a
grinning nod. "Cap'n, sir, you're a piker. I once seen a British
tar, Matagorda it was, do like justice to a like quantity of the
Royal Navy's rum."

" 'Ave you, then!" Trevelyan's laughter boomed again.
"Wager 'e scoffed it out of his skipper's overladen stores, then.
Rum dole's been abolished and a ship's master don't guzzle
rum like this berry pee, not 'n' keep his bloomin' head, 'e
don't."

"Or a cap'n of the Comanchero, either, eh?"

"Right you are, mate."

Trevelyan was arranging his somewhat disarranged clothing
as he spoke, sizing up Rhiannon in a shrewd sweeping glance
from head to foot. "Sorry to keep you gents waitin'. Business
upstairs." He winked bawdily, arching his blond brows toward

the ceiling. "Does tax a man's juices, gets 'im up a thirst." His glance touched briefly on the others. " 'Ere, for Christ's sake, there's chairs, don't be standin' about like lead dunces. Hope you brought your appetites; there's a whole sucklin' pig turnin' on the galley spit, Mr. . . . Ree-nan, the Comanch' 'ave it?"

"Rhiannon, Michael Rhiannon it is, and these are my friends." He introduced Bernal Rubriz, Blanco, and Warrington with the same fake names he'd given the Comanches—Telisfor Rodriguez, Jim Dowlett, and Henry Sandwick—and Trevelyan courteously acknowledged each introduction, waiting till all were seated before he flopped into a chair, stretched his long legs, and crossed his boots.

A large, strapping figure of a buccaneer he was, Rhiannon thought, not without admiration. That broad, ruddy, handsome face framed by a mane of rich golden hair, the walrus mustache, and spruce spike of beard put one in mind of a Viking corsair or, more like, one of Drake's swashbuckling privateers. So did his colorful and flamboyant garb: jackboots, leather breeches, emerald-green shirt with puffed sleeves, crimson sash around his middle, wide leather belt supporting two big revolvers and a Bowie knife. His teeth were big and square, his eyes the color of woodsmoke, twinkling and friendly.

"The sucklin' pig smells mighty fine," Rhiannon said. "But regretfully, we've just been the honored guests of a Comanche feast and are filled. Room for a pinch o' poteen, though . . . There's always that."

"Ain't there! As Stone Bull's brother-in-law, I hazard you've enjoyed his hospitality before?"

Rhiannon explained a little of his background, told of how they were scouting for buffalo and Comanche permission to hunt it, short and sweet.

"Bless me soul," Trevelyan said. "I'll wager yers is a life story to rival me own, Mr. Rhiannon! I'll look forward to hearing more of it when we're a bit into our cups. Nothing like booze to whet the confessional spirit and lighten the soul. That's still a mighty sticky burr on yer tongue, Shamrock. And from yer reference to tars and the RN, you've divined I was a seafarin' man?"

"Aye. The roll of your walk, and a kitchen ain't a galley, cap'n."

Warrington spoke for the first time. "You were born within the sound of Bow bells, sir?"

Trevelyan's eyes widened. "Why, pipe 'im aboard, men! If it ain't a countryman of finest feather. I'm a Cockney by birth and raisin', yes, and of blue blood by the qualified direction known as bastardy. At least if you can believe me sweet mar, who lived in the dives me old man frequented. Had a taste for low passions, 'e did, and per'aps I've that to blame for me own lifelong turn o' taste. Indeed, the Trevelyan she named is distant kin to HRM Victoria and a boozin' chum of 'is philanderin' 'ighness the Prince of Wales. However, all may be naught but Mar's aspirin' fancy if she even once bedded the cove. But w'ot the hell . . . Where's that blarsted square-face?"

He rummaged among the potables for a bottle of gin and filled a glass to the brim. "Flory, you fetch that box of fine Spanish cheroots from yon cabinet, there's a good lad."

Diaz, without hesitation or a flicker of resentment at being ordered about like a common *mozo*, rose and undulated to the cabinet. He passed the box of twisted black cigars around, and each man accepted one. Even the tough Bernal Rubriz, with all his proud sense of honor, seemed rather captivated by the magnetism of their host. As a man's man, Harry Trevelyan was almost impossible not to like, whatever gruesome deeds might rest on his soul. Only Warrington, eased by a half glass of brandy now, seemed to remain cool and measuring.

Trevelyan said he was pleased to see everyone managing to relax in his iniquitious den and began to wax volubly about his exploits. "Aye, shipped before the queen's masts for many a year, I did. And on more villainous craft. Consorted with the scupper scum of the seas, the dregs of a hundred ports. Across God's green globe from Canton to the Vatican I been, oh, aye, even served in the Swiss Guard for a time. Imagine—yers truly 'elpin' protect the pope!" He gave a hearty snort of laughter, drained his glass, and swiped the back of a big hand across his mouth. "Me last nautical turn five years ago, it were on H.M.S. *Edinburgh Castle*, I jumped ship off Galvez Island looking to revel in the last wild and degenerate stronghold of real piracy, tallyho! Alas, only a sorry handful of Jean Laffite's old cut-'n'-slash crew still 'eld forth there, aged householders the lot, gibbets retired and slave barracoons in ruin; the whole place deader'n Job and all 'is sorrows. So I struck for the coast . . ."

Avoiding the Texas ports and other signs of coastal habitation, for the arm of the queen was long, Trevelyan had made straight inland on foot with a canteen, a haversack of grub, and a compass. All that helped him do was keep straight north. A city-bred seaman, he'd no conception of the overwhelming vastness of the Texas plains. He had no map to go by, just sketchy hearsay. In three days he was thoroughly lost, his food and water gone, his compass broken. In a week he was tottering with hunger, half dead with thirst. When he was on his last legs, the Comancheros found him. A whim of the band's leader kept him alive. Overnight he was one of them, taking to their blackguard way of life like a fish to water. Within a year he was *segundo* to the chief, Martinez. In less than another year Martinez and an underling killed each other in a Bowie knife duel and Trevelyan moved up the last notch.

"It's all true, guv'nors, what they say about America! Here a man can rise from a guttersnipe to grand muckymuck of his outfit. A strong dream and hard work does it! All I wanted then was a fortress of sorts to indulge me kingly tastes and 'ere it was in the Palo Duro, waitin' for me."

Rhiannon said, "And if the army gets the wind up and ye get cornered in this fine crack in the earth with only one way out? It happened to Musketoon."

Trevelyan chuckled in his chest and reached for the gin bottle. "Life's a gamble, mate. Where's its savor if a man don't play it to the hilt? I catch wind of army movements, out I move. Meantime I got a nice hunk of the Comanch' nation between me and the enemy. Heigh-ho! The livin's high and if the price be high too in the end, what did the Bard say? Memorized it, I did. 'By my troth I care not; a man can die but once, we owe God a death. . . . and let it go which way it will, he that dies this year is quit for the next.' Flory, me boy . . . ain't it past your bedtime?"

Diaz rolled his eyes toward the ceiling, dreamily. "Of a certainty, *jefe*. I was about to suggest—"

"Go along up with you, then. Oh, drop by the galley or kitchen and tell 'em to belay supper. And send out the girls."

"*All* the . . . ?"

"No, no. The *dark* ones, Flory."

"Of a certainty. *Caballeros,* it has been a pleasure. *Vaya con Dios.*"

Diaz made his way unsteadily but gracefully from the room, calling dulcetly, "Ho-*zay*-hey . . ."

Trevelyan grinned at them. "If you wonder, José is the *mozo* who admitted you."

Rhiannon grinned. "Are we to be surprised, then?"

"Why, I'd hate for Flory to surprise any man. Gent'd get 'is throat cut in a trice. Deadly as a snake Flory is, 'specially with a pigsticker. And absolutely loyal to me, gentlemen. 'E's the eyes at me back. Don't mistake; me own taste in dalliance runs to the fair sex exclusive. Ah, and 'ere the ladies are . . . Come in, luvs, and say 'ello to our guests. Gents, meet Rosalita, and this is Dominga."

Rosalita was a delight to behold, an elfin sprite of a girl, dainty and mischief-eyed. Dominga was quite different, tall and supple and full-lipped, with very dark skin and a hint of an exotic tilt to the eyelids and cheekbones. A stunning beauty with sullen golden eyes, she moved with a feline grace. Both wore the costumes of Mexican peasant girls, and there were no prettier costumes under the sun. White scoop-necked blouses; bright-dyed skirts that ended below the calves; light thong sandals on bare feet. No damn fool stays or cinches and but one petticoat apiece, with lace peeping from under the skirt hems. Their hands showed that they did their share of menial work, but both looked clean and groomed and a bit pampered all the same.

"God, gents, ain't they *sightly*? Have your plains-weary eyes seen the like in a coon's age? 'Ere, Rosalita, perch on my knee, precious. Dominga, take that chair by Mr. Rhiannon, 'e's the big redhead. Impress 'im with yer vast learnin'. Talk."

Dominga said, "Nothing else is required by the *patrón*?"

Trevelyan's glance held a flicker of displeasure. "That's your choice and his. Sit and look pleasant, if you can manage as much."

Rhiannon rose with a flourish, held Dominga's chair for her, then sat down half facing her. "You are a lovely lady, indeed. May I pour you a glass of wine?"

"Yes."

"May I be inquiring of your, ah . . . antecedents, my dear?"

*"Qué?"*

" 'E means yer dad and mar, luv." Trevelyan chuckled. "To put it with the greatest charity and to pass lightly over details, Dominga is what we colonial Britons call a Chigro—half Chinese, half Negro—and she hails from the island of Jamaica. Got 'er education in the quadroon finishing schools of N'Awleans. Trained to all the brothel arts, very finest brothels. A very tony *puta*. And she'd as lief slip a knife between a man's ribs as bed 'im. You're warned, guv."

Dominga sipped her wine and was the image of sultry calm. Rhiannon sensed thunderstorms underneath. Interesting. Something between Trevelyan and her, strong and stormy but gone awry. He wondered . . .

But the wondering trailed off. Trevelyan knew how to make a congenial occasion shine. An endless repository of derring-do tales, ribald jokes, glibly hearty speech, he caught them up in the brawny whirl of his personality. He stimulated, he probed, he urged more drink on them. Rhiannon was aware of his tongue growing fuzzy. Blanco never said a word, never changed expression, just looked increasingly glassy-eyed. He had no head for liquor and presently began to slide down in his chair. Rubriz kept glaring at him unfocusedly, grimly shaking his head and muttering, "Filthy *puerco*," over and over. Warrington alone showed no effects of drink—as a real class gent he'd take pride in his belly for liquor—except that his face got redder and redder. His hand clenched tightly around his glass; he was a man waiting . . . for anything. He looked like an overdone pepper.

Funny as hell. Rhiannon wanted to laugh, but his stomach was beginning to churn. No more talk. Might say the wrong thing. No more drink. Best be hustling their hocks away from here . . .

His bowed chin snapped up off his chest.

Trevelyan was saying proudly, ". . . Miss Melissa Drago-man. Me royal consort, gentlemen, and me true love."

There she was, standing before them. Rhiannon sifted clarity out of the clouds to take her in: a slim, medium-tall girl with a sweetly distant air. She had a delicate heartshaped face, lips pursed in a childlike pout, and a faintly cleft chin. Guileless blue eyes and softly winged brows gave her a mildly quizzical look. Her hair was worn loose and spread like a soft chestnut fan on the shoulders of her rich rustling dress.

Trevelyan was making introductions.

"Please"—Melissa's voice had the chime of tender bells—"don't get up on my account, gentlemen. Don't even *try*. I declare, so you're Mr. Rhiannon. My father has spoken of you quite often."

# CHAPTER TWELVE

**R**HIANNON BLINKED HIS SANDY EYELIDS AND MOVED HIS head a little. "Christ . . ." It crawled out of his throat as a dry phlegmy whisper. He was lying facedown on a bed, his head tilted sideways on a pillow. The pulse of war drums in his head and the driving splinters of pain behind his eyes told him that he was emerging from a sodden sleep into the agony of that familiar comrade of old, the hangover.

Oh, God. It was another monumental one. Half a bleedin' day with that pounding in his bloody skull and a quaking belly lay in store for him. He contemplated the prospect with a vast and dreary calm, then rolled slowly onto his back.

He made it halfway onto his back, anyway. Then he bumped warm flesh and heard a woman's mild murmur. He twisted his head sideways. Rosalita blinked her long dark lashes and smiled sweetly. Her slim brown shoulder was the obstacle.

Rhiannon groaned.

Fine. Not a bloody shred of memory was left in his brain of what had taken place after the shank of the evening. An indeterminate time, that is, after Trevelyan had introduced his ladylove. Maybe all of them had gone into slow paralysis. Rhiannon's last thought had been of desperately trying not to say the wrong thing and hoping to God's blue eyes that Warrington wouldn't.

"*Caballero*," whispered Rosalita, "is there anything I can do for you?"

Rhiannon shut his eyes. "*Buenas días*," he said in a parched whisper.

"*Buenas días*."

"I believe you can, my dove," he croaked. "Something wet to drink, no, not ring-tailed wet," as she reached for a wine bottle on a bedside taboret. "The ol' *agua pura,* y'know, water?"

"Yes."

Rosalita slipped from under the covers and walked nimbly over to the marble-topped commode in a corner of the small chamber. She poured water from a pitcher into a glass. Sunlight slanting in through a narrow window skittered on the squirmy little muscles of her back and bottom, gilding part of her to a bronze turn. Gold on brown, a very becoming blend on such a delightful naiad.

Delightful, mmm. A man could only hope so, when he couldn't recall a damn thing. She came back with the water, and he sat up by tortured degrees—God how the old gourd did rock and roar—and took the glass. "Thanks." He drained it, tipping back his head, and shuddered as his stomach boiled coldly at the water's impact. Then he tilted down his gaze to the fallen covers on his lap. Yes. The whole snake-bed map of scars right out in sight.

"Rosie, lass. How does it feel to have bedded a monster?"

Rosalita perched quickly on the bed's edge and gave him a birdlike peck on the shoulder. So much mischief in those shiny eyes. He regretted his memory lapse all the more.

"Each is a holy scar," she said solemnly. "Only a holy man would know such words and so many of them."

"Ah, yes. Words like . . ."

"*Dios,* said many times, and bless my old bones and bless your young limber ones, *querida.* There were so many words, and sentences as well. Some not so holy, but *pues y que*? Do you want—"

"No, ahem, no catalog necessary."

Delightful. Confirmation and all blasted away. He might have known. "Rosalita of the dancing eyes, what time is it?"

"*Qué hora es?* Morning, señor. More water?"

"If ye please?"

Rhiannon drank half the second glass. "Thanks." She took the glass from him and sympathetically watched him strain up and onto his feet. He braced his legs and growled in his throat—still a raw kiln but at least wetted down—and peered about him. He located her clothes folded on a chair, the sandals squared off neat as pins on top, and his own clothes dumped on the floor beside it. There was a small crucifix on the wall, one of the terrible Spanish ones with thorn-browed head and side-thrust bloodstreams painted bright red on a plaster savior. He gazed at it for a bleary time, thought, Hum, life's all that, and wobbled over to the chair. He began to climb into his clothes and it took a painful while.

"Rosie . . . would ye know what became of my friends?"

"*Sí*, they left soon after Señorita M'lissa came in. You remember that?"

"Passing well, yes."

"The two older ones went out almost carrying the young one between them. *El capitán* sent along a man to pass them through the camp below and back to the *Indio* camp."

"That's good. Good."

Rhiannon stamped his boots on firmly, cinched his broad leather belt, shrugged into his old grease-stained hunting jacket, and gingerly settled his crushed-crowned hat on his head, scowling at the tall Arabesque mirror alongside the commode. He looked red-eyed and formidable. He felt grouchy and sick.

"And *el capitán* and I drank a wee more?" he asked.

"And roared funny things at each other. Funny but very mean. Usually only old *amigos* may talk so. Otherwise there would be killing."

"In life," Rhiannon said, scowling at himself, "there are magic moments. Ye meet someone and bang, *buen amigos*. Rosie, I want to—"

Someone rapped once on the door and promptly opened it. Florentino Díaz stood there, his smile demurely quirking the facial troughs that might have been dimples thirty-odd years ago. Rosalita hissed at him and went quickly to the chair, reaching for her clothes.

"*Buenas días, señor!* And did you enjoy—"

"Get the hell out of here," Rhiannon snarled.

"But, dear fellow, would you deny a man the rare diversion of watching a nymph of morning rousing from her drowsy *déshabillé*?" He kissed the tips of his fingers at Rosalita. "Ah,

the glories of her form, almost a symphony in sepia but a bit
bony across the—"

Rosalita yelled, "You get the hell away, you damn *medio
hombre*!"

"You heard the lady, Minceface." Rhiannon said it in his
throat, growling it low, as he turned from the mirror to face
Diaz, who had folded his arms and was settling his shoulder
against the doorjamb.

"Such a fuss. I merely came to extend a matutinal courtesy,
to tell you that the *jefe* desires your company—"

"*Out!*"

"—at breakfast, and you would deny a fellow *hombre* the
simple pleasure of—"

A red surge hit Rhiannon's brain. Not a black one. He was
furiously, savagely in control as he moved, quick as a
catamount, to grab Florentino Diaz by the shoulder and whirl
him around. He smashed the rock-hard edge of his palm
against the dandy's arm as Diaz's hand reached to seize one of
the sash knives. Diaz gave a shocked squeal, twisting.
Rhiannon fetched him a stunning clout on the head, then held
him upright as he jerked the pistols and knives, one by one,
from Diaz's sash and pitched them aside. He gripped Diaz by
the collar of his *charro* jacket and the seat of his *charro* pants
and carried him, feebly kicking, out to the hall and the head of
a stairs. Rhiannon set himself, then heaved up and outward.
Diaz hit the wood rises halfway down and clattered on,
bowling head over heels to the stairs bottom, where he lay
crumpled and moaning.

Rosalita came out of her room, wearing her petticoat and
holding her other clothes to her bosom. She looked down at
Diaz with mild apprehension. "Señor, I hope to heaven you
did not break anything in him."

Rhiannon said grimly, "I hope to Sheol your hope is
misplaced," and tramped down the stairway, arriving at its
bottom as Trevelyan entered from a side door. He halted,
looked down at Florentino Diaz and then at Rhiannon, and
sighed deeply.

"What did 'e do?"

Rhiannon told him shortly.

"Shamrock, now that was a bit drastic for the offense, you
have to own. After all, Rosalita—"

"Don't be telling me what Rosie is. Would you want *him* eyeballing you with your clout off? It's enough to make the flesh crawl on an armadillo."

Trevelyan arched his brows, tugged at his beard spike, and smiled just a little. "Well, let's on to breakfast. It's served up and pipin' hot. José," he said, as the liquid-eyed youth emerged from a chamber above, peering down at them, appalled, "get Flory up to bed and tend 'is hurts. Where are 'is weapons?"

"Rosie's room," Rhiannon said.

"Gather 'em up and lock 'em in me own gun locker." Trevelyan produced a key and tossed it up; José caught it fumblingly. "Any others in 'is duffle, too. 'E gets 'em back when Mr. Rhiannon has taken 'is leave. Foller me, mate."

He preceded Rhiannon through the side door into a small dining chamber, its big single window open to a flood of midmorning sun. A table was spread with snowy linen, chinaware, and a silver service. A fine rosewood sideboard held covered silver dishes set out in the top-crust English style. With a flourish, Trevelyan lifted the covers from steaming platters of eggs, muffins, and rashers of bacon. There was fresh-looking butter, a small pot of marmalade, a large one of steaming tea.

Rhiannon said in amazement, "God save the pound."

"There's a staunch Irish sentiment. Bacon's from a razorback boar and the muffins are cornmeal, but the tea and marmalade are the real homeland article."

"Where's the kippers?"

"Don't be picky, I try to make do in my humble way. 'Ere, let's pile our plates and dig in. Leave the teapot . . . best china in the world it is, no other way to steep tea to a flavor. You do ruffle hackles, Michael: Hardly settled in and you got two on the peck for you, Flory and yer Comanche chum."

Rhiannon puckered his brows. "Stone Bull?"

"Breaks Something, I think the gent's name was. Believe I've seen 'im about, the great ape? You do ramble on in ye'r cups, bad habit. Your ape and my lieutenant 'ud make a grand pair to dog a man to death. But that's *your* lookout, mate, long as you remain in the Palo Duro."

Trevelyan laughed heartily and carried his loaded plate to the table, yelling, "Dominga!" She came in from the kitchen, looking sulky and smoldering. "Got a bad head this morning, she 'as. Shame on you, Michael, pressin' all that berry pee on 'er. Temper's up, too. Gives 'er a brisk tongue betimes. Serve us our tea, dear, and keep your flamin' thoughts in your lovely head."

Rhiannon rolled his own tongue around the pasty inside of his mouth as Dominga poured the tea. She looked as if she might like to dash it in their faces. How much had been said last night? No way of being sure. Evidently Melissa had told Trevelyan of the enmity between Rhiannon and her daddy, but not that she was affianced to a crumb off the British upper crust. Or else, even if Richard Warrington was using the name Henry Sandwick, Trevelyan would have gotten the wind up at once.

Yet, who was to say he hadn't and wasn't just staying mum, being the perfect host and biding his time? After all, the Commanchero leader believed himself invulnerable in his fortress. Not without reason.

Dominga returned the teapot to the sideboard and stalked out of the room.

"Miss Dragoman won't be joining us?" Rhiannon asked.

"She likes to stay late abed. Damn, I've never indulged a woman so. But then never before have I . . . well." Trevelyan spoke around a stuffed mouth; he nodded at Rhiannon's plate. "That's a busy fork, Michael, but food ain't just for stirrin' about. Appetite lackin'?"

"Only due to putting away quantities of your more potent stores. Remember, Harry?"

"I do, and you shipped on enough to scuttle a man o' war, much less a plain man. Where was I? Melissa, now. She had an idea that, soon or late, 'er father would send to try and ransom 'er. But he'd not send *you* as an emissary, for sure. Listen 'ere, you eat a bit. You'll feel the better."

Rhiannon forked up his mixture of eggs and muffin hunks. He swallowed slowly and drank his tea.

Melissa. A few fuzzy strands of remembrance sifted through. Enough to leave him with the impression that she was much as Warrington had described her. Pretty enough, but no raving beauty. What would fascinate the hell out of some men, he supposed, was her capricious ways, her moods veering from color to color like a chameleon. From soft-eyed demure and gentle one moment, to laughing, bubbling wit the next. And her sudden turns from childlike innocence to bawdy turns of tongue as bad as the men's.

Also, she was plainly getting a tremendous thrill out of this whole sordid business, and was as captivated by Trevelyan as he was by her. God, there was a hitch they hadn't foreseen in their wildest calculations.

"Dominga," Trevelyan called, "more tea 'ere!"

Dominga, yes. Rhiannon ignored her as she refilled their cups, but he was thinking. Clearly Melissa had replaced Dominga in the Comanchero leader's affections. The Jamaican's vivid beauty made Melissa look pallid, but men could be dogs on the scent where the ladies were concerned. Get jaded and their tastes changed, their attentions switched. And Melissa had her special power. But . . .

But a jealous and hot-blooded woman might be the key to a fortress that otherwise seemed impregnable.

The thought sweetened Rhiannon's morning. A little.

Trevelyan laid down his fork and said quietly, "Listen, mate. Dead serious, now. I told you, Flory ain't just a sissy lad. 'E's the eyes at me back, now he'll be the dagger at yours. Speakin' of which, he don't carry them two big ones just for show."

"So ye mentioned. There's a place for both in his ruddy arse."

Trevelyan's smile was brief and thin. " 'E's a jealous cove. That's why 'e baited you just then. Couldn't help 'imself. 'E had cause. Michael, I ain't 'ad such a brawl of an evenin', nor met your like, in a lifetime. God, mate. If you threw in with me, as a partner not a lackey . . . God, how we two could make the welkin ring."

"That won't happen," Rhiannon said quietly. "I feel the same. But strong as the likeness is, it begins and ends there."

"Agh, I know. All that will stand with us hereafter is a worry and a warnin'. A worry that Florentino will go for your hide if he sees a way, and even I can't prevent it. A warnin' . . ." Trevelyan paused, tugging at a small gold ring in his right ear. "If Flory goes after you and you kill 'im, no matter the circumstances, I'll 'ave your head. Call it Comanchero justice, call it steadfastness to one's own. There it is. *Comprende?*"

Rhiannon entered the tipi, ducking through the door and straightening up, rubbing the heels of his palms against his eyes. "Whooof!" Sun dazzle had almost cooked his aching head to mush, or so it felt, on the long hike upcanyon.

Only Warrington was here, sitting with his back against a willow backrest and morosely gazing into the coffee cup he held. He didn't glance up. Rhiannon tramped over to the faintly smoking firepit, stooped, and laid a callused palm on the coffeepot. Good and hot it still was. Only the brown bean was fit to damp a man's hangover humors.

"Morning, sunshine," he said. "Shitty day, ain't it? Got pink-eye this morning?"

Warrington eyed him a touch murderously. "Haven't you? I suppose you caroused the night long with your newfound chum."

Rhiannon chuckled. "I found a couple o' those." He squatted on his haunches and gulped near-scalding coffee and felt better. "Where's Bernie and the kid?"

"I have no idea. Each, though barely able to navigate, went his own way this morning. Neither offered reasons."

They wouldn't, Rhiannon thought grimly, but each would hope to catch another peep of Consuelo. God grant they'd be discreet and not tip the game. He couldn't regulate two grown men's every move, especially not two like those.

"Let's clear the air, Sassenach. Aye, Master Trevelyan and me are birds of a bawdy, booze-bibbin' feather some ways. But our side is where I squarely am and remain. Good?"

Warrington nodded almost indifferently. "If you say so."

"Look, laddie buck," Rhiannon said gently. "I know ye got fetched a bitter blow last night. But the final heat ain't yet run. Not by a far cry it ain't."

"Isn't it?" Warrington's face was as wooden as a ceremonial mask. "I'm afraid I've dropped out of the race."

"Shame on you, then." Rhiannon poured another cup of coffee. "It's a large handicap, to be sure. But if I cared for a woman as much as ye've said you do, I'd run it, by God. I'd follow that woman to hell and run odds against Satan himself."

"Why?" Warrington's mask slipped; his eyes went livid briefly. "For what? To pick up the leavings of that gutter scum?"

"You didn't feel that way about taking up a Comanche's leavings."

"In that," Warrington said hotly, "she had no *choice*! God, man, isn't the difference as plain as a pikestaff?"

Rhiannon drank some coffee and juggled the remainder in his cup. Warrington was far more open-minded than the most of his breed. But last night's revelation would shake the mettle of the most forgiving of decent men. The Sassenach had kept his head. Topping it all, of course, was the fact of his rejection: the utter and shattering blow to a man's pride.

Rhiannon tipped his brows and shrugged. "Too bad you wasn't born a bloody Elizabethan. But let's talk it out, Sassenach. I've quite a lot of thoughts cooking on a few things, and I'd like the benefit of your own."

"Why?" Warrington was staring at a point on the tipi wall, his eyes as brittle as heat-fractured glass. "Why should I give a damn?"

"I'll tell ye why. Because you gave me an oath, boyo. You and Rubriz and Blanco. Because the fate of my two children hangs on your holding to it. That's reason enough, my fine English gentleman who prides himself on his goddam sworn word. If it means a solitary mote, you won't go doggo on me now. You'll listen. And you'll help. I can't force ye, though."

Warrington lowered his eyes for a long time. With a shuddering sigh, he rubbed a hand slow and hard over his face. He nodded his head once.

# CHAPTER THIRTEEN

"**T**HIS"—RHIANNON MADE A WIDE CIRCLING MOVEMENT with his hand to indicate the whole of Palo Duro—"is a trap, brother. Some day the soldiers will take you in it."

Stone Bull grunted. "If the soldiers move in force on the Llano Estacado, when they come, our scouts will tell us. It will be time to move. Besides, it is late in the year. Too late even for Mackenzie to be out. A few seasons ago he tried to follow the *Nenema* onto the Staked Plains. The great cold came and snow fell and Three Stars retreated. All the way he was followed by Quanah Parker's braves, who shot arrows and bullets into his men. Three Stars himself was wounded."

"Mackenzie will not come this year," Rhiannon agreed. "But the next?"

"He is a good enemy," Stone Bull conceded. "He fights us as we fight the Americans. The other soldier chiefs have not learned this."

"Look for him to come again. Sherman, the chief of all the soldiers, has come from the East. He would like to kill all the Comanches."

Stone Bull shrugged his bullish shoulders. "Always the winds carry his windy talk. Mackenzie does not talk. He hangs to a trail like a wolf. Yes. Three Stars is a fighter. I wish he was a Comanche." There was admiration in his voice. "But no. I like him better as an enemy. A good enemy is better than a good friend. All but for you, *haint*."

If you but knew the viper you're harboring in your bosom, old friend. Rhiannon's thought was sad, the sadness taking on a bitter glow from several cups of *waqui*, the Comanche brew

concocted from the juice of the mescal cactus. He and Stone
Bull sat cross-legged in the war chief's tipi, smoking cotton-
wood-leaf cigarettes and drinking. The firepit's aura ruddied
the tipi walls, a warm oasis against the chilly night.

After he had done what he had come to do, the old
friendship would be through. If he still lived, Stone Bull would
count him an enemy, for he had come under the blanket of a lie.

Stone Bull gazed about him, at his three wives busy at small
tasks, at his six children tumbling at play in the firelight. He
sighed. "The warrior's path is hard, Redbeard. Yet he loves to
make war, to fight. Why did the Great Power make him so?"

"I have never heard the Great Power pass your lips."
Rhiannon smiled. "Does Stone Bull follow Ishatai, then?"

"Coyote Shit? He is like Sherman. He has many words.
Many listen." Stone Bull took a swallow of *waqui*. "A man
fights because he is made to fight. Who knows what makes him
so?"

"Ishatai says it is so that he can rub out the white men."

"The *Nenema* fought other *Nenema*, and they fought most
other people, before white men came. How do you *gottams*
say?—Coyote Shit is full of it. He eats pieces of peyote and has
visions. So have I, but I know they are dreams. Yet words will
make men fight."

Rhiannon nodded. "They run to the cry of the pack, *haint*. It
is always so with most men."

"But a *man* will fight for his own reasons, Redbeard. Or
maybe none."

They sat in a shared silence in the middle of the chummy
family chaos. They had often spoken together in this manner in
the past, and this might well be the last time. Rhiannon's
thoughts wore a dolorous color. In Trevelyan he had found a
friend for one level of him; Stone Bull had long shared another
level. Soon, very soon, there would be neither.

Today the Comanches had held an entertainment. The young
men had wrestled, getting their blood up so much that they'd
fallen into the old-time sport of kicking each other. *Wakara*,
shooting at the mark, was played, with each contestant being
allowed four arrow shots to prove himself; and more elaborate
skills of *tisowoko*, throwing arrows at a mark, and *nafoteneisa*,
throwing arrows for distance, were also tested. The women

played their special games of shinny and double ball. The betting was fast and furious, men and women winning or losing nearly all they and their spouses owned—lodge covers, clothing, ornaments, weapons, tools and utensils, even slaves —on the drop of an arrow.

All of it was loud and barbarous and colorful, even Warrington having to own he'd not seen anything to beat it in all of his globe-trotting. It had given the four comrades a brief, irresistible lightening of their tense concerns.

Some of the Comancheros had drifted upcanyon to watch. Rhiannon and Trevelyan had chatted and insulted each other as cordially as they had the other night. Florentino Diaz, wearing a vast purple bruise across his forehead, had shown up, very polite and smiling with all his teeth while his eyes promised death.

At that, Diaz had looked only half as foreboding as Breaks Something, who lumbered wide of Rhiannon and his friends, giving them a cautious rather than fearful berth, though it was hard to tell anything from his badly bashed and swollen face.

Sumah had found it amusing that the great ape could hardly see to glare anymore, but at least, she laughingly told Rhiannon, his looks were markedly improved. What she was otherwise saying to him, both with her own mocking looks and a few sly suggestions, continued to unsettle him. As yet she hadn't made the more direct approach that he was braced for. Whether he was in trepidation of it or hoping for it, or both, he wasn't sure.

Either way, though, he sure as hell didn't feel indifferent. Damn and blast that brazen brown baggage.

Rhiannon stood up, limbering cricks out of his muscles. Stone Bull rose, too, picking up the jug of *waqui* as he came to his feet. "It is too soon to leave the fire," he said.

"It is late. My stomach is not good. My head is not so good. They have not been the same since they took in so much Comanchero firewater."

Stone Bull laughed heartily. No trace of suspicion showed in his manner anymore and Rhiannon felt another prod of guilt. No further reference had been made by either to scouting out buffalo, and Rhiannon knew that his brother-in-law was simply pleased to have him in camp once more, to share the good rounds of palaver they had always known.

"The night is cold." Stone Bull thrust the jug at him. "This will warm it and not make your head and stomach too bad. Share it with your friends as we two have shared it. They are good men, I think. When they come again, they will be welcome at the fires."

"I am glad to hear it."

"I will say it. There are a good American, good *Inglés*, good Meh-hi-kano. A few of them are good. Better than their firewater. Pagh!"

Rhiannon gave parting words to all in the lodge and took his leave. The prods of regret continued as he tramped through the camp, past the murmurous, bustling tipis of the night, and drink would not relieve them, he knew.

The frosty points of starfire were bright between the canyon rims. Deep in the canyon, at this hour, the moonlight rarely reached them. This was good. They'd want a clear night on which to make their move, stars by which to take their bearings. But they'd have to take whatever came when the right time presented itself. A clear night with no moon would be best.

They'd been in the Palo Duro nearly a week, waiting and watching. He and the others had discussed a loose set of plans over and over, knowing that like as not they'd have to improvise when the time came. Always expect the unexpected, Rhiannon's Comanche foster father used to say. Or what you tried to surprise would surprise you. The plans remained frustratingly incomplete.

Their tipi was somewhat isolated from the main camp now, relocated almost inside a deep wedge in the canyon wall. Here they could discuss things more freely. Also it was irksome for a civilized man to camp in a cluster of hide lodges with all their sounds and smells.

As Rhiannon passed into the black groin of shadow relieved only by touches of firelight from inside the tipi, he heard a low but sharp lift of voices. Extending his walk to a lope, he reached the door cover and lifted it. Taking in the scene, he ducked quickly inside and dropped the cover.

Bernal Rubriz and Blanco were on their feet, facing each

other tensely. The reason was plain. A girl stood almost
between them, her hands half raised as if to keep them apart.

Everyone froze as Rhiannon stepped in, but Rubriz and
Blanco barely glanced at him. Warrington, standing to one
side, said in a harried voice, "Thank God you're back!"

Consuelo Rubriz was not a tall girl, and she might naturally
be on the thin side or captivity had worn her to thinness. She
looked lost and waiflike in a voluminous buckskin dress. Her
features were small and fine-boned, a bit snub-nosed, and her
looks were about so-so. But her large black eyes, at least in this
moment, flashed with strength and spirit. Yesterday Rhiannon
had seen her briefly from a little distance when Blanco had
surreptitiously pointed her out.

She said, "Señor Rhiannon?"

"Aye, and pleased to make your acquaintance, Miss Rubriz.
Now what the devil is this?"

As if it wasn't too damned obvious.

Rubriz and Blanco continued to lock stares as she quickly
and calmly explained that she'd seized her first opportunity,
while the old squaw who usually watched her was sick from
too much *waqui,* to come here. It was risky and she had little
time, but how else could she learn what they planned to do? If
she had known her presence would be a spark to set off her
father and the one with whom she had a *promesa de
matrimonio,* she would have thought twice.

"Ye did right," Rhiannon said. "We could not get to you."
He looked his anger and disgust at Rubriz, then at Blanco, who
said gently, "Mr. Rhiannon, I told you before I don't hone for
trouble on't. But I'm getting a mite edgy from telling her pappy
so."

"All right—all right! Bernie, do I got to remind ye again—"

"*No!*"

Bernal spat the one word. That was all, but the situation
seemed damped for the moment. Rhiannon tried to jolly the
atmosphere with a quip or two, then told Consuelo they had no
firm plan as yet but brought her up-to-date on everything so far.
It took a while. When he told of Melissa's infatuation with the
Comanchero leader, she only gave a placid nod—obviously,
she knew her mistress—and said gravely, "It will make things
very much harder, no?"

"It's a large chuck hole in the road, girl. But we'll bound it somehow. Thing now is to keep ye apprised of what comes up so you'll know your part. But you'll not be sure you can slip away again?"

Consuelo shook her head. "*Quién sabe?* I might come again by dark and stealth, señor, but even that is dangerous to us all. Still, it helps to know what has passed so far."

"She's got ten times the sense of you together," Rhiannon grimly told Rubriz and Blanco. "You stay set and watch sharp, lass. We'll get ye the word."

"There is a thing you should know," Consuelo said slowly. "The brother of your friend, the chief. Kicking Bird?"

"What about him?"

"He has spoken often with me. He asks me to walk out with him."

"*Dios!*" hissed Rubriz. "Have you done that?"

Consuelo gazed at him for a long moment, her small resolute face contained against any shadow of hurt. "Is that what you think of me now?" She tipped her head at Blanco. "Is it because of him? It is not the same, Padre. Will you ever believe that?"

Rubriz glared at Blanco, who wisely said nothing. After a moment, Rhiannon said, "All right, lass. Thank ye for telling us. It might be useful to know. No matter how fine it wears you, stand fast."

When Consuelo had slipped out, both Rubriz and Blanco retired without a word, rolling into their blankets in their usual positions at opposite sides of the tipi with their backs to each other. Rhiannon and Warrington sat down by the fire.

Warrington said, "Whew!" and nodded at the jug. "Would that be a spot of, ah, something wet and ring-tailed?"

"A gift from Stone Bull. To share with friends, he said." Rhiannon proffered the jug. "It'll raise cactus spines on your gizzard, Dickie lad, but I'd say a touch of the tonic would do you fair right now."

Warrington took a short pull and screwed up his face. "God!" He took another, longer pull and passed the jug back. "Where do we stand, Mike? Did Stone Bull say anything that might help?"

"Not him. Oh, he says he likes you boys. Reckon that means you can come back sometime and hunt buffalo."

"Smashing."

"For the hell of it," Rhiannon said, "if you've a mind to sit up for a while, let's go over what we already have."

They did, but it came to no more than they already knew or had speculated. Almost surely Trevelyan was suspicious of them and had his people on the alert. He'd have no particular wish to do them ill, nor would Melissa, for all her terribly capricious ways. Trevelyan could wait them out forever. But Rhiannon thought there was a chink in his bastion and he kept circling back to it.

"The girl Dominga, yes," Warrington said. "But it's a woefully slim hope, seems to me."

"Well, but look at the whole of it. She'll want your lady out of her hair by any means. She'd not dare do her harm, so what remains? To help us spirit Melissa away but with no suspicion falling on her. If Dominga guesses who we are, what we're about, she's likely had the thought herself. Most like, though, she's heard naught of what Trevelyan and Melissa may have said of us, and they'd surely not confide in her or she'd have sought us out before this. Unless she's still weighing the risks or waiting on the opportunity, of course."

"And assuming," Warrington said, "that Trevelyan ever permits his coterie of servants, outside of the Diaz bloke, to stray from the Casa Grande. Also, if he had your own thoughts about Dominga, he'd see she stays put. We've been over all that. And a damned sight more is-or-ain'ts."

Rhiannon gave him a tired but friendly grin. "We have, by God. But, laddie buck, there's one thing we ain't touched on but the single time. I had another thought about Miss Dragoman, and it's none of my business. You needn't hear it if that's your wish, and I apologize for bringing it up."

"Why?" Warrington said curtly. "If it suited you to mention a crib trollop to me, you wouldn't apologize, would you? This amounts to considerably less. Say it."

"Well, then, it's this. I hardly met the girl, but I could see she's as strange a one as you said. Is it possible she's merely pretending a great fascination for old Harry? She might have deemed it the price of her survival."

"My God. Do you believe *that*?"

"I'm asking you. I'll allow it may sound unlikely, but you

know her if any man does. It would be a great act, to be sure. She could be an actress to outshine Bernhardt or Lavinia Booth."

"No. She's no actress." Warrington stared into the fire, his face a gray study. "What you see of Melissa is all of Melissa, moment to moment. Feigning her infatuation with that blackguard? If one could believe it for a second . . . But as little as I ever really understood her . . . that, no."

Rhiannon pushed out his lips, said, "Mmmhmm," and applied them to the jug.

Both men gave a start as something brushed the door cover outside. Rhiannon tensed on his haunches, half slipping his Bowie knife from its sheath.

"Who's that, now?"

"Sumah the Warrior Woman," said Sumah's tipsy voice. "Come out, *kumaxp*. Come out and take your bride to her lodge. The blankets are warm and they are waiting."

God, he thought, she's rolling in her cups.

Warrington gave him a startled look. "Why, I believe it's your sister-in-law. What did she say?"

"Never mind," Rhiannon said heavily. "She's a sassbox without a kiver, as my sainted mother would say. Stay set; I'll go out to her."

Rhiannon stepped out of the tipi and straightened up. Because he had been looking at the fire, a practice that could get a man's hair lifted in an unwary moment, he blinked against near solid darkness. Only the fire flickers from lodges off to his left broke it.

Sumah, to one side, giggled and touched his arm. He jerked it away and was just able to make her out, a statuesque figure in the dark. She took his hand in hers.

"Does Redbeard jump at shadows? I am no shadow. Here, lay your hand here . . . and here . . ."

He pulled his hand away from her guiding one. "What is Warrior Woman looking for? There are no enemies here."

"We are enemies of old, *kumaxp*. It is a war of love."

"You are drunk and foolish. Go back to your blankets."

"Not without you, *kumaxp*. The bridal night has waited too long."

She was quite intense, standing close and taut. A realization struck him. "You are not drunk."

"No."

"You are without shame, woman. Among my people, in a time long ago, you would have been put to death by stones thrown at you." Feeling his blood coming up at the animal warmth of her closeness, he lapsed angrily into English. "I told ye to stop calling me your husband in a double-tongued way, dammit! I was never that, nor will I be!"

"Does Redbeard desire a stone? Here, I will pick one up for him." She stooped and fumbled at the ground. Rhiannon seized her wrist and dragged her upright. Her teeth shone faintly in the dark. "You are hurting me, *kumaxp*. It will not do you any good. I will scream very loudly, over and over, and it will bring people. I do not care what they think, but you do. Many who remember why you left us do not like you. Think what they will see, a white man hurting a Quohada woman."

Rhiannon let go of her. As soon as he dropped his hand, she grabbed it again. "Come. We will talk, if that's what you prefer. We will sit on the warm blankets, the blankets that wait, and talk."

All his blood was up now. Wordlessly, he let her lead him through the camp to her own tipi. He felt like a marionette being guided on strings. They ducked inside the tipi and stood tall, facing each other. He saw with a minor shock that Sumah had decked herself out as a *paibe*, a female dandy. Sumah, who had always despised such affectation. She was wearing a fine costume of white buckskin: a blouse with wide butterfly sleeves, fringed and brightly beaded, a two-piece skirt just as fancifully decorated, and an ornamental peplum hanging in points to midthigh. The beadwork formed brilliant geometrical designs. Her hair was adorned with beads and silver. Her legs and feet were bare and her face was daubed with bizarre touches of red and yellow and blue.

Sumah motioned toward her neatly arranged blankets. "Sit, *kumaxp*. No? Then we will talk so. Long ago you wanted me and would not take me. Do not tell me again it is the way of your people. You do not care much more than I do what people think. Do not tell me it was because the thing you felt for Naduah you did not feel for me. This I knew. Still you wanted me. You could have taken me."

Rhiannon felt the familiar burn in his face. God, she could

cross up his feelings as no woman ever had. What he'd felt for
Naduah was as sure and certain as the sunrise. Naduah *was* the
sun. But Sumah . . . She was the daughter of darkness and
confusion. She pulled his thoughts one way and then another.

"Maybe," he said slowly, "I was afraid of you."

Sumah's eyes flew wide. But the usual mockery tinged her
look and he knew the admission wasn't a new idea to her.

"Afraid of *me*, Redbeard? The little Sumah you played
games with so long ago?"

Rhiannon sighed. Get it all out. "Yes, even then. I don't
know what it is, or was. In my language"—he paused, trying
roughly to phrase it in Comanche—"one would say you are too
hot to handle. Fire warms, but too much of it burns. Then it is
sickness. Maybe it is death. I do not know. I did not want to
find out."

Sumah whispered, "Would we kill each other, Redbeard? It
would be a thing to find out."

"No."

"Maybe I could be to you as Naduah was. I wanted it.
Naduah is dead. Maybe it can be."

"No. You are not Naduah. You are not a wife. You were not
made to be one. You love too much being what you are. So do
I. We are too alike. And too different."

Sumah's eyes went stormy. "You are playing with words,"
she said angrily, "*Hai!* There are better uses for mouths. You
showed us, remember?"

Only too well . . . those days of teaching the two girls
how white people kissed. Comanches did not kiss and it was
exciting for the girls to learn how.

One of them moved now, or the other did.

They clutched at each other, their mouths meshing deeply.
After a minute, Sumah wrenched away, panting, her hands
busy. The peplum, blouse, and skirt slipped to the tipi floor.

She was all glossy, all golden, polished by firelight. Lean
and muscled and finely shaped, neck to toe, the fleshy nuggets
of her small breasts with their large sepia nipples uptilted and
taut, seeming to challenge him.

"Now, *kumaxp*," she whispered, "you will teach me
everything. We have grown too old for games."

# CHAPTER FOURTEEN

**U**P IN THE BRANCH CANYON WHERE THE SECLUDED POOL was, the stream that fed the lower canyon began. A couple of other sparkling rills fed by underground sources joined it farther down and formed a lively, tumbling current that ran down past the Comanchero village and lost itself somewhere in the terminus of the big canyon. Rhiannon couldn't recall ever exploring the stream to its end, but he'd remembered that the Comanche women did their washing at a particular place that lay roughly between the Comanche and Comanchero camps.

In their timeless lives, there was no particular wash day. The women washed garments as they needed cleaning, pounding them with stones or using larger boulders as crude scrub boards. But generally they chose the morning hours when the sun's heat hadn't yet penetrated to the canyon depths, for as the sun rose higher the canyon walls at this narrow point became a bake oven, reflecting the heat too fiercely for comfort. There was little green foliage for shade, but the projections of big and small rocks were ideal for draping clothes to dry as the first sun rays touched the lower canyon. Though it was late in the year now, and the mornings were chilly, the women kept the same hours out of habit. They could wash and dry their hair while the clothes dried, and they could gossip.

Since the second morning after his arrival in the Palo Duro, Rhiannon had ambled down to the outdoor laundry every day and watched the ladies, giving them a top o' the morning and joining in their talk while he smoked one or two of the Spanish cigars Trevelyan had given him. They came to expect him there, liking his bold humor and infected by his large, hearty presence. Comanche men more or less avoided the place, as if this site of women's work did not exist in their world.

Rhiannon had a reason for the daily visit. It was really a vigil. The Comanchero women, too, came here to scrub their clothes, holding a little apart from the Indians. Although the prospect seemed dim after nearly a week, he kept hoping against hope that Dominga might show up sometime. Here, where no men usually came, would be the likeliest place to catch her unwatched, away from the Casa Grande.

By the end of the week he'd decided it was probably a futile vigil. Either Dominga did her washing at the Casa Grande or she was never permitted out. Then one morning, all the blessed saints and earth spirits be praised, he found Rosalita among the women.

"Top o' the morning, lass!" he bellowed, genuinely pleased to see her. "How are ye faring?"

Rosalita was equally delighted by the meeting, and they chatted for a half hour before she remembered that her time was limited and began to tackle her basket of wash.

"And does your beautiful friend, ah, the Chinese-Negro lady, cleanse her dainties at this place also?" Rhiannon asked.

"Oh, yes, once a week. I think she will come tomorrow. I will tell her I saw you."

"Mmm, fine," Rhiannon said, and quickly changed the subject, offering to help with the washing since he had delayed her. Rosalita said no laughingly, it was her own work to do, but she was pleased by the courtesy, most unusual in a man.

Next morning, soon after sunrise, Dominga came. She walked past him with only a glance of the gold-irised eyes, a fleeting nod to his pleasant greeting. Her lovely brown-black face was as still as a carved Toltec mask as she set down her basket, kneeled on a rock ledge, and began to sort things for scrubbing.

Rhiannon settled idly on his haunches beside her, looking around briefly. They were a good space away from any other women, and no men were in sight. He tucked one of Trevelyan's cigars into his teeth and lit it.

"And how goes it at the Casa Grande, Dominga? About as ever?"

"What did you expect?"

Rhiannon waved his cheroot. "Oh, nothing. Wondered how *el capitán* is, that's all. And his Anglo wench."

Dominga turned her head, looking straight into his eyes. "The Anglo bitch is the daughter of your enemy. This much I know. What do you care about her?"

Rhiannon shifted on his heels, glanced about him again, and lowered his voice to a conspiratorial murmur. "How well d'ye keep a secret, my dear?"

"What secret?"

"Well, I have a great feeling for Señorita Dragoman. It's what brought me so far from my native heath. See, the señorita and I were meeting by night. Very hush-hush, you understand. Her daddy never knew. He had me whipped once—ye know about that?—and he 'ud have me strung higher than a buzzard's neck if he knew I was courting his daughter. We were promised to each other, and would have gone away together, far away. My old compadre Stone Bull did me a bad turn, though unwittingly, by bearing her off."

Dominga watched him impassively for a moment. At length she said, "She was engaged to the *Inglés*. Why is *he* with you?"

Damn! How much else did she know? He'd have to back and fill and hope his rambling bullshit Irish glibness didn't trip him up again. "Well, he ain't aware of how things stand, y'see. He offered me a lot of money—he's a *very* rich *hombre*—to find her and help him effect a ransom of her from the Comanches, if it could be done. But I've my own reasons he doesn't know."

"Why did she promise herself to him if—"

"Ah, he has her daddy's approval, y'see? Naturally she goes along with the old *bastardo*'s wishes on the surface of it. Now, then, seeing ransom's out o' the question as things are, we mean to undertake a daring rescue of our lady from *el capitán*. Clear so far?"

"To be rescued?" Dominga gave a short bitter laugh. "You think that is the bitch's desire?"

"Mmm, no, not from what I seen. She's a one to change suddenly. But I'm a stubborn man. If we can be off and away from this place, I'll take me chances on persuading her back to my side."

Dominga tossed her head and took a small washboard and a piece of yellow soap from the basket. "That is impossible."

"My dear girl, I can be a terribly convincing gent when I set my mind to't."

"I am sure. I mean, to take her away against her will is not possible."

"Why, lass, when it's his very heart's desire a man's set on, nothing is impossible."

Dominga's slant-lidded eyes narrowed. "What kind of a fool are you?"

"A fool of the heart, my dear, maybe a big dumb one at that." He smiled winningly, not knowing if brash charm was the right tack to take, but apparently it worked nicely for Trevelyan. At least it was keeping her a shade off balance. "I'm determined to give it a try, at the least. Do I have to say that ye can help me? And why you'll be wanting to?"

Dominga bent her head and began to scrub furiously at a soiled blouse. "I should not even be listening to you."

But she was listening. Rhiannon went over the plan briefly, then again in more detail, stressing what her part would be. All the while Dominga scrubbed away and never lifted her head. But he knew from her silence that the seed was sown and his words were nourishing it. Presently, he was starting to repeat himself in the same low-voiced, persuasive way, wondering if she'd ever break her silence one way or the other, when Dominga raised her head suddenly.

"Yes. I will do it. We may both die for this night's work, Anglo. But I will do it."

Rhiannon tipped back his head, sniffing the air and studying the dingy sky. "Aye, well enough. But it won't be tonight. There's bad weather brewing or my scars are achin' for nothing. A storm'll be on us by nightfall and it's a clear night as well as clear heads we'll be wanting for this work. Now, my dear, I need some information from *you*."

The storm held off till late afternoon, then broke in all its fury. Networks of lightning filligreed the sky, and thunder cracked like cannonades of light artillery between the cliffs. Torrents of rain streamed off the rimrocks and turned the canyon floor into a sopping lake of mud. The denizens of the

Palo Duro huddled in their tipis and rude shelters to wait it out. Runoff from the upper canyon backed up below the Comanchero village and threatened to flood it.

By early darkness the rain subsided to a cold drizzle and the thunder to a sullen rumble. Rhiannon and his companions sat in their tipi and discussed plans. Now that Dominga's aid was enlisted, they could solidify and synchronize the separate actions that would involve each man. If tomorrow night was clear, they would cast the dice on one crucial throw and hope that the inevitable farrago of unforeseen hitches wouldn't ball up the operation too badly. At least not fatally.

Meantime at least one more day of waiting remained. Rhiannon meant to use tonight's rainy cover to make a final determination on which the outcome of their plan might hinge.

The Comanche remuda was pastured in a side gorge near the big canyon's upper end. The Comanches had turned their horses into it on the day of their arrival, and Rhiannon knew its layout pretty well from boyhood. The gorge hollowed into a great bowl farther up, the cliff walls forming a natural corral, and its spacious bottom had plenty of grass and a spring-fed seep of water. A strong fence with a gate was set across the gorge mouth.

Bernal Rubriz was a *jinete*—one who had developed master skills in handling horseflesh in his lifetime—and on him would fall the duty of managing the horses for their escape. It was essential that he have a chance to reconnoiter the horse valley carefully beforehand and it couldn't easily be managed by daylight when others might be about. Braves going out to hunt might come for horses anytime and return just as unexpectedly. A man might sneak there after dark, but he'd make out practically nothing. Rhiannon had planned for Rubriz and him to join a hunting party today, but the weather had canceled it. This way was better. They'd have all the time they wanted to cover the place thoroughly, with nobody about, and lightning would furnish all the light needed.

"We'll go there separately," Rhiannon told Rubriz. "There's enough Indians in this camp that got a sore eye for our presence that any little thing, even a sight of two of us being out after dark in the rain, might touch off a suspicion of something afoot. Everyone's in their tipis; maybe we'll neither of us be seen. But let's go apart. Move along easy and out in sight;

don't play the skulker till ye're past the camp. Then stay next to the canyon wall; it'll guide you when the lightning flashes don't. I'll go first; you follow in ten minutes or so. I'll be waiting by the gorge fence."

Rhiannon crossed the camp at a leisurely gait. All of the tipi firepits were aglow tonight, sending out wan flickers here and there, but the door covers were down. Even if anyone saw him, they'd reckon he was bound for Sumah's tipi. He'd paid night-long calls on her for three nights straight and that sort of business went the rounds quickly, no matter how discreetly you conducted it.

Not to disturb the routine, he would do the same tonight. A bit later. It would be a good-bye to Sumah, for good and all.

Danger put an edge on passion. So did a couple years of near abstention from sex, for a man in his prime and full of more lusty appetites than most. He'd had no desire to wed again and, bearing the children in mind, had never brought a female companion to the ranch. On those times that business had taken him to Bolton, there'd been drunken, unsatisfactory couplings in its few sorry fleshpots. Fasitidious in his rough way, he'd felt unclean afterward. The night with Rosalita remained a drunken blank, another crumb of regret.

Given that dismal record along with the pent-up force of what had always been electric between them, his nights with Sumah had been feasts to a starving man. Yet the hunger seemed unsatisfiable. God. Exploring the acts of love, losing himself in the sensual arabesques of her lithe, twisting body, the fever of her cries and moans, the storms of passion had racked them again and again. It was a drug of all-consuming intensity, fire feeding on fire, the drug he'd instinctively feared, and already he was addicted.

Nor had consummation solved any confusion in his mind. He was still unsure of what Sumah and he really were to each other. Shortly the forces of circumstance would break it clean and forever. And so he would never know. But that's for the best, he told himself with a gray half-conviction. It's for the best. . . .

Walking unhurriedly with the mud slushing underfoot, Rhiannon hunched his shoulders against the slowing beat of rain. It runneled off the back and front of his curl-brimmed hat; the poncho-serape he wore was greased to repel water. The wet chill ate through his clothes; visibility was rotten. The flecks of tipi light guided him well at first, but once he was beyond the camp and facing solid blackness, only the sporadic flicker of lightning picked out his way.

As he moved into the upcanyon darkness, keeping one hand out to brush protrusions of the rough cliff wall and to hold his course, he looked back at the camp. And saw a figure pass across the streaks of firelight, coming right along on his track.

Damn! Rubriz was following him up too soon. Had something gone awry? He'd go a bit further, past a bend where he knew there was an overhang shelter of rock, and wait for Rubriz.

Rhiannon passed the bend, and lightning briefly showed him the overhang. He moved beneath it and waited, resting a hand on his Army Colt under the serape, but with no particular thought of danger.

Then the muffled figure came suddenly around the bend, swinging warily out and away from the cliff wall. Lightning flashed and showed Rhiannon two things at once. The man's pistol was out and ready. And the face under the broad sombrero was that of Florentino Diaz.

Simultaneously Diaz saw Rhiannon and stopped in his tracks. They were equally startled. But Diaz was less than four yards away now, and he had the drop.

Rhiannon was the first to speak. "Flory lad, all this damp's bad for firearms. If yours misfires, I'll be on you like a tiger."

After a long moment, Diaz said, "I keep my guns clean. My shells have metal jackets. I do not often misfire, señor."

"I don't detect that fine lilt in your voice, sweet as a canary's ever was. I believe you're all keyed up, Flory. Ye've had a watch on me. Waiting for a moment, eh? Though how ye managed it, I can't fathom."

Another spurt of skyfire lighted Diaz's face. It had a vindictive set. "It was not hard. I know a young woman in the Comanche camp . . ."

"Why, Florentino! The thought brings a blush. What must your friends think?"

A flat hiss escaped from the dandy. "Damn your smiling teeth, Anglo! She owed me a favor not of the amorous sort. She has kept an eye on you. She knows you go to a woman each night."

"Ah, the picture clears," Rhiannon murmured. "It offered a chance you couldn't resist. Tonight, with all the rain to cover, ye'd catch me alone for a moment, and the moment would be enough. But the shot 'ud fetch people, Flory. Ah . . . but it'd be the knife, wouldn't it? Ye'd be on me in an instant from behind. A quick slip of the knife between the ribs. Would that be it?"

"Of course," Diaz whispered. "You are clever, you are quick, Anglo. Did you see me? Did you lead me out to the dark? But no, or I would not have caught you off your guard." Lightning showed Diaz's perplexed scowl. "You were waiting here. For *what*, señor?"

"Maybe for a tryst with you, dear Flory."

"Damn you!"

"Seeing me headed off from camp you were curious enough to follow and keep your gun out. But we're too close to camp still, m'lad. A shot will be heard. So you hesitate."

"Take one step toward me," Diaz snapped, "and you're dead!"

"Am I?"

"I can kill you and run upcanyon. There are rocks and shadows to hide me."

"No matter how well you hide, *amigo*, the Comanche camp'll remain between you and the Comanchero one. Stone Bull is my brother-in-law. He'll hunt for my killer. The canyon end ain't far and he'll search ye out with torches."

Rhiannon's brain was cold clear, working with the precision of a fine Swiss watch. Twist Flory's thoughts, get him off balance for an instant . . .

But Diaz wasn't easily shaken. His aplomb quickly back in hand, he said in a raking purr, "Do you have skill with the knife, señor?"

"I'm passing fair with a sticker," Rhiannon lied. "And ye carry two knives, if I catch your drift."

"Precisely. I believe I can kill you with one. I will give you the other to hold in your hand. Not a very good chance for you, but better than none at all, eh?"

Was it, indeed. Rhiannon wondered if going after his enemy now, taking his chance with the gun, might not be the better choice. But he thought, Play for time.

"Agreed. Here and now?"

"A little farther up the canyon, señor." Diaz motioned with the pistol. "Walk. Keep a distance ahead of me."

Rhiannon tramped slowly on in the rain and darkness till Diaz said, "Stop."

Rhiannon swung to face him.

"Take off the serape. Drop your weapons on the ground."

"Mind if I keep me own sticker? I know the use of it."

"As you will. Do as I said. Now turn around and do not draw it until I tell you."

Rhiannon turned his back again and waited till Diaz said, "Now."

Coming around with Bowie knife in hand, Rhiannon saw that Flory had discarded his sombrero, poncho, and *charro* jacket. His pistols were probably wrapped in his clothes. He stood with a dagger in each hand. In the fitful lightning flashes, his smile gleamed ferally, twisting the cheek scar. "Since you have no use for my 'sticker,' Anglo . . . On guard!"

Diaz lunged and thrust, feinting in and out cat-quick. Rhiannon's answering swing missed. He was only a shade less quick than Diaz, but he was no knife man. All he could do was swing his blade in great horizontal arcs, hoping his greater reach would keep his opponent beyond arm's length.

It worked for a while. They circled and shifted constantly, always facing each other, their boots grating on the flinty ground. Rhiannon did not have to worry about Diaz's two stickers against his one as long as he could keep the Bowie in continuous dogged play, ringing himself in lethal arcs of steel that the popinjay couldn't penetrate.

Diaz was patient. He made a few idle feints. Rain matted his hair and pasted his silk shirt to his wiry, rippling torso. Always the predator's smile stayed on his lips. Before long his enemy must begin to tire, his reflexes grow slower.

Inevitably Rhiannon felt a numb ache creep from shoulder to wrist. He tried to ignore it, but the mechanical rhythm was dulling his mind and muscles. So was the mutter of thunder and the fitful flashes of lightning, both confusing his concentration, with the nimble figure of his adversary hidden by total darkness for frightening moments.

God, his arm was tiring. The knife felt as awkward as a lead weight. *Soon, in God's name!*

Suddenly Diaz was in and out, feinting with one blade. The razor edge of the other scored with exact timing on Rhiannon's fist, slashing the knuckles where they were still half-raw from his beating on Breaks Something's face.

The Bowie knife clattered on the stones at their feet.

A moment's pause, both men poised in their tracks. Flory's smile was very wide. "Do not pick it up, señor. I think the game has gone on long enough. Now . . ."

"Now you drop yours, *cabrón*," Bernal Rubriz said quietly from behind him. "It will square things off."

Diaz pivoted on his heel, knives up. But Rubriz had halted a good five yards away and the gun in his hand was as steady as the rock of Erin's isle.

Rhiannon let out a long, gusty sigh. "Bernie, I'd swear you waited an hour and not ten minutes."

"I would not have waited one minute if I had known. *Cabrón*, I told you to drop the knives. Do it."

Diaz's blades clashed on the pebbly earth.

Bernal Rubriz said, "And now, señor."

"No gunplay. We'll keep it quiet." Rhiannon cuddled his injured hand against his chest, flexing it. "Now it'll be my choice of weapons, bucko. Which is none at all. Make your play."

Diaz turned slowly to face him, the slash scar by his mouth twitching. There was no fear in his haughty stare. But he didn't move.

"Then I'll walk up to ye and break your damned neck where ye stand," Rhiannon said. "Your choice, sissy lad."

Diaz rushed him. Rhiannon sidestepped just a handbreadth; Diaz's wild swing grazed his chin. Rhiannon's hands shot out, gripping and closing. Diaz let out a single lost wail as the hands closed on his neck and crotch, lifting him off his feet.

Then he was high above Rhiannon's head, helpless and kicking in that terrible grip. Rhiannon swung back and forward, putting out all of his strength and then letting go. Florentino Diaz's body smashed sidelong against the canyon wall.

It fell to the ground as limp as a rag doll. It did not move again.

# CHAPTER FIFTEEN

**R**HIANNON'S NEXT THOUGHT WAS TO CONCEAL THE BODY. He prowled a little farther upcanyon and found a huge chunk of scale rock projecting from the wall. It seemed loosely set, so he gave it a push and felt it grind in its mooring. He and Rubriz carried Diaz's body and clothes and weapons to the wobbly rock spur and laid them underneath. Rhiannon gave a powerful heave and then leaped sideways as the scale chunk came crashing down along with a spill of rubble. Diaz was covered except for his boots. Rhiannon piled on more rubble and then inspected his handiwork. The spur might have tumbled down naturally and the rain would quickly erase traces of fresh-turned rock and dirt.

Afterward he and Rubriz made their way up the gorge to the horse pasture. The rain had died to a light mizzle, but sporadic tongues of lightning continued to pick out their way. The light showed them a panoramic view of the big grass-floored valley and its flanking cliffs. They tramped around it, reconnoitering the cliff walls, rock monuments, mottes of cedar and tall brush, the contour of the ground. Now and then they spooked bunches of horses. Both men commented on the layout as they went along, Rubriz mentally charting it all.

As they swung back to the gorge mouth, Rhiannon said, "What d'ye think, Bernie? Can it be done?"

"I can do it," Bernal Rubriz said, "with the help of torches I will set in various places. Also by the grace of Our Lady of Guadaloupe and with the assistance of various saints."

"Ye've a becoming case of modesty. I've heard it said you're a pure wizard with horseflesh. Think like 'em and outthink 'em. Like you're half horse your own self."

"Mule is the word," Rubriz said thoughtfully. "I am more stubborn than any horse."

Rhiannon thought: Amen to that!

They returned to the encampment, Rubriz going ahead first. Rhiannon waited a spell and then followed, heading for Sumah's tipi.

With his guts and head rattled by what had happened with Florentino Diaz, he knew how it would go. At first Sumah was puzzled and mildly solicitous at his impotence. Presently she grew angry and spiteful. Rhiannon merely nodded wearily to her taunt that he'd herded Texas steers so long he had become like one and, when she pressed him to tell what was wrong, said his stomach was bad from *waqui*. He agreed to her bitter accusation that he drank too much and suggested that maybe his powers were a wee drained. Might come back all the stronger for a couple nights' abstinence . . . Hurt and still puzzled and a touch solicitous again, she seemed willing to settle for that.

Next day he and his companions stayed on a hair-trigger alert for anything. Trevelyan would have a pretty good idea of why his *segundo* had disappeared and he might send to find out why or come himself. But either he did not or he made private inquiries that didn't reach their ears. Throughout the day no hint of anything amiss reached them.

Tonight would be the night, then.

Hardly any more surreptitious preparations had to be made. Over the past week they had quietly and casually conveyed all the gear and grub supplies they would need upcanyon to a point near the mouth of the pasture gorge. Any idle stroll by one of them in that direction sufficed to smuggle out bridles and compact oilcloth-wrapped stores of jerky and hardtack and parched corn, which they could hide under their clothing.

Only their saddles and bulky canteens presented a problem. Rhiannon had solved it by making periodic rounds of the Comanche encampment, chatting, admiring the possessions of friendly families, cannily trading here and there, larding his negotiations with so much boisterous on-rolling bull of jokes and small talk that his true activity was easily covered. He was forever tramping around burdened with one trade article or another. In this manner he sold off three of their saddles but acquired six Comanche rigs, making up the necessary eight. Watching his chance at odd times when the camp was drowsy with midday doldrums, he'd managed to sneak the saddles and canteens and a few blankets, along with the oil-and-pitch torches Rubriz had prepared, to their supply cache near the gorge. All of it was hidden by being crammed beneath a large slab of rock tilted against the cliff, its open sides concealed by smaller boulders that were easily moved.

Altogether it was a precarious and scary piece of business. Casual as his trading activity was, there was enough of it to be conspicuous. If it were brought to Stone Bull's attention . . . Apparently, though, other concerns occupied the war chief's thoughts; at least he gave no overt sign that he'd spotted anything amiss. Day before yesterday Rhiannon had filled out the cache, and he'd heaved a sigh of relief and braced for the far trickier business that lay ahead.

They sat in the tipi as darkness closed down, eating a supper for which nobody had any appetite. The night was clear as a judge's head, the stars etched against it like a casting of white-fire gems. The weather signs were irrevocably correct.

They went over the plans a final time.

"That's it, then," Rhiannon said. "All is fixed as well as we can make it." He paused, looking from one to the other. "I've never inquired of any man his beliefs—in a higher power or the like. Each to his own. Whatever any of you has inside him to make his peace with himself, hold it like a torch this night."

It was the nearest pronouncement to the blessing of a venture he'd ever made. And likely the very last.


Rhiannon and Warrington crept along the high rimrock of the Palo Duro, making detours around yawning gaps in the upper cliff walls. They were muffled in poncho-serapes and a couple of wide sombreros that Rhiannon had secured in trade dickering. Both wore parfleche-soled moccasins obtained by the same means. They were armed with revolvers and knives and three sturdy lariats hitched together. The ponchos and sombreros would serve the purpose of a rough disguise, if any were needed.

There'd been a touch-and-go feeling to things as they'd slipped out of the encampment one by one. They could not avoid being noticed idly by a few people, but not all at once and, they hoped, not by the same people as they took separate routes among the tipis. Nobody spoke to them, none showed more than passing curiosity. In short, they didn't look like men up to anything in particular. They carried their rifles hidden under their slickers and left the bulky weapons at the cache point.

Rubriz collected his torches and headed for the horse valley. Blanco took up a station in hiding. Earlier, Rhiannon had managed to catch Consuelo briefly alone when she was sent to fetch water. She knew her part.

Rhiannon and Warrington met at the foot of the single trail to the rimrock. They ascended it by faint starlight, picking out every step with the utmost care. The climb would have been impossible with last night's rain-slick footing. In this still night even a bit of shale rattling down might give them away. Rhiannon tried not to think of how it would be when they made the breakout, trying to beetle up the bloody cliff with horses in tow while possibly a great hue and cry was being raised below. If they got that far. After coming onto the rim, he and Warrington paused briefly, cocking their eyes and ears toward the canyon floor. Everything seemed normal; there was no sign they'd been spotted on the dim starlit ascent.

Now, working along the rim upcanyon from one vantage point to the next, they saw the fire spots of the Comanche lodges slide in and out of view, then fade behind them altogether. The Comanchero fires came into sight and these, too, fell behind but remained partly visible as the two men eased onto the bulge of rimrock above the Casa Grande.

They crouched on their heels, scrunching down as far as possible. A guard unseen from up here would be stationed at the foot of the trail to the *casa*. If the man chanced to look up, they might be dimly skylined. Just the outer edge of the building showed from its deep niche under the rim. It was all they needed.

Rhiannon cast an eye over the rugged scattering of boulders roundabout, pale under starlight, their lees drenched in black shadow. He chose a massive, roughly squared-off one close to the rim and looped a lariat noose around it. He and the Englishman tested both the anchor and the three hitched ropes by moving back from the rim grasping the end lariat and throwing their combined weights on it. Rhiannon dropped the rope end over the rimrock and paid out line slowly, till it brushed the roof of the Casa Grande and hung a couple of yards down its front wall. He grunted with satisfaction. Just about right for length; no need for the spare lariat he'd packed along.

Rhiannon slipped his watch out and made out the time by starshine. Warrington had given his watch to Blanco, who had none, Rubriz had his own, and the three were synchronized.

"So far," he murmured, "we've time and to spare. Not too much. I'll go first. Wait'll I'm on the roof. In case ye can't make out my wave of hand, there'll also be three tugs on the rope. Then you come down like a bloody beetle. After, there'll be no more talk 'cept what's absolutely called for."

"Spot on," Warrington said, and thrust out his hand. "Mike . . . just in case."

Rhiannon grasped the hand with a grin. "Why, good-bye to you, too, then, Dickie."

Gripping the rope, he walked slowly backward off the rim and down its bulging slant till his feet fell free. Then he twined his legs around the rope and slid downward. The line creaked tautly, rasping along his sweaty left hand, rubbing the cloth wrapped around his injured right one. His toes touched the flat pole-and-thatch roof. He held tightly to the rope as he settled his weight, feeling the roof good and solid underfoot. He waved a hand and jerked the rope three times.

Moments later, Warrington stood beside him.

Rhiannon leaned out and peered down past the eaves. They were right above the middle second-story chamber, Dominga's own, and its window shutters should be open. They were. The room was unlighted, as it should be. It shouldn't be occupied by a soul.

Rhiannon seized the rope again and let himself down hand over hand to Dominga's window. He peered into darkness that was total except for a pencil of light under the door opposite the window. Setting his foot against the sill, he gave himself a hard push, swinging his body out and then inward. He landed in a crouch on the sill and paused, listening. No sound in the room. He climbed through the window and gave the rope a jerk.

Warrington descended quickly. Rhiannon assisted him across
the sill. Revolvers out and ready now, they crossed to the door.
Rhiannon cautiously opened it a crack, then pushed it farther.
A wall-mounted lamp sent a sallow glow down a narrow
corridor between two flanking rows of chambers. All of the
doors were closed.

Noise came faintly from below. Women's voices and a clink
of dishware as if they were cleaning up in the kitchen. No other
activity that he could single out. Sounded normal for the hour
from what Dominga had told him of a typical evening in the
Casa Grande.

Still . . .

Rhiannon couldn't account for the cold prickling at the back
of his neck. But he'd felt it on other occasions. Sometimes it
presaged a thing about to go wrong. Other times it seemed to
mean nothing. A man's own keyed-up nerves could work him
into a fancy. No question of not going ahead now that they'd
come this far.

But he whispered, "Small change in the plan . . ."

Warrington listened to it and nodded once. They'd loosely
anticipated several contingency actions.

Rhiannon stepped from the room, his moccasins noiseless as
he crept to the head of the stairway. Warrington remained
behind, the door partly open. On guard for the least thing
amiss, Rhiannon went down the stairs and turned left through a
short, half-dark corridor. Other closed doors lay to his left and
right, but his sole concern was with the slightly opened one at
the corridor's end. Light shone out.

Trevelyan had a kind of study or retreat there. It was a rare
evening, Dominga had said, that he didn't spend two or three
hours reading or going over his crude accounts.

Rhiannon heard the rustle of a book page being turned. He
prodded the door with his moccasin toe and swung it inward.
Trevelyan was seated in a comfortable chair with his legs up,
boots crossed on the edge of a littered desk. He glanced up,
saw Rhiannon and his revolver, and showed a broad welcoming smile.

"Evenin', Michael," he said. "You're expected. But
where'n'ell did you dig up that shoddy greaser outfit?"

# CHAPTER SIXTEEN

**R**HIANNON HEARD THE TINY SHUFFLE OF A MAN IN STOCK-inged feet at his back. He didn't have to turn to know that he was taken as soundlessly as he'd taken Trevelyan, and might be killed on the spot if he did turn. A gun barrel touched his spine through the thick-weave serape.

Trevelyan laid his book aside. "Come right in," he said genially. "There's two behind you. Either or both will spill your tripe if I say or if you make an unfortunate mistake. On your peril, mate."

Rhiannon took a few steps into the room and half turned his head. The front man, filling the doorway as he stepped inside, was the tall, burly guard who had admitted them on that first visit. The other one, slight and wiry, was the man who usually watched the trail below. Both had their big Colt revolvers out. The slight one moved far enough around Rhiannon to take his gun.

Trevelyan dropped his boots to the floor. "No smart words, Michael? No ribald Irish witticism to improve the occasion? Come now, man. You must be dry."

Rhiannon said in a contained voice, "Where is Dominga?"

"There's a bright turn o' tongue. Well . . ." Trevelyan lounged to his feet and reached over to a shelf that held a decanter and two small glasses. "She didn't betray you, if that's your thought." He filled the glasses as he went on, "Dominga got found out. Rosalita mentioned you was at the rustic laundry and that you asked about Dominga. Had me a thought or two about that. Dominga has a dark brooding mind, that lass. I told one o' the ladies from the camp below to 'ave a lookout for you next day. You and Dommy had an uncommon long chat. Asked 'er later what about. Cool as a wellspring, that lovely 'un, but 'er answer didn't ring just right to me. So . . ."

Trevelyan came over and held out one of the glasses. "Come now. Whet or wet your wit."

Rhiannon didn't stir. He said again, tonelessly, "Where is Dominga?"

"Dominga's no longer in our company. It weren't vindictive, mate. Though she came clean about your little plan, I couldn't trust 'er again, that's all there was to it. Disloyalty is a bad trait that might have *me* dead were it ever repeated. Could be contagious, too. Did what I 'ad to do. Quick and almost painless, I assure you. Take the bloody glass."

Rhiannon looked straight into the iron-colored eyes that masked a soul. They seemed unchanged except for the vanished twinkle. He had an impulse to reach out and smash them. He let it glide in and out of his mind. He took the glass.

"Drink it. Let us 'ave a toast to Florentino. The late?"

Rhiannon drank the whiskey and let the glass fall to the floor. It broke in three pieces.

Trevelyan swallowed his drink. "How much did m'lud the toff pay you to undertake this daring sortie? Or was it Melissa's dad's money paid to you through the toff? Either way it must've been a bloody young fortune. Bloodier'n that long-ago whipping?"

"Even bloodier," Rhiannon said.

Trevelyan shook his head slowly, regretfully. "You disappoint me, Michael. It takes something from a man your size. And for mere pelf. Now, about Flory . . ."

"You got your pick of guesses."

Trevelyan sighed and moved back to the desk, half sitting on its edge, folding his arms. "You must've hid the body damned good. A couple o' my bravos scoured the canyon one end to the other today. Well, 'e made the play on 'is own, and dead is dead." He shrugged and settled his shoulders. "By that token alone, so are you. Pity your friends are about other business. But I'll merely slip a word to Stone Bull—"

*"Don't turn."*

Warrington said only the two words. The big guard jerked as

if something had rammed hard in his back. Warrington was in the half dark behind both guards, who stood a little apart in front of the doorway. He had moved up silent as a snake and maybe as swift. One moment he wasn't there, the next he was. He hardly raised his voice, it hardly carried, yet it was cold-steel crisp.

"Don't turn," he repeated. "Two steps forward. Then stop. Both of you, *ándale*!"

The guards were caught in their tracks. They moved with stiff obedience, their swarthy faces immobile.

Warrington cast one glance back over his shoulder, then stepped into the room and closed the door. "Bend over. *Quietly* lay your guns on the floor, Mr. Rhiannon's too. Very quietly. Then walk across the room and lie down on your faces."

The guards stood frozen, looking at Trevelyan for a sign. He said mildly, "Better do as you're told."

Warrington's blue stare, and now his gun barrel, was trained on Trevelyan as the guards followed orders. Rhiannon knew what was running through his mind; he also knew Warrington would control it.

"So there was a thing the blinkin' wench didn't tell me," Trevelyan said wryly. "Well."

"She didn't tell ye because I didn't tell her," Rhiannon said. "That there'd be two of us, not one."

"Ah, Michael. Then you trust nobody, either."

Rhiannon reached under his serape and pulled a crumpled wad of rawhide cords and pieces of cloth from his belt. "Down on your belly, Harry."

Trevelyan obeyed without a word. In a few minutes Rhiannon had both him and the guards trussed up securely, hand and foot, gags stuffed in their mouths. Afterward he and Warrington went out to the *sala*, encountering no one on the way. Warrington took up a post by the door to make sure that no one tried to slip out while Rhiannon began a room-by-room search of the *casa*'s lower story. The first place he looked was the kitchen and he netted nearly all of his fish right there. Dominga had told him the household staff consisted of Rosalita, José, and a half-senile old woman who was the mother of Martinez, the late chieftain of the Comancheros.

Rhiannon surprised all three, although none appeared too

surprised at that. Obviously they'd been apprised of his coming and had been told to go about their usual business. They broke off their nervous talk and scullery work and gave him round-eyed looks as he loomed in the doorway.

"Oh, señor," Rosalita said in a tremulous whisper.

"All right. Rosie lass. Nobody's been hurt, and nobody will be, if ye do as I say. Lie down on your faces. Snap to, now."

José scrambled to obey. The old woman looked misty and confused. Rosalita shrilly repeated the command in Spanish, twice, and the old woman obeyed it. Rhiannon tied up and gagged all three.

That left Miss Dragoman.

Earlier, Warrington had flatly declared that he had no word to say to her. So Rhiannon tramped dutifully up the stairs to the room that Dominga had told him was shared by José and Florentino Diaz. He dug out a set of the *mozo*'s spare duds: cotton shirt and pants, a serape, and a sombrero. Then he wrenched open the door of Melissa's room and strode in.

She lay on a comfortable bed, wearing a flowered silk robe, a book in her hands. She blinked at him drowsily and then her eyes widened.

"I'll make it short and not at all sweet," Rhiannon said. "Your handsome Harry is taken. Him and his two gun-toting buckos and everyone else in the place. Your daddy is waiting for you back south, Miss Dragoman. Will you come quiet or do we have a shindy on't?"

There were a few tears and remonstrations, such as she was happy where she was, happy for the first time in her life, couldn't he understand that, and so on. Rhiannon cut her short brutally by chucking the *mozo*'s duds at her and saying that if she wasn't in them in two minutes flat he'd dress her himself. He turned his back while she struggled with the clothes. She was weeping forlornly but moving briskly all the same.

They went down to the study. Rhiannon cut Trevelyan free and herded both Melissa and him out to the *sala*.

"What we're going to do now," he told them, "is go out this door and past your gang of rascals and through the Comanch' camp. Me and Harry are going to walk real close. My gun'll be smack in Harry's ribs the whole bloody way. One little thing goes wrong—either of you makes a wrong sound or a bad move—Harry'll be swallowing his own innards. That's all there is to it. Any questions?"

Melissa threw a tearful, appealing look at Warrington, who avoided her eyes. "Richard," she said almost inaudibly. "No—"

Trevelyan cleared his throat deeply. "No question'd change your mind, that's plain. But God, Michael. You're running a long tight race against all odds just for Dragoman's sorry pelf."

"Dragoman kidnapped my two children," Rhiannon said quietly. "He'll hold them till his daughter's returned to him. That's my stake in the matter, my only stake. I want ye to understand that, Harry, old *camarada*. So you'll understand why I've not a damned thing to lose. You, on the other hand, have the prospect of going free and unharmed once we're safely out of this."

A kind of wild and murderous fury filled Trevelyan's face. In that moment a man could tell with a certainty how he was able to hold sway over his half-savage band of brigands. Trevelyan turned his stare on Melissa. She was biting her lip, slowly shaking her head. Maybe he's got the stake of his life riding, too, Rhiannon thought. Or thinks he has. Same thing.

It was a thought to bear high and sharp through what lay ahead.

They left the Casa Grande and began the descent of the broad trail. Rhiannon walked beside Trevelyan and just inches behind him. The drape of Rhiannon's poncho hid the gun that prodded Trevelyan's side now and again. Warrington and Melissa were close behind them.

Except for one brief hitch, all had gone as it was supposed to. So far. He and Warrington had come in by the back door, so to speak, to avoid passing the Comanchero camp and the two guards. The touchiest part of the gamble would have been to have to overcome the guards, one inside and one outside, without gunfire, which would have wrecked the scheme. By letting Rhiannon come in through Dominga's window as planned, Trevelyan had neatly checkmated himself.

One question was still unanswered and Trevelyán could simply give a cool lie to it. Had he shared his foreknowledge with any of his precious bravos below? Probably not. His arrogance had directed him to play out a personal hand.

Otherwise, likely enough, men would have been posted to riddle Rhiannon with bullets as he came down that rope to the roof. By the aid of torchlight, it would have been easy as swatting a fly. That being so, it was doubtful Trevelyan had any contingency measures rigged. . . .

They reached the canyon bottom and were briefly hidden in its deep gulf of shadow as they tramped on. Squares of light showed ahead. The Comanchero village was settled for the night, but spills of light issued from a few open doors and windows. If anyone looked out, they would see their leader and three others—maybe the two regular guards and the *mozo*—in ordinary bulky ponchos and sombreros that put their faces into shadow. Trevelyan himself wore a blue seaman's jacket and a Stetson tipped back on his head. If they were hailed along the way, he would do the talking, tell people to mind their own business or, if necessary, come up with a glib reason why he was out at an unusual hour.

Before an open doorway of one dwelling a couple of drunken women stood screeching at each other. They paid no attention to the four people going by. On the ground in front of another a dazed-looking man sat clutching a demijohn to his chest. He said nothing, just followed them with an owlish stare as they went past.

They entered a lengthy stretch of darkness, guided only by the stars and the stream's chuckle over its rocky bed to their right. Rhiannon warned them to go slowly on the uneven canyon floor. He stumbled off balance a couple of times; after each he gave Trevelyan a warning prod to ensure that he wouldn't be encouraged to seize a fancied opportunity.

A fan of wan orange light grew ahead of them. At last they walked straight and bold into the Indian encampment. Past the lodges of various bands, meeting no more than quizzical looks as people peered out of their tipis. There were outside fires that plainly picked out the Comanchero leader and three of his followers. Four Comancheros going about some inscrutable nocturnal business of their own. Saints and spirits grant that nobody thought he saw anything more. If any night pickets were out, they weren't immediately in evidence.

It seemed like the longest walk of Rhiannon's life. Even with the last tipis—those of the Quohadas—behind them, he felt no abating of anxiety. Just before they passed from firelight's aura into darkness again, he checked his watch. The timing was almost perfect. They hiked on toward the canyon's end.

Now Rhiannon used the familiar shape of upcanyon rimrock against the sky to keep his bearings. But he couldn't see the mouth of the horse valley gorge as they approached it. And Blanco's soft, questioning word coming out of the darkness startled him, though he expected it. He heard the snuffle of a horse.

"Stop," Rhiannon said. "How did it go?"

"Mostly right," Blanco drawled. "Okay if I make a light, sir?"

"Yes."

A match was struck. The sulphurous burst of light showed the scene. Several horses stood ready with the necessary gear lashed to their saddles. A picket line strung between two wide-spaced rocks secured their bridles. Blanco was holding the sputtering lucifer high in his hand; Consuelo stood beside him. On the ground, tied and gagged and out cold, was Kicking Bird.

"He gave me an argument," Blanco said laconically.

Consuelo's part had been to tell Kicking Bird she would walk out with him tonight. Where she had taken him was up the canyon to the place at which Blanco was stationed.

"He did not want to come so far," Consuelo said soberly. "So I told him there were blankets waiting there. And we would go such a distance from camp because I am a modest girl."

Blanco dropped the match before it scorched his fingers. He said into the darkness, "There was me waitin' and he wanted to argufy that. Buffaloed him 'fore he could give out a whoop."

Rhiannon said, "Not too hard, I hope."

"No, sir. You know how, you can rap a man above his ear with a gun barrel and he'll sleep a spell and come out no worse but for a headache."

"Light up another, will you, lad?"

By the flare of the second match Rhiannon looked over the seven horses and shook his head, grinning, as he took out his watch again. "Bernie did a job of it, for sure. Caught up the number of nags we need, three of 'em our own at that. I suppose he found his mount, too? Damn, I only half believed he could, even with torches to help!"

"Yes, sir," Blanco said. "Mr. Rubriz came back same time me and Connie got here with the Comanch', who I toted on my shoulders. Had the horses on as many halters. We helped him get the rigs on and he went back in on his own horse."

Consuelo said, "*Padre* is a *jinete*." Her sober face was wearing a small, proud smile now.

The match went out and Rhiannon, having noted the time, tucked away his watch. "Five minutes," he murmured. "If Bernie can bring off the rest on time, there'll be all hell poppin' about then."

They waited in the cold blackness, Rhiannon keeping his gun muzzle pressed to Trevelyan's side. They had the two necessary hostages, Kicking Bird and the Comanchero leader. All that remained was to get out of the Palo Duro. Down here they were lost in canyon shadow. Up above, as they climbed the lone trail to the rim, starlight would pick them out. Their progress would be agonizingly slow. The horses' hooves, if nothing else, would make enough sound in the crisp stillness to carry between the canyon walls and alert the Quohada end of the encampment.

Their own party would never make it to the rim unless there was a diversion to give them extra minutes of time. Enough or not enough. It would be running on the thinnest of margins . . .

From up the gorge came the sound of horses on the move. Faintly at first, then growing as the sound came near. A clatter of echoing hooves between the cramping walls. How many horses? As many as Rubriz had managed to bunch together and drive into the funnel-shaped valley end of the gorge.

They were coming fast now; Rubriz was pushing them hard. His shouts urged them on and now his pistol sounded, pressing them harder and faster.

By now Rhiannon's eyes were slightly accustomed to the dark. He saw the rush of horses pour out of the gorge mouth, thundering past the seven humans on their left. Blanco and

Warrington fired their revolvers in the air and yelled at the top of their lungs to turn the animals downcanyon.

They were pointed for the encampment. Unstoppable in their panic, they would hit it like a blizzard of flesh and bone. Fires would be scattered, tipis bashed in, a chaos of unutterable confusion would prevail for an unguessable time. And while it did, eight people and eight horses would be beetling up the bloody cliff. . . .

In his excitement, Rhiannon's attention strayed by a hair; the press of his gun against Trevelyan's side relaxed.

Suddenly a powerful arm whipped around his neck, a hand grabbed for the gun. Trevelyan tried to wrestle him to the ground, but Rhiannon braced his legs. Trevelyan's hand had found his wrist and locked onto it, trying to turn the gun against Rhiannon's body.

Rhiannon roared "Araaagh!" and thrust savagely against the hold.

The gun went off between them. Trevelyan's grip relaxed, his weight fell away, as he slipped backward to the ground.

Melissa gave a piercing scream.

"Let's get—" Rhiannon choked and swallowed. "Let's get the bloody hell out of here!"

# CHAPTER SEVENTEEN

**T**HEY PRESSED A STEADY PACE THROUGH THE FIRST NIGHT OF their flight. The ruse had worked. They were clear of the Palo Duro, and Rhiannon's first goal was to put as much distance between them and immediate pursuit as they could. Not that it would matter in the long run. The Comanches wouldn't follow by darkness, but they would be coming on tomorrow and they would have spare horses. So almost certainly, sooner or later, there would be a showdown fight.

Just before the flat rays of sunrise cut the horizon, Rhiannon ordered a halt. Everyone but Melissa and Kicking Bird piled stiffly off their horses and unlimbered aching muscles. Rhiannon inspected their backtrail. A light dawn wind combed the far brown swells of buffalo grass. Nothing stirred out there. It would be a while.

About the Comancheros, there was no telling. Yet. They might join the Comanches or they might not. Given the tooth-and-claw ethics of Trevelyan's rogues, his loss as a hostage might make no difference at all. Sentiment had no part in whatever loyalty the Comancheros gave a leader. With both Trevelyan and Florentino Diaz dead, there'd be an immediate scramble for leadership. In that case the main danger was that one bravo might shrewdly implement his bid for power by inflaming his fellows to a blood quest for vengeance against Trevelyan's killer. But any protracted squabble for chieftainship should lessen the likelihood.

Wait and see . . .

He turned his attention to Melissa Dragoman.

After seeing Trevelyan shot down, she'd turned from

apparent tractability into a wildcat. It had taken precious seconds and the combined efforts of Warrington and Blanco to subdue her kickings and strugglings, gag her, bind her hands, and get her on a horse, lashing her feet together with a rope passed under the horse's barrel. The unconscious Kicking Bird was thrown across a saddle and similarly secured, a line beneath the horse connecting his bound feet with his bound hands. Once they were out of the canyon and well away from it, the revived hostage was permitted to sit his saddle, hands tied in front of him. He was too groggy to make a bid for escape. Melissa's gag was removed, but she remained tied fast to her horse.

Now Rhiannon cut her free and said flatly, "Get down."

She didn't stir, only looked a pure and lively hatred at him out of the windblown tangle of her hair. A thread of dried blood ran down her chin from a split lip. She said in a slow, cottony croak, rolling each word carefully off her tongue, "You stinking brush bastard. I'll see you dead for this. I'll see you in hell and I'll dance on your damned grave."

"Tut, tut," Rhiannon said wearily. "You'll get down all the same. Or I'll dump you off."

Melissa slipped painfully to the ground. Nobody made a move to assist her. Her long nails had left a set of red furrows down Rhiannon's cheek and Blanco was limping slightly from a kick to his shins. *Frail!* Warrington had once called her that. Now, at least, she was too stiff and sore to do anything but glare at them. She stood massaging her wrists and said to Warrington in a voice of hate, spacing her words distinctly, "God damn you, Richard. God damn your prissified stiff-collared little soul."

Warrington's face was stony; he turned away.

"Cheers for the little lady," Rhiannon said. "The man only risked his bloody neck to save yours from what's laughingly termed a fate worse'n death."

Melissa tried to spit at him. She managed a dry hiss.

"A little moisture for the purpose?" Rhiannon uncapped a canteen and held it out. He jerked it back as she tried to bat it from his hand. "Later, then."

"I had everything," she whispered. "All I ever wanted . . . with him. You could tell that much. You could have left it alone."

"If not for my children," Rhiannon said grimly, "nothing would've given me greater pleasure. Harry had a few good points, but I'm doubting constancy was one of 'em. How long before he tired of your flighty ways? Tossed you to his boyos for a plaything? Did that ever cross your gnat of a mind?"

"It wasn't like that!" Melissa half screamed.

"You're a damned spoiled chit of a rich man's daughter," Rhiannon said brutally. "You're as much a moth of the affections as Harry was. Flitting here, then there. *That's* how it was. I'd not care a pinch of owl's dung if your bloody infatuation got your stupid neck wrung. Now, nobody but your bloody old dad does. So have the sense to behave. There's nothing else you can do, no place else you can go. Digest that along with your venom, sweet one."

Rhiannon tramped over to Kicking Bird's horse and gave the lad a boost to the ground, leaving his hands tied. The youthful Quohada's face was still unshaped by the stoicism of manhood. It held a mingled anger and hurt and bewilderment.

"I do not understand this thing, *haint*. Some of it . . . I think. But not all. Tell me why you did it."

"It is a long story," Rhiannon said tiredly. "It will come out as we ride. I will tell you and then you will hate me and spit on me for a traitor. There is no help for it. Come now, let's work the lameness out of our joints and rest and have a bite to eat. We'll need all our strength."

They tended the horses, walking them up and down while they munched on jerky and pebbles of good army hardtack, the kind that had to be beaten with a rock or a gun butt to reduce it to an edible consistency. Concentrated food might be all they'd have to carry them through, depending on the conditions that lay ahead. Even at a steady pace the horses would be pushed hard, beyond any ordinary horse's stamina, and they had only one spare mount, the one intended to bear Trevelyn.

Rested and fed, they mounted up and rode on.

At midday the Comanches appeared in the distance. Rhiannon trained his field glasses on them. As he had hoped, no Comancheros rode with them. But it was a large party; he made out fifteen riders and Stone Bull's distinctive white-plumed bonnet.

The Quohadas had taken up the trail early this morning, and it was a plain one. They'd come on fast to overtake the fugitives, and now they were in no hurry. Having reached a measured distance from their prey, they held in and kept to the fugitives' own pace.

So far, not too bad. Stone Bull's eagle eye would tell him that his kid brother was alive and unhurt. Still, there'd be no predicting his actions. Comanches were high on blood honor and clan loyalty, but next to those qualities the individual life often counted for little. Stone Bull was a moody fellow, not one to be predicted lightly, and Rhiannon could only gamble that his depth of personal feeling for Kicking Bird would outweigh any other consideration.

If so, the chief wouldn't launch an outright attack. But his brain would be seething with ideas. They would center around avenging himself on a treacherous brother-in-law while not endangering the life of a cherished brother by blood. . . .

The days plodded by like a train of sullen mules. The flight continued and so did the pursuit. The Comanches clung to their backtrail at the same unvarying distance, halting when they did, resuming the trackdown when they moved on. The whole business began to assume a nightmarish quality. It ground on like a treadmill of the gods till even the harshest edge of reality slipped into a blur of abstraction. Sometimes Rhiannon's Celtic-blooded fancy made him feel he was guiding a band of grim and gritty-eyed specters across a tawny unknown dream-scape.

But it was all real. The landmarks that informed him of what seemed like an inchworm's progress. The few streams or waterholes where they could slake thirst and refill their canteens. The deadly broil of sun that baked their heads and innards. The few overcast days, cooling toward deep autumn, that cleared their heads and made the traveling easier, even as the slate-gray skies depressed their spirits. The deadly stultifying weariness that soaked deeper, day by day, into their bones. At times, the vast, lonely reaches of country seemed to swallow a man's thoughts and hopes, to dwarf them to antlike significance, while the endless prairie winds blew them away to powder, to nothing.

Overriding all else was the knowledge of stalking death at their backs.

They stretched their food carefully. Blanco supplemented it by killing an occasional jackrabbit suddenly spooked to flight. The ordinary Colt revolver, notorious for inaccuracy at any slightly respectable distance, was a live and lethal thing in his hand. Blanco was quick as lightning, never missed a shot, and usually bored his target through the head. Spitted and broiled over coals, even tough and stringy jack meat was a strengthening respite from their dwindling supply of jerky, hardtack, and parched corn. So were findings of edible roots and barks.

Rhiannon set long hours for a day's travel, driving his companions and the horses as much as he dared, not neglecting carefully timed rest stops. When the time came for bivouac and sleep, he chose each campsite with an eye to its natural advantages. Whenever it could be managed, he selected an isolated cluster of rocks, with a wide scan of surrounding open territory, where they could hole up and defend themselves if necessary. He and Warrington and Rubriz and Blanco took turns at two-hour guard duty, with two of them standing each watch. It was hard on them, but it reduced almost to nil any danger of their being taken by surprise after dark. It would be easy even for a man fully vigilant, ground fine by exhaustion, bad nerves and sheer monotony—and none of them was quite that vigilant any longer—to miss a crucial sight or sound. Having two men on watch pretty well coppered the bet.

Comanches disliked moving about by night, of course, but Stone Bull's hands were never tied by impractical customs. At the same time, he would be unutterably patient while he awaited his chance. His war chief's prestige as well as his brother's life was at stake. He and his seasoned warriors could drag out the game indefinitely while knowing their prey was gradually being worn down, body and nerves, the whole while. Only when the prey neared their own country and were in danger of eluding his reach was he likely to make his move. God knew exactly when or how it would come.

Rhiannon made early camps while daylight still held. He never waited until full dawn to resume the trek. As early as the light of each chilly morning permitted, he had them up and on the move again.

Both Melissa and Kicking Bird seemed to have accepted their present lot, if only provisionally.

As Rhiannon had expected, the young Comanche's early bewilderment had changed and hardened into an implacable hatred for his captors, particularly his old *haint* Redbeard. His black looks and unbroken silence told of the humiliation and fury boiling in his randy young breast. But he was canny, too, never creating a fuss. From time to time Rhiannon loosened his wrist bonds to restore circulation, keeping a careful watch on him till he was securely tied again. Kicking Bird's pony stayed on a lead rope attached to Rhiannon's saddle. At night the youth's feet were also tied and part of the guards' duties was to check on him now and then.

Rhiannon left Melissa's hands free after extracting from her a sullen promise not to make another commotion. Even if a typically perverse whim made her decide to try a break again, where could she go? As a precaution, however, her pony was fettered to a lead line on Rubriz's saddle. In camp everyone kept a general eye on her. Meantime her attitude of smoldering and unrelaxed hatred was a match for Kicking Bird's. Like his, most of it focused on her lover's killer, Rhiannon. In this, at least, she proved herself capable of a sustained emotion. Given an opportunity, she might still try something harebrained and dangerous.

Still, she was hardly as stupid as he'd named her. She was being returned to her daddy and her old, spoiled-rotten life. Given her present condition, it had to be a welcome prospect. She was saddle-sore and crushed to the same steady exhaustion as all of them. Her limp white cottons were stained and gamey with grime and sweat; her hair was filthy and matted; her face was sunburned and peeling. She shared her companions' nerve-drawn awareness of danger and her obsessive grief, or whatever, could only exacerbate it. Even those driven days of her Comanche captivity must seem a paltry candle to what she was undergoing now.

So the days and nights passed. Minor irritants rubbed everyone the wrong way. Snappish bursts of acrimony were exchanged now and then. But nothing very serious occurred until they made camp on the evening of the twelfth day. Then, like a delayed storm compounded of the building tensions, several kinds of hell began to break loose at once.

Rhiannon had chosen a rock-strewn site on an eminence of land from which he could see the Comanches settling down for the night. Their fires spattered the twilight prairie at the usual distance.

His own party was arranged in its usual disposition. They sat on the ground or squatted on their heels, none of them keeping close together or saying much. Warrington was sunk in his own chosen isolation, hunkered down and cleaning a revolver that didn't need cleaning, his blond head bent to his work. Rubriz crouched with his arms folded on his knees, staring grimly at nothing, contracting his thick, dust-powdered eyebrows now and then. Consuelo was preparing supper, turning a rabbit carcass over a small fire, while Blanco had ranged out a short distance to hunt up more wood.

Mostly, out of respect for her father's barely leashed antagonism, the two young people had stayed apart, exchanging few words. Their unhappiness was almost a tangible thing. But Rhiannon could see no help for it. They and Bernal Rubriz would have to work it out for themselves. The whole situation held a feel of impending tragedy.

Kicking Bird sat stoic and silent, his bound hands between his knees. His black eyes were withdrawn but alert; they unceasingly weighed everything and sized it all up and never showed a trace of what he thought.

Melissa seemed less sullen than usual. She was sitting cross-legged, tugging on her matted hair with her fingers. It was the first sign of arousal from her wickedly contained hatred to an interest in the neglected grooming of her person.

Might be she's coming out of it a little, Rhiannon thought. Might be a good sign.

Melissa said in a cold and abrupt voice, "Connie!"

Consuelo looked up in surprise. Melissa hadn't given her a word, hadn't paid her a lick of attention, in all these days. "Yes, señorita?"

"Help me straighten my hair."

*"Que?"*

"You're still working for us, aren't you? For the Dragomans? You are my personal servant. I have given you an order."

Consuelo looked at the spitted rabbit she was turning, then back at Melissa. She made a small confused motion of one hand. "But . . . I am cooking."

"Let that mick do it. Or your father. He works for us too, doesn't he?"

Consuelo said hesitantly, "But we do not have a comb."

"You have fingers, haven't you?"

Warrington said, without looking up, "There's a bloody comb in my bloody saddlebag. Use that."

Consuelo rose uncertainly to her feet, smoothing her palms on her buckskin skirt, then looking at Melissa, at Rhiannon, at her father. Rubriz gazed fixedly at a rock, unstirring, not changing expression.

Rhiannon said quietly to Consuelo, "That meat'll scorch if it ain't turned, lass. I'll take it over if that's your wish. Just be sure it is."

"Señor?"

"If ye care to follow her bidding, do it. That's your choice, no one else's. Just be sure it's the right one."

Consuelo bit her underlip. Slowly she shook her head. "I think it is not. I am no longer in your service, señorita. I am going to marry Jack Halleck. We are going away together."

Melissa's brows arched. She smiled, her tongue lolling gently in her pink mouth, then passing lightly over her teeth. "Jack Halleck? He's the albino boy? Is that his real name?"

"Yes. We are going to be married."

"Well, I vow." Melissa laughed. "And you"—she looked at Rhiannon—"expressed a lofty, censorious view of *my* taste in men. Very well, Connie. At least I can offer you a wedding wish. I give you a long and happy life in hell, sweetheart."

Rubriz turned his face toward her. "You will not speak so to my daughter."

"Why not, Bernal? I haven't received an impression that you unqualifiedly approve of that bleach-faced killer she's set her cap for." Melissa laughed again. "They were playing out their little tête-á-tête practically under your nose. Months before you ever realized it. From what I saw, a lot more than *you* ever did, I'm pretty sure you're almost an *abuelito* already. A lovin' old granddaddy."

"You," Rhiannon told her ominously, "shut your damned face. Or I'll shut it for you."

Blanco had returned from his search for fuel. He stood at the edge of the camp holding a stack of brush in his arms. He'd heard most of it and now he watched Rubriz unbend and rise to his feet.

"What have you done?" Bernal Rubriz said. "What have you done?"

Blanco let the armload of brush fall. Rubriz's eyes were fixed on him with a bright and terrible intensity. He looked like a man about to spill over a tenuous line into madness.

Slowly Blanco drew his Colt. He looked into Rubriz's blazing stare as he flipped the weapon over in his hand and tossed it. The revolver landed in the dirt at Rubriz's feet.

"You can pick it up," Blanco said, "and you can use it. Or leave it like it is and use your own hogleg. I've had enough, Mr. Rubriz. I am sick to my soul with taking it off you. If you got the guts to kill me, do it. Now. You won't get no other chance. Now, or there's an end of it."

Rubriz stood unmoving for a long moment. Then he bent stiffly and picked up the revolver. He held it in his hand and looked at it. A muscle squirmed in his cheek. Then he looked at Melissa. Firelight made red flecks in his eyes.

"I would like to do it. But I think you are the one who should be shot now. What you said is not true."

Melissa smiled perkily. "Of course it is."

"I watched you grow up," Bernal Rubriz said. "I taught you how to ride and how to shoot a gun. But I have never understood you. I have seen you ride a good horse to death. I have heard you tell lies to me, to your father, to others, and never turn a hair. To have fun. To have your own wanton way. To be cruel. Or is it that a devil entered you at birth? Something in you is unclean."

"Oh, come now, Bernal. Really."

Rubriz looked back at the gun in his hand, then at Blanco. "Now is not the time." His voice sounded reedy and old and tired. "Another time, *bastardo*."

With a sudden repelling gesture, as if the gun were a snake in his hands, he flung it sideways away from him.

Rhiannon had been as frozen to the spot as any of them. A

gusty relief shook him. He cleared his throat and started to speak.

Then Melissa moved. The gun had hit the ground a scant six feet from where she stood. She moved and pounced, then straightened up and whirled, Blanco's Colt in one hand, the other hand bracing it. She held it at arm's length and pointed it at Rhiannon.

"Brush bastard!" she shrilled. "I told you I'd see you in hell!"

She double-thumbed the hammer as she cocked it.

She was facing them all, except for Warrington. In the three seconds it took her to drag the hammer to full cock, he had time to gather himself and dive at her back. He hit her in back of the knees and spilled her to the ground. The gun roared and exploded a flurry of sparks from the fire.

Warrington wrestled the gun away and let her up, spitting and cursing. She spat sand and turned on him, cursing him directly.

Warrington slapped her. A flat, open-handed clout that swiveled her head and knocked her staggering. She swayed to and fro on her feet, blinking unfocusedly and shaking her head.

"Why, Richard," she said softly, dazedly.

"Shut your mouth. Say another word and I'll do it again." Warrington's tone held all the steel of which Rhiannon had seen glints in him from time to time. "Rubriz never understood you. I never did. Doubt any man can. Woman or wanton or child or devil . . . Lord. I don't know what you are, Melissa. I loved you, that was all I ever knew. God help me, I still do. Suppose I always shall. Is there more in you than I've seen . . . than anyone has? I would like to find out."

Melissa's lip was split open again. Her tongue licked up the blood. She blinked at him with a kind of gentle uncomprehension.

Warrington said, "Mike, take off your shirt. Show her what her father did to you."

A cold prickling ran over Rhiannon's flesh. "Man, now I'm not just sure—"

"Do it. Show her. And turn around. Show her all of it."

Rhiannon sighed heavily. He shed his jacket and then his shirt, pulling it off over his head.

"Oh, *Dios*," whispered Consuelo. The others were silent with shock, their eyes riveted to the network of ridged, discolored, smooth and puckered scars. Rhiannon slowly turned full circle and faced Melissa again.

"Note the *C*, my dear," he said in a moderate voice. "The heart would be a bit to your left of it, if Dick will loan ye back the gun."

"No," said Melissa. "No, no."

"That's what your dad gave the man for accidentally straying over his line and branding an unmarked steer," Warrington told her. "It wasn't enough. Now he's kidnapped the man's children, to hold for God knows what if he fails to bring you back. The same cruelty must be in your blood, Melissa. *But how much does it take to satisfy your peculiar taste?*"

She pressed her palms flat to her cheeks, still gently shaking her head, her eyes wide and naked. "Please . . . put on your shirt."

"Be damned to that," Warrington said. "Take the view a while. Glut your eyes. Even you may have your fill after a bit. *Even you.*"

Rhiannon said, "I think that'll be enough. You can cross even the devil's eyes, Dick." He bent and picked up his shirt. "That rabbit is burning up. Maybe it's as well. After this great blather of emotion, aren't ye all a wee too tired to feel like eating?"

# CHAPTER EIGHTEEN

**T**HE NEXT DAY DAWNED COLD AND CHEERLESS. THEY were on the move again. The monotony of a nightmare pattern was resumed. Something had been broken among them last night, like a festering sore laid open. They had changed some. But not very much, altogether, when a man got thinking on it.

Blanco was really Jack Halleck. But Bernal Rubriz could go on hating him under one name as well as another. The boy's mettle had been shown to Rubriz a dozen times beyond need, yet he could hate as insensately as ever. How a man could be so just and reasonable otherwise and so utterly intractable in this, beat the hell out of Rhiannon.

Well, a lot in human nature went that way. It was sad and puzzling and senseless.

Melissa. Who the hell could tell anything about her? Seeing his mutilated flesh had struck a psychic chord in her that nothing else had touched. Not too surprising, at that. The sight of his hideous scars was certain to brand itself forever on the viewer's brain. But how much did it really count for? The cocoon of withdrawn silence in which she now rode hadn't changed, except that the hate was gone. Melissa was still Melissa. Whatever *that* was . . .

As midday drew on, the Brushthorn Hills came into sight. A rugged stretch of country they had crossed on the way north, it could be widely skirted by taking a roundabout way. But one that would lose them a lot of time. And time was snapping at their heels.

Rhiannon had given a good deal of thought to detouring toward any agency post that wasn't unreasonably distant and finding sanctuary there. But that wouldn't resolve the problem, only dump it on someone else's doorstep. It would mean besiegement and certain bloodshed. They and any hapless allies could be starved out. Stone Bull's men, with all of their horses, had a whole commissary on the hoof. Driving fiercely on a war trail, a Comanche had no qualms about riding a horse nearly to death, then eating it.

Push straight on, then. Tackle the Brushthorns with your innards knotted in the knowledge that the enemy, no longer hampered by open country, could steal up on your rear, spread out along your flanks, lay an ambush almost anywhere.

By late afternoon they were climbing into the broken hills, inching through coulees choked with brush, pushing as fast as they could but held to a miserably slow pace. Now all that mattered was staying ahead of the Comanches.

They came to a long, bare escarpment that was so steep that everyone had to dismount and lead his horse up it. Here, at last, Kicking Bird made his desperate bid for escape.

It was hard enough for a single person to urge one animal into the climb. Rhiannon detached the Quohada's lead halter from his saddle and told him to lead his own pony up the rock-studded rise. He, Rhiannon, would be right behind him. That seemed precaution enough.

Halfway up, Kicking Bird whirled and sprang astride his pony in a twisting leap, the halter clenched in his bound hands. A wrench of the pony's head, a drumming of heels on its flanks, and Kicking Bird was wheeling past Rhiannon and plunging downslope at a headlong run.

There was no time even to think of catching him up. It all happened too fast. Almost at the slope's bottom the pony stumbled, its forequarters crumpled, and it crashed on its side. Dust moiled up as it struggled to its feet.

Kicking Bird lay motionless. Rhiannon scrambled down to him. The Quohada youth was sprawled faceup, his head resting against a boulder and twisted at a grotesque angle to his shoulders. His neck was broken, the side of his skull crushed.

Rhiannon tramped back up to the others. They watched him soberly, waiting. He took off his hat and sleeved caked dust from his face, trying to collect his numb thoughts.

"We have lost a hostage," he said slowly and thickly. "A

very precious hostage." He didn't have to add that he had lost a brother, a brother he'd betrayed. "And now we'll have all hell on our heels."

There was no way to hide the body so that Comanche plainscraft wouldn't quickly and easily discover it. Not without losing a lot of time at the task, and every minute counted now. In any case, as soon as they were in the open again, the trailing enemy would swiftly note that a member of the party was missing.

Once he knew of his young brother's fate, Stone Bull would come on like an irresistible force. Caution would go to the winds. He'd be a driving instrument of red vengeance against a foe his forces outnumbered several times over.

All they could do was keep a step ahead for a while, before the Comanches' remuda of extra horses enabled them to close the gap swiftly.

There was no camp halt tonight. They pushed on through the near darkness, often proceeding on foot over the bitter terrain, Rhiannon picking out their way largely by memory. Around dawn they would emerge from the Brushthorns, almost dead on their feet maybe, but close to a place of which he knew, a decrepit but solid shelter where they could at least make themselves damned hard to kill. . . .

Full daylight brought them into a country of gently rolling prairie hills. The sky was drab and overcast; a biting wind chilled their bones as they approached the abandoned place where a forgotten hardscrabble settler had broken his back and his hopes, then died or moved on.

The walls of the old fieldstone house stood firm against time, though the roof had fallen in and the few sod outbuildings were sunken ruins. There was a well, a sagging windlass, and a leaky bucket that still served the purpose, and the water was good, not a tinge of gypsum in it.

While the others tended the horses, Rhiannon examined their situation and decided it was no worse than he'd expected. They could hole up in the house as long as their food and ammunition held out. With a doorway in front and a window centered in each of the other walls, they could defend all sides. Water would be no problem for a long while. The single large rock-walled room held two big oaken casks, obviously placed by the former owner against a possible siege. Still intact and unrotted, all they needed was filling up. The house was set in a broad hollow between the smooth open hills to break somewhat the prevailing winds; nobody could come up on any side without making himself the plainest of targets.

The Comanches would know of this place as well as Rhiannon did. The track would tell them how, after leaving the Brushthorns, his party had made for it on a beeline that diverged from their expected route. Stone Bull would realize that they meant to use the place as a last-ditch fortress. And he would lay his plan of attack accordingly.

Disregarding their dead-weariness, Rhiannon set everyone to preparations for the siege. They cleaned out the remains of the collapsed roof, pulling down its jackstraw tangle of pole joists and rotted sod chunks. They'd not be burned out or smoked out by fire arrows arching over and down into flammable debris. The one leaky bucket made many trips between the well and the oak barrels. One or another of the girls kept a watch atop the tallest rise, spelling each other while the hurried work went on. Finally the horses were herded inside the house and picketed along one wall.

God knew what they'd do with the horses. There was limited water and no feed. They'd end up eating them, maybe. But Rhiannon didn't expect a long-drawn siege, just a short and terrible one that could have only one finish. If it went on long enough for them to be ankle-deep in horse dung and their own, it wouldn't matter.

They settled down by the door and the windows to watch . . . and to wait.

The sky was still sunless, the day chilly. They huddled in whatever warm clothing they had, dead tired and too nerve-strung for sleep.

Posted at the doorway, Rhiannon gazed drowsily at the wind-pressed grass on the rises. Waiting to feel the ravening fury of his former kinsman. *Comanches,* he thought with a twist of obtuse pride. Even the name, given to them by the Utes, meant enemy. The greatest fighting men on earth, some called them. In their time they had dominated all of the country south of the Arkansas River and east of the Pecos. The

Pawnee, Osage, Tonks, and Navajo had all tried conclusions with them. The Sioux had invaded them from the north, the Apaches from the south. All had been soundly defeated.

*And they'll be nearly four to our one.* He didn't count the girls.

Melissa sat half asleep with her back propped against a wall, head tipped down on her chest like a drooping flower. Warrington settled himself beside her, saying gently, "May as well lie down and let it all go. Sleep. We all need a bit of that."

She stirred her head sluggishly, back and forth. "Don' . . . wanna . . . sleep. Can't."

Warrington slid an arm around her shoulders. She pushed weakly and wearily against him. "Don' . . . Richard. Lea' . . . me . . . 'lone."

"I'm afraid I can't do that, my dear. Tried and I can't. Let yourself go. Some sleep will do you wonders."

Melissa gave a kind of nestling sigh. Her head tilted against his shoulder; her body curled bonelessly into his embrace.

"We should all sleep," Rhiannon said. "All but two, a man to the front and one to the back. It'll give each enough vantage so we'll not be surprised."

Blanco, already crouched by the rear window, said, "I can keep awake, sir."

"Fine. For an hour, anyway. Then Dick and Bernie can spell us."

Consuelo was sitting apart. Now, she rose wordlessly and walked over to Blanco, limping a little. She sat down next to him and smiled, twining her hands around his wrist, lacing her fingers lightly together. Blanco smiled, too. Their eyes were for each other and the two of them might have been all alone.

Rubriz jerked out a rusty, chin-down chuckle. "Do you like his touch, daughter?"

"Very much," Consuelo said.

"I wonder why. His skin is like a snake's. It does not take sun properly."

"Do you blame him for that, too?"

"Is he Catholic? I do not think there are Catholics where he comes from."

"What he is, he is. That is what I care about."

"It could put your soul in jeopardy."

"I do not know. Does anybody know?"

"You are a child. He turned your head."

Rhiannon glanced around at them, grinning. "There ain't no baby women, *amigo*."

Rubriz exhaustedly lifted his head, glaring. "What does that mean?"

"It means," Consuelo said clearly, "that if we live, I will go away with my man. We will go so far from you that the sight of us will no longer pain your eyes."

"Can you go with a dead man? That will be interesting to see."

Rhiannon said roughly, "Get your sleep, Bernie. It's an order. Ye'll have to spell one of us in a while."

An hour later, Rhiannon was relieved by Rubriz. He stretched out on the dirt floor, his saddle for a pillow. The moment his head touched it, he went out like a light. It might have been an hour or a minute later that he came groggily to wakefulness. Somebody was gripping his shoulder, shaking it hard.

Rubriz was bending above him. He said nothing but jerked his head sideways. Everyone but Warrington, now on watch at the back window, was asleep. The Englishman gave them an expectant nod. Rhiannon rose and moved softly to the empty rectangle of doorway, exposing one eye as he peered around its edge.

The wind gusted in cold little flicks, whipping up the grasses. He saw nothing else. Heard nothing else. But he sensed beyond any physical knowledge that something was beyond those rises. Something couched and waiting . . .

Rubriz murmured, "I did not see anything. But I am sure I heard a click of metal. Then another. They are out there."

"And getting around us on all sides, like enough."

"Yes."

"Get everyone up. To the windows and lose no time."

In moments they were all set, a man to the door and each window, rifles ready. Revolvers at their hips and ammunition close to hand. Melissa crouched beside Warrington, Consuelo beside Blanco. Rhiannon gave them one terse order. Each was to take her man's revolver. Not for any such bloody nonsense as saving a last bullet for herself, unless she chose to. Both knew how to use a pistol. Bullets should be saved for any foe that got inside pistol range. Rhiannon had his big buffalo rifle in readiness, but the weapon's great firepower and one-shot capacity would be of little advantage at this short range. His Winchester repeater was far better for the purpose.

Giving his companions a last swift lookover, Rhiannon felt an unexpected sting of pride. Sturdy as rocks, the lot, now that the danger was on them. These, too, were his people.

Now he gave his full attention to the rises, taking in as much of them to either side as the periphery of his vision would permit. *Come on*, haint. *Come on, old comrade.* . . .

Stone Bull, unseen somewhere to his front, gave a sudden shout. At his signal, the Comanches came pouring over the low hills on all sides. The fragile stillness was shattered by the cries of battle, the roar of gunfire.

As neatly as Stone Bull had planned his surprise charge, he had failed—perhaps in a fine excess of grief and rage and impatience—to weigh into account what he, as much as Rhiannon, had learned at his Comanche father's knee: "Always look for the unexpected, my son. Expect the unexpected."

The wave of warriors came over the brows of the hills in a fierce, spread-out line, and their timing was perfection.

It didn't matter. They knew the enemy was laid up in secure cover but had expected to surprise and overwhelm them in a brief charge. Instead they raced head-on into the withering fire of a foe prepared for them on the instant.

The charge was broken at once.

Rhiannon fired and saw a brave go down, crumpling and kicking. Then his rifle sights crossed the broad chest of another and he hesitated for a strained moment. The man was Stone Bull.

Breaks Something . . . He was there to the war chief's left. And on her brother's right was Sumah! God. In the same instant he saw her, Rhiannon pulled the trigger. Stone Bull went down on his face like an axed steer. Breaks Something whirled, bent and seized the war chief, flung him across a shoulder, and retreated upslope in great, loping strides.

Sumah hesitated long enough to pull a bead on Rhiannon, on

his exposed head and shoulder, and fire. The slug screamed off the doorway edge, chipping a sting of rock dust against his cheek. Then she turned and raced after Breaks Something. But not before Rhiannon actually glimpsed the whites of her eyes, the sheen of rage and hate that varnished them.

He had time to bring her down, Breaks Something, too. But his hands froze around his rifle as he watched them plunge out of sight across the rise. A warrior somewhat to their right had also turned tail. Rhiannon shot at him and missed.

Already, on the other sides, the deafening din of sustained gunfire had slacked off. But the churning chaos of shots and war cries still rang in his brain. The horses were still snorting and stamping in panic. Jesus and Mary, he thought, hardly able to believe it.

The Comanches were gone, unable in the teeth of that withering fire to follow their usual perilous practice of bearing away the bodies of their dead and wounded. Except for Stone Bull.

# CHAPTER NINETEEN

**R**HIANNON PULLED BACK FROM THE DOORWAY, QUICKLY reconnoitering their situation. Blanco had taken out a man; so had Warrington. Their bodies lay unmoving on the slopes. The first man Rhiannon had brought down had ceased to kick in his death throes. On Rubriz's side two other braves lay wounded halfway up a rise. Other wounded ones had managed to escape.

Warrington's lips wore a crazed fighting grin. "Awfully good," he said. And repeated: "Awfully good. Doubt the beggars expected anything like that, what?"

Rhiannon shook his head back and forth once, in a stunned and mechanical way. He hadn't expected anything like it, either. Half or more of the Comanche force had been devastated. Dead or crippled in less than one shattering minute.

Rubriz, his back to the room, was bracing himself with one hand against the sill of the window from which he'd been firing. His other hand still clutched his rifle, but the forearm was pressed hard across his middle.

*"Padre?"* Consuelo said softly.

Rubriz let go the sill and turned slowly to face them. The side of his brush jacket was soaked with blood. "It is nothing," he said between his teeth. *"Nada!"*

"The hell it ain't," Rhiannon said. "That needs tending, and now. Lie down, Bernie."

Rubriz swept them with a fierce, almost contemptuous glare. He turned back to the window. One of the braves he'd shot had struggled to his feet and was trying to flounder up the slope.

Rubriz drew a bead, his hands as steady as iron, and fired. The brave sprawled out and was still.

Rubriz staggered away from the window and Rhiannon caught him before he fell and eased him to the dirt floor. Consuelo gave a little cry and dropped onto her knees beside him.

Rhiannon's nostrils burned with the sting and stench of powder smoke. He turned his watering eyes back to the slope where the other live, moaning brave lay. The Quohada was belly-shot. Do it, Rhiannon thought, and brought the Winchester to his shoulder and fired once.

Feeling sick to his marrow, he said, "Reload your weapons. Dick, get up front by the door. Blanco, stay by the back window."

Melissa was trying to raise Rubriz's shoulders while Consuelo removed his brush jacket. Rhiannon motioned Melissa aside, saying, "Spare shirts in our saddlebags. Tear 'em up for bandages. Here, my knife'll help."

He lifted Rubriz to a sitting position; he and Consuelo got the jacket off, then the shirt, and spread them underneath before easing him back down. It was bad, all right. The bullet had gone clean through. Rubriz would bleed to death in minutes if the wounds weren't tied off at once. After that . . . God only knew.

Rhiannon's first instinct was to plaster the bullet holes with flour, the frontiersman's favored means for caking a hard-bleeding wound—which a physician had once warned him was a hazardous practice. But they had used up their flour, he remembered, during the trek northward. Next best choices, he'd heard, were cobweb or mud made by mixing dirt and urine. They had no cobweb, either; he searched the corners for some in vain. The mud seemed an anodyne as stupid as it was indelicate; why dirty an open wound? Cloth plugs seemed about as bad. Christ, what did they have?

They had knives. They had gun barrels, spurs, belt buckles. Any metal object heated red-hot would do for the purpose.

"Yes," Rubriz said huskily. "That will do it, *amigo*. Touch-on-touch cautery, eh? Have you done it before?"

"Aye," Rhiannon said. "To horses and calves with bleedin' hurts. After they was tied down. But Jesus, Bernie. We got no laudanum, no ether, not even a swallow of whiskey for ye."

"No. Well, then, *amigo,* we have a man's will. Do it."

"We also have the girls to hold ye down."

"No. Do it."

Rhiannon built a compact fire and heated a knife blade. And then he did it. Rubriz gripped a hunk of strap leather between his teeth, chunks of rock in his fists. His face went gray with agony; his bloodshot eyes started from their sockets; sweat ran off his brown skin in rivulets.

When it was done, he spat out the leather and the rocks rolled out of his hands. His eyes were glazed from the pain of the ordeal, but he smiled. "See, *amigo?* The spirit is stronger than any flesh."

Rhiannon wiped sweat from his own face. The sizzled stink of burned skin clung to his nose and throat. "Ye've proved that," he said. "God's eyes, Bernie, but ye might have had the grace to pass out, at the least."

"Women faint," Rubriz whispered, but he smiled again as he glanced at Consuelo. "However, my daughter does not."

Consuelo had held him in a sitting position, and he had not objected, while Rhiannon sealed the back wound. Tear streaks penciled her face, but no other streak of emotion had touched it.

"You should have had a son, *padre,*" she murmured. "He would not be so much trouble."

"Ah, the sons. Well, they did not live. I will be with them soon enough, I think."

"Man talks like that," Rhiannon said, "he's got himself half dead already. Where's that spirit, now?"

"Back in the flesh, *amigo.* For a time." Rubriz's gaze held a hard steady burn. "You must get me back to Corazon. I will live that long." He looked again at Consuelo. "I suppose you'll want my blessing now. . . ."

"It would be good to have"—her lips quavered, then settled firmly—"*padre.*"

"Yes, yes," Rubriz said tiredly, his eyes half-shuttered with pain. "And I must include the *cabrón,* I suppose."

"His name is Jack. Yes. That would be good."

"All right. I suppose it is all right now." He lifted one hand and made a vague motion. "There you are. . . ."

Rhiannon helped Consuelo with the bandaging, then returned to his position at the doorway, again assigning Warrington to a side window. Slumping on his heels, Rhiannon replaced the spent shells in his magazine and forced his muddy brain to cogitate.

Melissa was crying softly; Warrington was saying low, comforting words to her. There was no other sound but the wind, no shadow of sound that might hint at what the Comanches were up to beyond the rises. Rhiannon hardly dared a hope that they might have pulled out.

Still . . .

Five of the fifteen lay sprawled and silent on the tawny slopes. Still others had been wounded in the charge and retreat. Badly or slightly incapacitated. Stone Bull was dead or dying or badly hurt. Rhiannon had pulled his shot a little at the last moment; he couldn't be sure. Stone Bull was out of the fight, anyway, except maybe to give orders.

*If he died?*

Ordinarily a war chief's death would cause Comanches to give up a fight. Even if he were untouched, so savage a loss as they'd just sustained meant his medicine had gone bad.

Yet there was nothing to indicate the Comanches were giving up. They had stolen up in silence, but departing, their horses would make giveaway sound. Probably they were talking it over.

Sumah . . . full of the madness of love turned to hate.

He could picture her taunting the braves with insults about the quality of their manhood, appealing to their warrior's pride. She would do that. By God, that's exactly what she'd do if he knew her. And in some ways he knew her only too painfully well.

Could a woman rally the wavering but able braves to hold fast? He had heard of such things. A woman's taunts could sting men's pride as nothing else on earth could. And Sumah was no ordinary woman. Her driving iron will, her terrible passion that could infect men to rage as easily as to lust, might turn the trick.

If it did, the braves would settle down for a real siege. No more foolhardy daylight charges. They could starve out their foe. They could try more circumspect means of attack, such as closing in by darkness . . .

The tendril of a thought snaked through Rhiannon's brain.

He blinked, pulling his shoulders erect. Here he was, thinking solely on the defensive side. For days, and right up until now, all his thinking had fallen into that pattern.

But why?

They had wiped out a third of the Comanche force. Others would be unable to make a good fight. Their heads were still reeling with the blow of unaccustomed defeat. All of a Comanche's training was directed toward never letting an enemy surprise him. When one did, he had a hell of a time rallying his senses.

Why wait? Carry the fight to them! Take them in their shoes—moccasins—while they were dazed and demoralized. God, it would be the last thing they'd expect!

Rhiannon stood up and turned, a smile on his lips. "Boys, if you're game, let's finish this now. What d'ye say?"

The three of them, Rhiannon and Blanco and Warrington, tramped slowly up the front-facing rise. They kept a few yards apart, their rifles held ready, their nerves keyed for anything. They slowed even more, crouching down a little as they neared the summit of the rise.

Just short of it, Rhiannon motioned the others to halt. Bending over deeply, he inched onward until his field of vision topped the summit.

The hill's opposite side peeled off in a long, easy slope. On the flat beyond, at a good distance, the Comanches were assembled. Their big remuda was picketed nearby. Five braves lay on the ground. Three showed signs of life; the other two, one of them Stone Bull, were unconscious or dead.

The remaining four braves and Sumah stood in a group. Breaks Something was among them. They had their rifles in hand but seemed passive. Sumah was speaking in a low voice, haranguing them no doubt, and gesticulating fiercely.

Nobody was looking this way. Rhiannon motioned his companions up to his side. They eased their rifles to their shoulders. The Comanches were at a goodly range, but they were plain and stationary targets.

Sumah looked up suddenly. She saw the white men. But she did not shout an alarm.

Rhiannon, his mouth open to give an order to fire, bit back the word.

Sumah's hand had been raised in a gesture that froze at shoulder level. Slowly now, she lowered the hand and spoke quietly to the men. It would be a warning and perhaps more than a warning. Whatever, Rhiannon sensed no threat in it. "Hold your fire, hold your fire," he muttered.

As if following her command, the four braves turned their heads simultaneously. They watched the white men—what little of them showed—in silence.

Sumah walked slowly forward until she was at the bottom of the long slope. She stopped, her rifle in one hand pointed downward. She said in a clear voice, "Redbeard, come down and talk."

"Yes, Warrior Woman. I will show myself and all of you will shoot me. It is not a good offer."

"No." She raised the rifle above her head. "I will throw away my gun. You will do the same. The other *gottams*, too. These"—she turned slightly and gestured toward the braves— "will throw away their guns."

Breaks Something let out a low rumble as he lumbered around to face the rise. His mashed, badly scarred face was contorted as he brought his rifle up. Quick as a flash, Sumah whirled, thumbing back the hammer of her rifle before she was half around. With no time to take aim, she pulled the trigger.

Breaks Something grunted hard. A welt of blood sprang across his right arm. By chance she had only creased him. He did not stir a muscle, just stood holding his partly raised rifle. He stood there stupidly as Sumah, lifting her rifle to her shoulder now, drew a precise bead on his giant chest. She did not say a word.

Break Something dropped his rifle to the ground.

"Get away from it," Sumah called to him. "Get over by the horses."

Unspeaking, the big warrior shambled unhurriedly over to the remuda. He folded his massive arms and tried to assume a stance of composed dignity. It was not easily accomplished by one who looked as if he'd been designed to get about on all fours.

"We will do this," Sumah said. "You *gottams* will come out into full sight and throw away your knives and small guns. So will we. One of our men will drop his long gun and walk away from it. Then one of yours. We will take turns till you and I are the last. We will throw our guns away from us at the same time. Then you will come down to me."

It sounded almost reasonable. Rhiannon translated for his companions. And it was done. He had a qualm as Sumah gave the word for both him and her to heave their rifles away. But she did it and so did he.

Rhiannon tramped down to her and halted two yards away. "I did not think Warrior Woman would want this."

Sumah's face was a coppery mask. "We could all kill each other. But Stone Bull's hurt will not kill him. If we other *Nenema* are all dead or hurt as bad as he is, who will care for him?"

"I did not kill Kicking Bird."

"This we know. But he would be alive if not for you. I would like to kill you, Redbeard. I have never wanted anything so much."

Rhiannon said nothing.

Sumah stood for a moment with her eyes boring into his face. The wind flicked up the heavy fringes of her buckskin dress. Otherwise she was as still as stone.

Finally she said, "The hardest thing after Kicking Bird is that you came to us with treachery in your head. Next to that is that you made me think you had a feeling for me."

"I did not say so. But there is more to everything than you think."

"I do not doubt it. But you are too full of lies for me to know what is true and what is not."

Rhiannon told her the only mitigating fact he knew: that his children were in Dragoman's hands. With her feeling for family, Sumah would understand that even if she did not believe it. The one time that she had seen her sister's children, she had been delighted with them.

"I do not have to lie now, Warrior Woman. My tongue is straight."

"It does not matter."

"It does matter. And what we had, you and I—"

"Matters even less." Sumah's words cut his off like a knife. "We will go now, Redbeard. But we will see you again. When we come, it will be in war. Red war. And you will know us."

# CHAPTER TWENTY

Bernal Rubriz had his wish.

The only thing he had wanted when his time came was to die on Corazon land and be buried there. Only his God could say how he managed to cling to the raveling shreds of life across the last days and miles of the homeward trek. Wasted by pain and fever, he jogged along day after plodding day in a tarp sling made of two ground sheets and suspended from cedar poles strung between two horses that had to be led and driven at a regulated pace. At the end he was a scarecrow of skin and bone that could no longer take nourishment and only sips of water. His eyes were sunk to living sparks in their sockets.

Rubriz was deep in a coma when they crossed where they reckoned the boundary line of Corazon was at sunset of the last day of their trek. The ranch headquarters was only a few hours away, but their bone-deep exhaustion forced them to halt for the night. They were all too strung-out and belly-tight with the pleasurable apprehension of homecoming to clean up the scraps of their remaining grub. The sun's last red flare heeled down and faded as they tried gently to rouse Bernal Rubriz to his minutes of final knowledge.

They succeeded. His lips formed three soundless words, a question. Less than an hour later his heartbeat threaded away.

At first light they were rested enough to be on the move again. Just barely, for they were all worn as fine as shadows, dirty and gaunt. Only Rhiannon felt like a tiger on the leash, wanting to push on at a heedless pace, hungry for the sight of Cully and Norabeth. His horse Donegal wasn't as tired as the rest. But going early to Corazon headquarters would get him

nothing unless Melissa Dragoman was with him. He rode
slowly beside his friends, sharing their quiet grief for Rubriz.
Sharing, too, the last hours of a camaraderie that only danger
and hardship could forge among different people. Knowing
that none of them, going their separate ways, would ever know
the like of it again. And with them to the end, blanket-wrapped
and tied across his saddle, went the body of Bernal Rubriz.

Margarita Tenoval, the matronly housekeeper of Corazón,
took a short break at midmorning from her weeks'-long duty of
watching and tending the two Rhiannon children. She was out
on the patio enjoying the sun when she saw the group of riders
coming around the maze of corrals.

Margarita's hands flew to her mouth. For a moment, she
only stared. Could it be?

One of the riders gave a lilting cry and waved a hand. *Hijo
de María!* It was. She looked like an unscrubbed urchin, a
sadly unkempt *mozo*, but it was indeed she, the Señorita
Dragoman. Margarita caught up her billowing black skirts and
hurried into the *casa*, crying out the news in a loud voice over
and over.

Rhiannon's children came running out of the house before
the riders were within a couple hundred feet of it. He almost
fell climbing out of his saddle, sweeping the two of them up in
his big arms.

Saints and earth spirits, if he weren't weeping like a woman
himself. He was as full to bursting as a man could be, but
damned if he'd show it while he remained in eyeshot of this
hated place.

He set Norabeth and Cully on their feet and dragged his
greasy jacket sleeve across his face. He snorted once.

The others were piling off their horses, too. Several *mozos*
were coming from the house at a run to gather round, jabber
greetings, and make a great to-do.

Melissa stood beside Warrington, holding his hand tightly,
her face flushed and radiant. "Oh, Mike . . . won't you
come inside? Only for a moment, please?"

Rhiannon's lips stiffened, but he managed to shape them into
a smile. "I've told you before I will not. I'd not take a step
under that roof if all God's angels and all the demons of Sheol
were hauling at my shirttail. But you get along to your daddy,

child. Tell him I'll be needing a horse apiece for my children. The horses will be returned."

"Yes . . . good-bye, Mike. Thank you, thank you, for everything. Come on, Richard! Come along."

Warrington gave a wry grin and a shrug, saying across his shoulder, "See you a bit later on, then, take care," as he was dragged away at a half run across the patio and into the *sala*.

Rhiannon turned to Consuelo, who was helping two *mozos* unlash her father's body from the saddle and warning them to be careful.

"Connie, there's little a man can be saying. I reckon you'll know anyway."

"Yes, señor." Consuelo's face was solemn as she gave him her hand. Then she gave him a smile, too. "Go with God all your days."

"And you, lass. Be happy." Rhiannon said to Blanco, "Jack, would ye do me a favor? A last one, I should say. Take Donegal's reins and come to the corral with us."

"Be pleasured to, sir."

A *mozo* was already looking to the animals. Blanco picked up the big black's trailing reins and walked beside Rhiannon and his children as they crossed the compound. Norabeth and Cully capered along on either side of their father, their small hands curled tightly in his. They were as happy as monkeys, not a sniffle or a tear between them, and were babbling more questions than a man could rightly answer at once. He gave them nonsensical replies and felt like capering himself.

More people were coming from the Mexican dwellings beyond the *casa*, men and women and kids, converging toward the group of horses and *mozos*. A passel of curious crewmen were emerging from the bunkhouse. Ah, it was the Sabbath, then. Rhiannon felt his mind budge almost unwillingly back into this other world, one where time's ticking was measured and held sacrosanct.

Blanco said, "Sir, it's been a mighty piece of road to ride together. I'm proud to have sided you on it."

"I'm proud to have sided with you, Jack. But, dammit, will ye quit 'sirring' me at the last?"

"Not likely." Blanco smiled a little. "Man catches the habit, sir."

They passed into the shade of the long, rambling stables, going around them to where the holding corrals abutted against them.

"Boo," a man said amiably.

Rhiannon came to a halt. On their right a stable door stood open and a big, yellow-haired man was leaning against it, thumbs tucked in his belt. A gunbelt sagged below it and its holster was fixed at an angle so that the rubber-butted Colt revolver slanted out to leave the butt free and clear.

Herb Mansavage raised his left hand, took the cigarette from his lips, and grinned his great shark's grin. "Hey there, Rhiannon. Seen you ridin' in. Mighty glad to see you-all. Safe and sound. Not too tuckered, I hope. Hey there, Blanco Jack Halleck." He gave the hint of a sleepy wink. "Ain't had to guess why *you* went a-kiting off all a-sudden. Well, boys, howdy. Welcome back."

A cold shadow glided over Rhiannon's day. He remembered something Mansavage had said during his forced visit here. At the time he'd taken it about half seriously. If the man wanted to push a fight, he'd not do it here and now, would he?

"I'd not be doubting the heartfeltness of your welcome, Herb. Whatever its reason. If ye'd be so good as to say it out?"

Mansavage dropped his cigarette and scuffed a boot toe on it, taking his time. "Well, it's kind of a private thing. Might be better we discuss it alone. Say, off behind that clump o' cottonwoods yonder?"

Rhiannon shook his head almost imperceptibly. "There is no business you and I got that I know of. So there's nothing worth the discussing."

"Hey there." Shark's grin. "I beg to differ. Course it don't need to be now. Not the best time or place, I'll allow. But, man, we have got business, you and me. Don't you play possum up a gum tree 'bout that. Now or later." Herb pushed away from the door and stood with his shoulders high, his thumbs belt-tucked. "Either way's fine with me."

Norabeth made a little sound in her throat. Rhiannon looked down at her wide, scared eyes. He smiled and lightly squeezed her hand, then looked back at Mansavage.

*Not the time or place.* But, God, he had come back with a heavy sickness in him, wanting only to get his children and return home, all the trouble and terror behind them. And here trouble was, waiting for him all over again. It would wait on, biding its time. He would never know when or how it might strike. He might be dead before he knew it had struck.

No. He was worn fine as goose down. Let it be now or never. Get it over.

"Jack lad," he said wearily, "take the children along, will you? Ready the horses for them. I'll be along in a minute."

"Mr. Rhiannon," Blanco said gently, "I don't think I will do that."

"Ye will, dammit!" Rhiannon half bellowed. "Do like I say!"

Blanco met his volcanic stare calmly, then nodded. "All right. I'll take your kids to Miguel, he tends the stables. Got a little hut yonder."

"And you stay with 'em, dammit!" Rhiannon gentled his voice for the children, both of them fidgety and frightened. He smiled at them. "You two nubbins go along with Mr. Halleck. Now don't be shedding tears, Nora." He nipped her chin lightly with his thumb and forefinger. "I'll be back in a trice and we'll be going home, all of us."

They knew something was wrong in the half-comprehending way that children did, finding it all the more terrifying for that. But his warmth and power of assurance actually checked their fear for the moment, as it always had.

Wordlessly and reluctantly, they followed Blanco and Donegal, looking back over their shoulders.

"Now, Herb. The cottonwoods, ye said?"

"Uh-huh, nice and private." Mansavage fell into step beside him. "Real sorry if I gave your young 'uns a bad turn, Rhiannon. It was a thing needed saying, was all. Best it get said now."

"Well, they might get a worse turn, Herb. 'Pends what you got in your head. Is it just talk for now? Or can't you wait to even up for that headache?"

Mansavage chuckled, throat-deep. "It was a skull-splitter right enough. But, laws, no. Headache's all cleared up. Could be we'll just talk some. For now."

"But it won't be the end o' things, will it?"

They reached the grove of cottonwoods and skirted it,

coming to a stop on its far side. The trees cut them clean off from any sight of Corazon's buildings.

"I have a thought," Rhiannon said. "If it's no grudge you're holding, why don't we shake hands? Or work off any loose ends, if that's the case, with a friendly bout of fisticuffs."

Mansavage walked a few yards away, halted, and turned to face him. "No, that wouldn't be a good bet for me, Rhiannon. I like Dame Luck sitting *my* shoulder. Is that gun you're packing clean? Man should always clean a piece after he's used it. See it's loaded up fresh. He never knows."

"It's clean. It's loaded. If it-ain't killing you want, Herb, and you have fear of breaking your hands—ain't that why your kind of coon cat avoids fisticuffs?—maybe ye'll settle for busting an arm or a leg? A bullet can mess things up real nasty that way."

For the first time Mansavage's smile seemed genuine. "Oh my, Rhiannon. I swear, I think you're hard on to begging."

Rhiannon said softly, "That'd be a mistake ye can afford to make only once, Herb."

"You wouldn't beg me to let you off that easy, huh? Not even for your kids' sake?"

"Not even that. For then it'd never be over. Me and my children both 'ud have a lifetime with it. Only tell me one thing, if you please."

" 'Pends what."

"Did Dragoman put ye up to this? Is he paying you a mighty bonus? Is that your reason?"

Mansavage gave a hearty, whickering laugh. "Hey. We're talking a pretty long streak here. Why-fors don't matter none. What does, you want to settle it now, quick and clean? Or . . ."

His voice trailed off as his gaze moved past Rhiannon's shoulder. A trick, thought Rhiannon, and didn't take his eyes off Herb. But he heard steps behind him and twisted his head enough to see Blanco coming around the trees at a run. Now he slowed down, walking easy, and came to a stop beside Rhiannon. Though not too close.

"Could matter a lot, Mr. Mansavage," Blanco said mildly. "Other hand, one minute from now it might not matter to you any longer. Not one damn little bit."

# CHAPTER TWENTY-ONE

RHIANNON SAID WRATHFULLY, "DAMMIT, I TOLD YOU TO stay with the kids! This is no mix of yours!"

"Some ways it ain't," Blanco half agreed, watching Mansavage. "But I ain't working for you, sir. I don't take your orders 'less it so suits me. Just now I wanted to see your young 'uns safe out of the way. They are. Mr. Mansavage . . ." His tone turned soft as butter, then steeled like a blade sliding through it. "This man said you and him got no business needs talking about. That's what I believe."

Mansavage's face had gone totally cold and unreadable. "Damn, now." He gave himself a light slap on the thigh. "All my born days, I ain't knowed a young man so cussed mulishly respectful. Back yonder, when was it, I had you broke down to Herb for a goodly while."

"That was back yonder a goodly while."

Mansavage lowered his eyes, took the makings from his shirt pocket, and began to shape a cigarette. "Who *are* you working for, boy?"

"Myself," Blanco said mildly. "I reckon I forgot to give you my notice."

"Ah-hm." Mansavage passed his tongue along the cigarette, sealing it. "Think you found reason to strike out on your own again, huh? You won't stay that way. Man can only lone-wolf it so long."

"So I have found," Blanco said. "Why I am about to marry and settle down. Not far from here, neither, way things have worked out. Fact, I will be a neighbor of Mr. Rhiannon's. Nearest one he's ever had."

"Is that right."

"Fact. Tell you what else. Mr. Rhiannon is no gun tipper. He would not stand a Chinaman's chance agin you. But me, now. I'd have you leaking from the belly, the heart, the head, before ever you cleared leather. We both of us know that, don't we?"

Mansavage pushed out his lips, then compressed them. He reached into his shirt pocket for a match, snapped it alight on his thumbnail, and touched it to his cigarette. "Ah-hm." He didn't seem to know what else to say. Blanco watched him unblinkingly. The seconds dragged. Herb said finally, "Well, it's a sorry pass of things when a man don't scrape the shit off his own boot soles."

"Keep your poker face," Blanco told him. "It's all the hand you got left to hold, *Herb*. You gave Mr. Rhiannon a threat, sort of, back after you took his kids off. He told me that much, short and sweet, as it never entered his head to ask for help. He ain't about to now and he don't need to."

"Goddammit!" Rhiannon roared. "I had a bellyful of you talking about me like I ain't here!"

"You be still, sir. *Herb*, that's 'most all that needs saying. Maybe one more thing. Meant to hang up my gun and never take it down evermore. But I changed my mind. You hark now. I ever catch wind anything has happened to Mr. Rhiannon— anything at all, mind you, even of natural-seemin' causes—I am a-going to look you up. And you can believe this. You will die as godawful hard as ever a man has died."

Silence except for the cottonwood leaves rustling overhead. Mansavage eyed the mouth end of his cigarette as if it had a bad taste.

The challenge had been made. Rhiannon didn't understand the why-fors of it any better than he understood Sanskrit. It belonged to a closed and deadly world that these two men inhabited and he did not. A world of dark and savage pride that could push a man knowingly to his own certain death. If he refused to pick up the gauntlet flung down, it would take something out of him. For a while only? Or for all of his days?

"Well, all right. You feel that hard about it."

Mansavage tipped a shoulder in the faintest shrug. He tossed his cigarette to the ground, turned on his heel, and walked away, vanishing around the arm of cottonwoods.

"All right," Rhiannon growled, "you saved my life. I'm honest. I owe you more than a man can rightly say. But, boy, you just remember, I never asked for your put-in."

The cigarette was smoldering in some dry leaves. Blanco walked over and carefully ground it out with his heel, then looked up with a small smile crinkling his eye corners. "Begging your pardon, sir. You never asked, just rightly so, but you sure-hell accepted my put-in."

"What double-talk is that, now?"

"Back a spell you told us your troubles and we all give an oath you and your young 'uns 'ud go safe and free. Mr. Warrington give it first and Mr. Rubriz followed suit on the altar of God and, me, I just given a nod on't. But it was said, sir, and you never gainsaid it."

Rhiannon tugged his beard, scowled, and shook his head. "There, ye've got me where the hairs are short, I'll allow. But could be you put yourself on a jack spot no married man's got a right to be. You got that little lady to think of."

"Herb? Sure, he'll think a spell 'bout dusting me some way. Likely in the back."

"Just think?"

"Just that. He ain't above taking a man from behind if he can't do it up front. Only he won't. All Herb's yellow ain't in his hair. He was always scared of me—a little. That makes me a jinx, sort of. In a kind o' way that he won't dast try anything. Not even if he's ordered."

*Ordered.*

The word beat thinly in Rhiannon's ears. Herb had a cheeky mouth, but he was a man who used his gun for wages. He took orders. And who gave the orders on Corazon?

"Jack lad, get back to where you left my children—Miguel's hut, is it—and tell 'em I'll be along directly. I got to see a man."

"Not—"

"Uh-uh. Not Herb. No . . ."

Rhiannon tramped unceremoniously into the *casa grande*, through the *sala* door, halting in the stone-walled coolness.

Dragoman was seated in his wheelchair, drumming his fingers pleasurably on its arms. Smiling and nodding as his daughter paced excitedly up and down, talking a blue streak. Warrington was sitting slackly in an armchair, an untouched glass of whiskey at his elbow. His eyes were closed, his head nodding a little. Then he jerked sharply erect, his head turning.

"Well, Mike!"

Dragoman's smile faded and so did Melissa's eager run of talk. One look at Rhiannon's face was enough to check-rein them both.

"You set Mansavage on me," he said quietly. "Do it again and he's a dead man. So are you."

A flush seeped into Dragoman's tanned face. "Did he tell you that?"

"He didn't need to."

Melissa looked in shock and bewilderment from Rhiannon to her father. "Oh, no! You're wrong, Mike. Dad—"

"Ain't that kind of a man? You don't know your old pa by now? You worn blinders all your life?"

Melissa opened her mouth and then closed it. If she flushed or paled, either way, it was lost in her grime and sunburn. Warrington rose to his feet, disgust and distress in his face.

Rhiannon said, "Herb tried to brace me and Blanco stopped him. Blanco will shoot him dead if he ever tries the like again. And I'll come after you, old man. I'm fed clean up to my craw with you."

"You blame me?" The loose flesh of Dragoman's face shook. So did his voice, a little. "You been waiting for years to take me some way. God damn you, Rhiannon. You think I want to go on waitin' for it? I took your kids, now I'll stick in your craw all the harder. You'll bear me a double grudge and you won't let go of it. Your rock-head kind never will, not in a lifetime."

"Oh, no," whispered Melissa.

Warrington said quietly, "Is that true, Mike?"

"I ain't thought on it. He didn't leave me time to think."

"Well," Warrington said judiciously, "there's this, if you can take another view of it. He's far worse off than you. You have scars, old comrade. But you also have legs. If it came to a choice, which—"

"Difference is, I didn't order his legs broken."

"Stop it!" Melissa cried. "Stop it now!" She whirled on her father, hands clenched at her sides. "If Mike Rhiannon ever comes to harm, no matter how you try to cover up your part, I'll *know*. I'll hate you the rest of my life. You'll never see me again. Ever!"

The blood had drained out of Dragoman's face. He half raised a hand and then dropped it. He sagged back in his wheelchair looking tired, defeated, older than his years. "All right, Melly. I'll give my promise. My promise that I'll never do a thing to harm him or his in any way. Will that suit you?"

Melissa looked at Rhiannon. "Will it *you*?"

Rhiannon rasped a hand slowly across his mouth.

*Revenge.* He had lived with the black thought of it for so long that it had marbled into a part of his brain, a reflex as natural as eating or sleeping. The purpose of it, he realized murkily, had turned so dispassionate and unthinking that it hardly had meaning anymore.

Maybe Dragoman would remain his personal demon until he died. Burned out of his mind, Dragoman's mark would remain burned into his hide, an everlasting reminder he couldn't escape. But pain and hate and loss and grief were the lot of life, along with all the good of it. And they never ceased. Out of his recent vicissitudes had come more to be borne. *Sumah . . . Stone Bull . . . Kicking Bird.*

And still there were Cully and Norabeth. Those things that would feed and nourish a man's soul, not drain and corrode it.

*Man, thank God you've a future to live for!*

"All right." Rhiannon settled all his weight on his heels. "Done. I'd shake your hand on it, Dragoman, if I could abide to touch you. But ye have my word."

He pivoted and strode from the *sala* out into the sunlight. As he crossed the patio, Warrington called, "Hold up a bit, Mike. I'll walk with you."

As they fell into step, heading for the stables, Warrington stumbled and swore sleepily. "You," said Rhiannon, "had best be going bed-a-bye."

"In a little. Need a whiff of something fresh, after all that."

"Aye. Like horse shit, say?"

They didn't speak again until, just short of the stables, they came to a stop as if by mutual consent. Warrington grinned in a crooked, bleary-eyed way. "Altogether, quite a marvelous go, wasn't it? Once was enough for a lifetime. What great lesson of life have you drawn from all of it, Michael?"

"Well, I reckon there's something to be said for the English. Ain't sorted all the rest just yet. Except"—Rhiannon quivered a brow upward—"you're going to have your hands full, Dickie lad. For the rest of *your* life."

"Righto. Melissa will still be . . . Melissa, eh? But that's the jolly way of things." Warrington gave a wry tug on his ear. "Suppose, along with all the rest, I'll have to live with the onus of not being Captain Harry Trevelyan."

"Oh, I dunno. Got the idea she now sees a cut of old Harry in you. Maybe a wee more. I'll wager he never batted her one in the mouth."

Warrington laughed. "You think that's what's called for? On a regular basis?"

"Now, now, don't be playing the brute. As if a prissified, stiff-collared limey gent could ever be that. Who knows, a word of reminder now and again might suffice." Rhiannon thrust out his hand. "Be seeing ye, Sassenach. . . ."

Riding homeward beside his children, Rhiannon stretched his tired muscles, liking the crack of vigor—or did it come of getting older—in them. God, the sun felt hot and good. Older than tiny man and all of his tiny, steamy passions, older than the earth itself, and it stayed hot and new and clean. Restorative.

Yet an ongoing coldness shaded his thoughts. The breaking of his last link with the Comanches. The forging of an undying enmity. When Stone Bull came again, would his former brother-in-law's ranch be the prime target of his raiding? Would Sumah the Warrior Woman come with him?

Rhiannon swallowed, feeling the raw scrape of regret in his throat. The seed of decision had been sprouting unacknowledged even before Blanco had taken Mansavage to account, before Melissa had wrung a pledge from her father. They'd have to send far to threaten a man who tore up his roots and moved a thousand miles away. It was a big country and the Comanches' range was wide. But who'd heard of Comanches on the warpath as far up, say, as Montana? Someplace, anyway, well to the north?

The children were prattling away as children would. He cleared his throat roughly. "Shut up a moment, will ye? I want to tell you what I been thinking on."

"Daddy," Cully said, "I want to hear 'Minstrel Boy'!"

"Right now you do, eh? It's a song for bedtime, nubbin. Too old for lullabies, are ye?"

"Oh, sing it, Daddy!" Norabeth said. "You do it so *beautifully.*"

"Why don't you be saving all that syrup for griddle cakes?" The kids laughed and Rhiannon harrumphed. "Well, then. 'The minstrel boy to the war is gone. . . .'"